A Penny Lost

Aspen Bassett

World Castle Publishing, LLC

Pensacola, Florida

Copyright © Aspen Bassett 2017

Hardback ISBN: 9798891263796

Paperback ISBN: 9798891263802

eBook ISBN: 9781629898544

Second Edition World Castle Publishing, LLC, January 15, 2018

http://www.worldcastlepublishing.com

Licensing Notes

Cover: Karen Fuller

Editor: Maxine Bringenberg

Table of Contents

To Mom, for teaching me about auras and chakras. Thanks for singing us to sleep to Danny Kaye's *I'll Take You Dreaming*.

To Dad, for supporting me through all my endeavors. I've always got a hug for you.

Chapter 1

My knees complained from sitting in a cross legged pose for too long. My hands rested on my thighs, palms up, thumbs and forefingers together. I had my eyes closed as I focused on my breathing. In. Out. Don't get mad. Just breathe, I told myself. Don't think about the fact that your family has forgotten you and you'll probably die of thirst on the steps of your high school. Just. Breathe.

I'd been doing that for an hour and a half. It had gotten old like two seconds into the meditation but, hey, when your ride forgets to pick you up and your only option is to stay put and hope they remember, opportunities for entertainment aren't high. I got so bored, I even started thumbing through my homework. Now, halfhearted attempts at math problems and history definitions crowded around me, just waiting for me to calm down enough to focus. But, angry as I was, I had two choices: 1: Fume and stomp around and prep the yelling of a lifetime for when they rolled into the parking lot, or 2: meditate before I gave myself a stomachache.

Technically, there was a third option. I could close my eyes and read all the energies around me within a two block radius. Like the old swing set to my left and down a block, which clung to a child's long aged joy. It radiated gold. I mentally gave it a little tap and a weightlessness washed through me…that moment when the swing had gone as high as it dared before gravity rushed it back to Earth. Or the jilted bracelet thrown into the ditch after a lover's spat. A green jealous energy shone brightly through the mud, despite the owner's rejection. One house was like an espresso shot straight to the veins, yet had an undertone of exhaustion as the owner stumbled through life under the weight of two jobs and night school.

I opened my eyes when a car honked its way into view. A green Volkswagen Bug climbed the parking lot curb and slammed to a stop three feet from me. I had to admit, I was relieved to see the driver. I stretched my legs out to get the feeling back in my toes, and slowly got to my feet as I stuffed all my homework into my backpack. I also had my dad's tablet…I had snuck it into school while he was out of town on business. I stuffed it between two textbooks so it wouldn't get scratched.

The driver of the ratted old Volkswagen stepped out of the driver's seat and looked at me over the short car roof. Her name was Dinah. We shared a birthday, a face, and two parents who couldn't tell us apart. A little Chinese, some Jamaican, and a whole lot of Scottish, Dinah had long thick hair up in a textbook perfect messy bun. A few delicate tendrils framed her angelic face. One curl in particular swirled across her right eye. It was a consistency with her, no matter the ever-changing hair style. She told herself it was a flirtatious curl, but I could always hear the id's stifled whisper over the ego's scream. She knew she wasn't perfect. The curl was the shield she hid behind, in case anyone ever found out the truth of her imperfection.

A part of me wanted to give the whole "even though we look alike, we couldn't be more different" rant, but the truth was there was only one big difference between us. She cared, and I couldn't afford to. Because caring about the people who couldn't be bothered to remember me had always been exhausting. A recipe for disappointment. If it wasn't for Dinah, sometimes I'd feel like I didn't even exist. Meanwhile, everyone expected so many great things out of Dinah that she ran around with her energies going in all different directions. A panicked yellow chased a lingering problem in the back of her mind, while a bumptious green sneered at anyone who might compete. I could never decide which one of us had gotten the worst end of the stick.

Dinah's heart chakra blazed red in anger as she flopped her arms in a hopeless shrug and shook her head. "I just got the text from Mom. Listen to this." She pulled her phone out and read from it in an exaggerated bratty tone. *"Were you supposed to pick Penny up after your practice? Because I'm in a meeting until five and can't make it."* Dinah tossed the phone back into the car and rolled her eyes. "Seriously? She's going to be paying for this in so many ways."

There was a rush of red in my own soul, which was very adamant that I join in on this anger/pity fest. After all, Mom had promised to pick me up. She'd insisted when I said I could just take the bus… not to worry. Then she dug her heels in when I suggested she might forget. But I couldn't afford to get mad about this again. And again. And most likely, again. Dinah could because it wasn't her problem. It was sympathy anger. Maybe a little frustration that her drive home had a detour. But she didn't have to worry that another fight would just make her and Mom grow further apart. She didn't have to watch every single thing she said in case she mentioned something she only knew because of her unnatural ability to read one's soul. She couldn't see everything as clearly as I could. And she was an optimist; in other words, someone who refused to see the world for what it is. She had bet me ten bucks that Mom would remember, because she honestly believed this time would be different.

I shouldered my backpack and stepped to the poor excuse of a car. "It's no big deal." But then I tossed a smirk her way. "Except now you owe me ten bucks," I said, and plopped myself proudly into the passenger's seat. Technically Dinah and I shared the car, but she was a social person and I…let's just say I learned to love my alone time. Despite the rusty look of the car, it always smelled of sweet peas. I didn't know what my sister did to make it always smell so nice. There were no air fresheners in sight. Did she just spritz some perfume in here every once in a while?

"I owe you ten bucks?" Dinah asked as the car started. "No. I don't think so, my little, naïve cabbage. That deal was never finalized."

"Because you're wimping out."

"I'm not wimping out! I just…." She paused to think. Then she spoke in slow intervals, as if each word came without full promise of another. "I don't like gambling. It's not appropriate behavior, and I don't want to condone it in my younger sister."

"I'm not your younger sister," I pointed out. "Just because the midwife got us mixed up doesn't automatically mean you were born first."

"But it doesn't *not* mean that."

"What?"

"Exactly." Dinah wiggled deeper into her seat in satisfaction. "I win."

"I hate it when you do that," I said.

"You know what I hate?"

"What?" I set my elbow on my knee, cupped my chin in my hand, and blinked at her like some five-year-old at story time.

"When you bottle your emotions up and don't deal with them. It's not healthy."

"Ugh." I dropped my sarcastic kid act and glared at her. "You went serious. That's a cruel joke." I slouched back in my seat but gave her aura a quick look over. Dinah said bottling emotions led to health issues. Well, she should know. Dinah's thick fear of disapproval acted like quicksand around her kidneys, strangling the blood flow and already starting to give her some trouble.

"Penny—" she started again, but I interrupted her.

"I'm fine. Seriously. I'm freaking awesome, actually…and, speaking of awesome." I bent down, largely without my seatbelt's approval, and scrambled through my backpack. "I found this awesome YouTube video. It's hilarious. Just wait until…." I forgot the rest of the sentence.

Where was Dad's tablet? I'd put it between the two textbooks so nothing would scratch the surface. I distinctly remembered putting it there. My fingers traced the frayed book covers, the metal notebook spiral, and even the plastic pencil holder. No smooth screen, though. I pulled the backpack up to my lap for a better angle.

"Just wait until what?" Dinah asked.

"I can't find it." I could barely get the words out before a rush of fear clogged my throat.

"If anything happens to that thing, Dad'll disown you," Dinah teased. "Check under the textbooks."

I forced a calm smile to trick the flush in my energies to cool down before I could check again. Was that it? A smooth corner, yes. My fake smile popped like a balloon under too much pressure. It was just my phone. "I swear I put it in my bag."

Dinah slammed on the brakes. "Are you joking?" She took one look at my face. "Oh geez. You're not joking." She quickly checked the roads and did a U-turn. The Volkswagen seemed as anxious as me as the engine growled along the way. "That thing better still be at school," Dinah warned. "If someone stole it—"

"I took it out to do some homework, but I distinctly remember putting it all back in my bag," I insisted. "It must have just fallen out.

It'll be there."

Lying worked like an emotion. A unique mixture of guilt and regret and fear all tossed together like homemade stew. Everyone had their own recipe, but everyone knew the stew by smell. And my lie-stew was boiling. Even then, I think a part of me knew it wasn't in my bag. And that it wasn't at the school. But then, where else could it be?

I jumped out of the car before it came to a full stop and stumbled back to where I'd waited for the last hour and a half. My heart pounded, but it was the energy around my heart that rolled around like an avalanche stuck on a loop. The black tablet would have been easy to spot against the gray cement. I gripped my necklace with nervous energy, my thumb rubbing the old penny charm like a worry stone. Dad was coming home tomorrow. "I'm dead," I whispered. "Forever. It'll say on my gravestone 'I swear I put it in my bag.'"

"When did you last see it?"

"When I put it. In. My. Bag."

"Don't get snarky with me," Dinah snapped. "I didn't lose Dad's brand new, top of the line tablet."

"I'm grounded. Forever. My freedom's gone." I gaped at the tablet-less view.

"Nah, you're not grounded," Dinah said with a knowing shake of her head. Her curl trailed back and forth in emphasis. "This will be the lamp all over again. They're going to make you work it off."

I cringed. She was right. My future was now riddled with mowing lawns and fixing fences to pay off the debt. "That danged lamp," I said. "Still can't believe they didn't listen when I said you were the one who broke it."

Her charcoal-lined eyes widened at me. "You pushed me into it!"

"We were playing pirates and you decided to mutiny. What was I supposed to do, hug you?"

"If you hugged me, you would have been able to keep your allowance."

"Yeah, and I would have gotten stabbed by your sword."

"Okay, it was foam, let's not get dramatic here." Dinah put her hand up like a diva and made an exaggerated disgusted face.

My stress faded into humor. My stomach stopped burning and the stress in my shoulders eased. Yes, I would have to work it off. Help the neighbors for a lousy price for a bit. Then it would be over. No one would remember it for long. I couldn't quite decide if I should be bothered with that knowledge. Mom and Dad couldn't even remember the *bad* things I'd done. Sometimes it felt like their brains had a leak whenever I was concerned.

I mulled over the pros and cons as I walked back to the car. A cold breeze zipped up my spine, making me shiver. "Dines, do you feel that?"

"My youth flickering by while I wait for you to get in the car? Yeah, I feel it."

"No, the chill."

"It's eighty-five degrees outside. There's no chill."

I frowned. Rubbing the tense hairs on the back of my neck, I turned around. The trees weren't bending under any wind. Physically, the world was perfectly still. But the colors drained from the emotions around me. I couldn't even blink as, in a flash, all those energies were doused with gas and set on fire, only to choke out and fall to dust. Dust that collected like sand in an hourglass, pooling on top of itself higher and higher until it towered over me. In all my years of seeing what no one else saw, never before had I seen anything like this. No energy I knew moved like this whisper of darkness as it reached through the air, like smoke through light, the sharp lines inching closer and closer. Never before had energy been malicious. So I didn't duck as that smoky arm touched my cheek.

Pain exploded in my head, the kind that sears down your neck and burns your eyes. My vision went black in an instant. Everything gone, just like that. Not just the physical world, but the emotional too. All colors destroyed.

Chapter 2

My scream brought the colors back. Sometime during the pain, Dinah had grabbed me. I was leaning against her, eyes wide as the color sifted back. The pain faded as the darkness dissipated from my sight.

"Penny!" Dinah snapped. "Talk to me. What's happening?"

Good question. The energetic world had blacked out, then reappeared as quickly as if someone had taken the cap off the camera lens. I blinked around, disoriented. The colors seemed off. I kept blinking, squinting even, as if that would put everything back into focus. It was like I was wearing glasses with the wrong prescription… but it was so similar, everything still looked more or less the same. The shadow. I twisted my neck as I looked all around, trying to locate it before it attacked again, but the block was empty. There were only normal colors.

"Are you okay?" She tipped her head down to regain my attention.

I wanted to say no. No, I wasn't okay. Something just attacked me, invaded me, and yet nothing had. "I'm fine." I kept blinking, but my eyes stayed unfocused. "Let's just go home."

"Honey…," she started, but her voice trailed off when my face tightened. I didn't want to talk about it. I didn't want to even think about it. It was nothing. A fluke.

Dinah nodded and let go. She opened the car door for me and I stepped in. I could barely feel anything, as if my skin and I were still disconnected. My backpack tipped over as I shoved it to the floor, notebooks and pencils spilling out. I watched it fall but didn't move to correct it. I looked out the window as the car started the drive home. The houses looked normal, but I still felt the energies of the owners. My energetic senses were still there.

Dinah drove slowly through the neighborhoods. I thought I had freaked her out, but I couldn't find the strength to find my "I'm okay" mask. Instead, I did the only thing I could do when things got overwhelming. I studied the energies.

The third house from the school was the only one with strong enough energies to knock me out of my self-pity. I'd labeled it the grieving house about a year back. I didn't know anything about the family, but I knew the energies of that house the same as every other. It used to be a tickled yellow, like a teasing chuckle and a safe hug. Then, in the space of a weekend, it had flipped a switch. I had connected with its energies only once since, but once was enough. The grief was so strong it had knocked me out of whack for a solid hour. There used to be four active souls running around in there, but then there were three. All just trying not to cry.

I had never lost anyone before, but I could tell who had and hadn't without even looking at their energies…something in the way they held themselves. A pseudo-strength to cancel out the cracks within their souls. Some people were able to move on, let go, and embrace the happy memories instead of the sad ones, but not always. Not all the time.

As we drove by a guy sat on the porch steps, sipping a Mountain Dew. He looked to be about my age, and when we passed, he glanced up. We looked at each other for a second. In the corner of my eye something dark stepped onto the side of the front porch. My eyes went straight to the movement, but Dinah turned and they disappeared behind us.

"Honey…," Dinah started again, but her voice went too serious, reminding me why I wanted to be distracted.

"What's your plan for the evening?" I interrupted. What was that flushing my cheeks? Embarrassment? Maybe. It was hard enough convincing people there were things in the world that only I could see. It would be another to claim those things had attacked me.

"A lot of homework," she said, playing along. "Have a history report I have to write about Shakespeare. Then I need to memorize some lines." She gasped and grabbed my knee. "You can help me!"

"No." I made a face. "I'd rather keep waiting for Mom to pick me

14

up."

"Oh yeah, you owe me!" She grinned. "I saved your butt picking you up today. Being that sweet, wonderful sister that I always am." She fluttered her eyelashes at me in exaggerated emphasis.

"I'm not falling for your guilt trip." I reached down and grabbed my backpack. As I stuffed my school supplies in, I chanced another look for Dad's tablet, but no luck.

"Are you sure you're okay?" Dinah asked again. "You seem a bit off."

"Yeah, I am," I answered, but wasn't quite sure which part I most agreed with. "I don't know what happened. Just some weird energy in the air."

"Energy? Like your, um...." She fluttered her hand at my head. "Your thingamajig?"

"Yeah."

"So, what was it? Like a nightmare or something?"

That was the thing about my family. They never believed what I saw was real. They just thought I had a great imagination. "Maybe," I allowed. "Either way, maybe we could keep this between ourselves? I don't think Mom or Dad need to hear about what happened."

"Oh no," Dinah kept her attention on the road, but her voice did the eye roll for her. "I'm sure two loving parents wouldn't care to hear that their daughter screamed in pain today."

"I don't want another psychiatrist telling me I'm seeing things, okay?" I didn't mean for it to come out as harsh as it did, but it was the truth. Odds were I was technically insane, but the title didn't make the colors go away.

Dinah didn't respond for the length of a block and a half, her aura weighing back and forth between the loving pink and an analytical, dispassionate yellow. If I had to make a guess, she was trying to decide whether now was a good time to say I needed therapy or if she should just be supportive. I kept her aura in my peripheral vision, waiting to see which won out.

"You know what you should do?" she said finally. Her aura beamed like the sun. I held my breath, waiting for her to recommend her favorite of my past doctors. "You could help me memorize my lines from *As You Like it*. It'll take your mind off things."

I actually guffawed. "Leave it to you to twist this into a way to help you," I teased, but I was relieved. *Thank you, Sis, for taking my side even though it's the crazy one.* "No," I said, and folded my arms across my chest in emphasis. "You're the one taking AP classes. Not my teacher, not my problem."

"Please!" She forced her voice to crack in false desperation, and I turned to see her lower lip sticking out as far as possible. "I'm not asking you to write my paper. I just need help getting down my lines for the scene my group has to act out."

"Ugh. That sounds horrible," I teased. "Shakespeare will only make me feel worse about my day."

"But doing a good deed to help those around you always makes everything sweeter." Dinah gave me her signature eyelash flutter.

I didn't really have a choice in the matter. After all, she had driven out of her way to pick me up. "You owe me," I sneered as I grabbed her homework from her bag.

"Okay." Dinah did a little head toss to get the curl out of her face, licked her lips, and looked at the road as if the lines to the play were written out in the concrete. "Let me just think about this for a second so I can remember." I leaned back into my seat and stretched my neck.

Something flickered in the corner of my eye. Something black and fast. I sat straight up and looked out the window. Nothing. But whenever I glanced away, darkness danced in my peripheral vision. I twisted as far as I could and looked behind me, prepared to see a pedestrian hurrying past, but the streets were empty.

"All right," Dinah said. She started spouting out Shakespearean dialogue like it made sense. I grabbed the paper and pored over the meaningless words, trying to catch up.

There…it appeared again, just out of sight. It looked tall enough to be human. The more I focused on the white sheet of paper, the sharper the figure came into view. Definitely humanoid, parallel to the passenger seat window. Keeping pace with us. I whipped my eyes to the darkness again. Nothing. No one.

"Different people travel at different speeds through time," Dinah said. I did a quick check.

"Eeeehhhhhh." I made a sound like a game show buzzer and Dinah cringed.

"What is it?"

"Time travels in diverse paces with diverse persons."

"Oh geez, that was way off."

She mouthed the words to herself. I glanced at the window again, but still nothing. A tingling sensation of a gaze whispered down my neck. If only my eyes could focus, I might be able to see what it was. I squinted at the muted colors of reality. A headache grew from the effort and spiked down my neck when I tried to push through. Dang it! Whatever happened back at the school had better wear off soon.

"Time travels in diverse paces with diverse persons," Dinah continued. "I'll tell you who time ambles withal, who time trots withal, who time gallops withal, and who he stands still withal."

The car went silent. I still couldn't see anything unusual. Unless it wasn't something in reality at all. Maybe it was an energy, one strong enough for me to see, even if just a little, without having to zero in on it.

"Ahem. Your turn," Dinah said.

I forced my lips together until I could squelch the frustration. I needed to see what lingered out there, but I couldn't focus like this. If only Dinah saw the world like I did, we wouldn't run into problems like this. I took a deep breath to stay calm and looked back at the paper. "Okay, no, who says prithee?" I snapped. "I don't care how old this crap is. No one ever says 'I prithee, who doth he trot withal?'" I quoted the line with a sarcastic British accent.

"Actually, there's a theory out that no one did. That's what made him so popular. The other writings from that time are more...." She weighed her head back and forth as she searched for the right word. "Understandable. And yet I still need to memorize this."

"Fine. I prithee, who doth he trot withal?"

"Marry, he trots hard with...." Dinah kept going, but I returned my attention to the darkness lurking on the other side of the car. I closed my eyes and let in all the colors around me. Dinah's studious blue aura as she worked to memorize her homework. The lavender colored aura of an older man wrapped in a hammock, daydreaming his afternoon away. Then I noticed how the neighbor's dog didn't bark. Its energy twisted, tight and red, pure fight or flight reflexes. Everyone in town knew this dog. The little thing barked up a storm if you changed perfumes. What made it quiet now?

Then, just as if a camera had refocused its lens, everything sharpened. And there it appeared. Staring at me. This...void. Like a hulk-shaped hole in a wall, only the wall was reality and the other side was nothing but starless space.

Dinah cleared her throat again. My eyes popped open, and just like that, the darkness disappeared. "Umm...who ambles time withal?" I

17

rushed the words out and reclosed my eyes. It was gone. Could that be the shadow that had attacked me? I searched for it but to no avail… if it had even been there in the first place. I wished I could say that I was confident in what I saw in my mind. But that was the problem with seeing things no one else saw…there was always the chance I was actually crazy.

Dinah went silent again. "Who doth he gallop withal?"

I closed my eyes one last time. One more check, just to make sure. Because I couldn't be crazy. It couldn't just all be in my head. Right?

There. Not a humanoid figure, but a cloud of smoky nothing over the sky. Just a little one. Kind of the shape of a cloud Pooh Bear might ride to reach the honey bees. It wouldn't have seemed particularly menacing if it hadn't been for the way it felt. Like the only reason I could sense it was because of the gap it created in the energies. Energy was everywhere, bouncing off each other in various vibrations, but that cloud stood completely still, like a bubble floating through water, spreading apart what was real to make room for the silence. It hovered for a moment before heading back into town. Out of my range.

I opened my eyes. The setting sun whispered its descent through the window. "Who stays it withal?" I quoted on autopilot to keep Dinah occupied. Whenever I wanted to think about the world no one else saw, it was best to make them believe I wasn't thinking at all. I stared at the distance where the invisible cloud had disappeared away from the setting sun. My stomach lurched, but I couldn't decide if it worked in warning or in excitement. Because I'd never felt this way before.

I'd felt everything, by proxy if not from personal experience. Joy, loss, confusion, peace. I'd felt the memories of hundreds of kids as I walked past them in the hallways. I knew which kids felt loved at home and which ones were in desperate need of a hug. I knew when Mom felt guilty for missing my games or when she decided it was worth it to put food on the table. I knew when Dad truly missed us or just felt obligated to treat us to dinner. When it came to emotions, energies, life, I'd felt it all. Age sixteen and nothing surprised me. But this…this was new.

And it had taken one long look at me before heading the other direction. Away from us. I twisted my back as far as it would go, trying to keep it in sight until we turned a corner and it was gone.

"You know what?" I smacked my forehead with the Shakespeare notes as if an obvious idea had just popped into my head. "I just thought of another place I might have put the tablet. We should turn around."

"Back to the school?"

"Go that way, yeah. I'll tell you if you need to turn."

"If? Are we going to the school or not?"

How should I know? I was chasing an energy I'd never seen before. But she didn't know that. I imagined explaining that to her. A possible response might be, "Oh, that's really interesting, Penny. Here, I found this white jacket I thought you might like. It lets you hug yourself all day long!"

"This isn't about the tablet, is it?" Dinah asked. "It's about your… thing."

"Oh, for crying out loud," I groaned. "Never mind. You know what? I just remembered I love marathon walking. You can just drop me off here and head home."

"Oh, sure, and then everyone will blame me when you disappear forever or turn up dead in some creek ten years later."

"Wow."

"Just saying if anything happens to you, it's not my fault. But if I'm going to humor you, you have to humor me too. Call Dr. Fredrick when we get home. If nothing else, he might have something for that nightmare vision thing. I, for one, don't want that happening again."

I shot a puff of frustrated air into the sky, but nodded to keep the car moving. This weird void energy had better be worth it. I knew how to handle psychiatrists, but it still took a lot of time. But at least I got to go on a treasure hunt for an invisible energy only I could see with a sidekick that didn't believe in my abilities. It was Christmas.

Dinah took the road to the school. I closed my eyes and pretended to be resting, but actually searched for The Void once more. It didn't take long to find. The thing stood at attention like a beacon. *Oh, that's always a good sign,* I thought as my stomach cringed. From excitement or anxiety only time could tell.

"Stop the car."

Chapter 3

We were outside the grieving house, the one that used to be happy. The porch was empty now, but I still remembered the face of the kid that lived here. And the darkness next to him. I stepped out of the car and walked to the white painted fence. The cloudy smoke moved as if an air current had sucked it into the house through an open window. I'd never seen energy move that way before.

"Why are we here?" Dinah asked as she stepped up beside me. "Do you know these people?"

"No," I admitted.

"So I'm guessing you left the tablet in there because you were in a hurry to get out with your stolen loot?"

"Sure," I said, not paying attention. Because this house was different now. It wasn't just the grieving house…it was dark. Sharper than mourning, just like that gap in the energies I'd seen earlier. Like peering into a deep empty pipe with a narrow lip. I knew there was something in there, but the light just couldn't make it. It didn't give off any energies either. None of the delicate reds or the raging greens. No happy yellows or peaceful blues. Just black. Just empty.

"Come on. Just tell me what's going on," Dinah pressed.

"Do you feel like something's off?" I asked. Because I didn't just see the unnatural gap anymore. I felt it…this pull, like a vacuum on low. Unsettling, unstable. Every cell shuddered at it, like a whisper from the depths, a promise to tear me apart. It could be just in my head.

I could have been crazy, and in that moment, I would have preferred going insane to the alternative. So I looked at Dinah, waiting for her answer.

Her face scrunched up in confusion before she gave an exasperated huff of realization. "If you're talking about all that energy crap, I don't know." She flew her hands up in the air. "Just tell me what's going on."

"You don't feel anything?" I asked.

She shook her head, but her expression turned worried when she glanced at the house. Or maybe it had been there since we parked on this block, and only now deemed exposure. But was it more than my strange behavior that freaked her out? "Are you okay?"

"I don't know. I've never felt this way before, Dines."

"Hey." She stepped closer and grabbed my elbow as if to steady me. Was I swaying? The pull of the darkness had started to make my blood scream in my ear. "You're okay," Dinah said. "Just take it easy. Breathe. It's not real." But I couldn't catch my breath. The vacuum sucked it away. "Calm down." Dinah's voice got lower in seriousness. "You're starting to freak me out."

"Are you sure it's me?" I asked. "Is it me, or is something else freaking you out?"

She hesitated. Didn't see that coming, I'd guess. Even I had to admit I had been acting weird. But if there was one thing I'd learned about my quirk, my weird tendency to see and feel what other people didn't, it was that, when people said they didn't feel the same things, they may not have been telling the complete truth. Sure, they might have thought they were telling the truth, but there was always a hint, a whisper in the back of their head, that said something else. Like their subconscious or their intuition knew exactly what I was talking about, but they'd forgotten how to listen to it. So when Dinah's eyes flickered to the house, I knew it wasn't all just in my head.

"Dines, if I said let's go knock on that door, what would you say?"

"I'd say we need to leave that poor, random family out of this. Okay, if you're feeling a panic attack or something, let's get you some help. I'll drive you to the emergency care or back home. I can run to the grocery store and grab a paper bag if you think you're going to lose it soon, but we can't just go knocking on stranger's houses without a reason."

"There's something wrong with that house," I explained. "The energy's off. I've never felt anything like this. It's not real. It's unnatural.

21

You feel it too, don't you? Doesn't that house make you nervous?"

"Well, it does now!" she snapped. "You made it sound all creepy! And now some poor old couple probably lives there, wouldn't hurt a fly, and you're making it seem like the witch's house at the end of the lane!"

I looked at the house again and frowned, eyes opened. It was one thing to lose myself in the colors around me. It was quite another to…to what? What was my grand plan? Play Sherlock without the evidence? Definitely not drag Dinah along with me. If it was real and did hurt me, it could hurt her too. And if it was fake…. Giving my sister more ammunition for teasing was never a good idea.

"I'm sorry," I said. "I was just…I don't know, being crazy. We can go home now." I stepped toward the car.

Dinah sighed in relief. "Thank you. I began to wonder. I know the tablet's somewhere. We'll find it. Or, I'll help you pay it off. It won't be a big deal, I promise. We'll sweet talk Dad so well, he'll thank us for losing the—"

"Help!"

Dinah and I stopped cold at the same time. I didn't want to turn, but the sound had come from behind me. Maybe I didn't hear it. Maybe it was just in my overactive imagination, and Dinah only stopped because she noticed I had stopped and—

"What was that?" Dinah spun around. "Did that come from the—?"

"Help me!"

Dinah was running before the scream finished wafting through the front door. With every step she got closer to the darkness. The blackness that stung my eyes.

"Stop!" I screamed.

She froze in her steps, her skin inches from the bubble. She turned back and looked at me, just long enough for me to see the look in her eyes, that wide eyed, tight jawed look she got when nothing could stop her. Someone was in trouble. She was going in. My mind raced to think of an excuse. "It's just the TV!" "Don't you know that's the scream from *Sharknado*?" "Don't take another step, because there's a weird gap in the energies and it makes me nervous!"

Dinah bounded up the stairs in two short leaps and reached the door. She stood in the gap of energy now. I couldn't see her aura, her energies, at all. As if she wasn't even there. Except I could see her.

Literally. The light from the setting sun still bounced off her skin as she knocked hard against the front door.

"Hello!" she hollered. "Is everyone okay in there?!"

No answer. I didn't remember moving, but I stood at the edge of the darkness. I wanted to step through, to be by my sister's side. After all, I had brought her here. Only the force of the bubble made my skin crawl. It felt so unnatural, like opposing magnetic pulls zeroing in on my cells, making them jittery. My muscles tensed up, and a part of me felt like the tension was the only thing keeping me together. How was Dinah so fine in this? Was it really all in my head?

"Dinah, you should go back to the car," I said.

She leaned her head against the door. "I think I hear something." She turned the door knob and I cringed, closed my hands into tight fists, and raced after her. The first step was the worst—nausea, pain, and fear all in one solid whack—but then all sensation numbed. Not to a dull desensitization, but rather a sharp, shocked numbness. As if I were about to fall down a bottomless cave and time slowed down so I could feel every sensation of shock settle into my skin. As if at any moment I'd fall and never land.

"Hello!" Dinah hollered, just in front of me. "Is anyone there?"

"I'm stuck!" the male voice screamed, and it came from the bottom of some stairs.

The basement. He was in the basement.

I grabbed Dinah's arm before she could start the descent. "It's a trap," I hissed. "Go call the police."

She blinked at me. I wished I could read her energy so I could know exactly what she thought and how to convince her to leave. But every time I reached out, nothing answered. All I could see was the hesitation in her eyes, like maybe I was right, maybe this was a trap. But what if it wasn't? Her thick lips tightened, and I didn't need to read her aura to know what thought ran through her head. Because I thought it too. What if the cries for help were real? What if we turned our backs, and then whoever was down there got hurt? Or worse. What if tomorrow I read the newspaper headline and it said "Boy Bleeds out in Basement"?

Dinah's arm slipped from my loosened grasp. I wanted a reason for her to turn around, any reason, but all I could muster to say was, "They're always in the basement in a horror film," and led the way.

The basement was large, the kind people usually turned into TV

23

rooms or recreational game rooms, with computers set up for online gaming and foosball tables. But there were no games here, online or table-set. Instead, the walls of this room were lined with white boards splattered with equations and monitors bleeping in warning. Cords leaked from the walls and pooled in the center of the room, where a whirring metal frame sputtered electrical sparks. Dead center in the room and over six feet tall, three bars of solid metal jutted out of the floor. And tucked between the frame was a thick metal door, the kind of double-layered vault door in old 1900s post offices or something. It looked so out of place in the middle of the modern tech.

The boy lay on the floor, his leg pinned down by a fallen metal shelf. It was the boy I'd seen earlier on the porch, the one who'd stared at me as we drove past. His dark blond hair stood out against his pale skin as two sharp pale blue eyes closed in relief when he saw us. Broken vials of chemicals littered the floor, steaming with unnatural speed. Dinah and I shared a dismayed face before running to his side.

He nodded at his leg. "It's stuck."

"We can see that," Dinah said as she and I assessed the situation. His leg didn't seem to be bleeding...that was a relief. In fact, luckily for him, most of the weight rested on a large stack of fallen books. Of course, if we tried to lift the bookcase and something went wrong, the books could dislodge and we would end up making the situation ten times worse.

"We should call for help," I said, and pulled out my cell phone. The screen was black and, despite the many times I slammed my finger into the power button, it remained dead. "I had a full battery."

Dinah pulled out her phone. "Mine's dead, too. Looks like we're doing this on our own. Grab that side and we'll just...." She motioned lifting it up.

"We should be cautious," I warned. "Let the professionals handle it."

"Not to rush you or anything, but I'm losing feeling in my legs," the boy said. Dinah hurried over to the other side of the bookcase, ready to start lifting with or without me. "Careful," the guy said. "There's a control box right behind you. Whatever you do, don't bump it."

I glanced behind Dinah. By the looks of the sparking box, the controls were compromised to a dangerous level. It fizzed with light and shook without warning.

"What kind of mad scientist's lab is this?" I complained as I bent down onto my knees and prepped my hands under the bookcase.

"Don't worry," he said with a half-smile. "The liquid's Mountain Dew."

I struggled to get a decent grip under the sharp ends, but Dinah didn't wait before lifting. The metal was heavier than it looked, and my fingers screamed as the corners dug into my skin, but I kept lifting. "Go, go, go, go…," Dinah and I both chanted at the boy.

He shuffled away. As soon as he freed his foot, Dinah and I dropped the shelf. It hit the floor with an echoing thump, which knocked a live wire out of place. The wire jerked toward Dinah. She stumbled back, trying to avoid the live sparks, only to collide right into the control box.

Everything happened at once. The control box fell to the floor. It whirred to life with a vengeance and shocked Dinah, who collapsed to the floor, out cold. I screamed and jumped to her, kneeling down to check for a pulse. No, no, no. Don't do this. A pulse. There. Okay. "She needs help. We gotta…."

I turned to the boy but saw something else instead. The metal door had burst open.

And there it was, the gap that had led us here. A vacuum of black, sucking in all the loose glass and stray papers. A targeted vacuum that sucked in everything not nailed down. The rest of the room, the corners too far away, were quiet. My hair whipped past my face, reaching for The Void. I tried to call out, but the vacuum caught the sound waves before they could reach my ears. Everywhere around me, sparks flew. Books and notepapers collided with each other on their way into the endless space, and yet I didn't hear a thing. The silence acted as a roar in my ears, so loud no other sound could survive. The corners of one or two white boards peeled away from the wall. The air got thinner by the second.

I saw the boy's lips move, how his hands waved for me to get out of the suck zone. But then Dinah's leg moved. Not with purpose, but because the vacuum had gained strength. Her leg twitched again, as if something had a grip on her ankle and was trying to yank her to them. The third time her whole body inched toward the space.

"No!" I screamed, but I couldn't hear myself. I reached out for her, only the vacuum was stronger than I'd anticipated. As soon as my foot left the ground, the force dragged me across the floor. I slammed my foot back down, my tennis shoes burning rubber as I struggled for a grip. Helpless without something to hold, I'd be lost to the darkness in seconds.

Then two hands slammed into my back, knocking me out of the vacuum, back to where the air was still. My hair slammed into my face, my ears popped, and I could hear again. I heard the clanking of the glass, the shocks of the sparks on Mountain Dew. And the boy's yells once more. I turned around but it was too late. Two sharp pale blue eyes disappeared, snuffed out as soon as he passed through the door frame. He was gone. And soon, Dinah would be, too.

I got on my hands and knees, trying to be as small a target as possible so the vacuum couldn't grab me again. I leaned forward into the mess and reached out for my sister. The vacuum whipped air against my face, stunning me, but I kept my eyes opened, tangling my foot into the bottom of a shelf as a brace. I reached for Dinah one more time and got her silky blouse with two fingers. My fingers clenched together as I tried to keep a hold of her, to yank her closer. I managed a whole fistful of fabric, then an arm. I couldn't hear my own cry as I heaved her against the wall.

Her purposefully messy bun exploded in every corner. Bobby pins stuck out the sides or just hung down her neck in defeat. She still didn't move, but she breathed. That was enough for now. Electricity continued to cackle behind me, but what was I supposed to do about it? The stairs were on the other side of the frame. It would be impossible to reach any exits without getting sucked into the darkness. Even if I could, I couldn't leave Dinah there.

I looked back at the door shaped hole. The boy was gone. We'd come down here to save him. How had this happened? The black swirled within the frame. As soon as anything got caught up in its emptiness, it disappeared. But not like through a veil or fog or anything so solid. It was like…like the materials were torn apart so seamlessly that for a moment they *were* the fog, and then…nothing. My stomach churned. Did that happen to the boy? Did he just die for me?

Then something stirred in the blackness. Eyes on me, studying me. Like something lingered in there. I stepped closer to get a better look, staying clear of the danger zone. Yes, there it was. A movement.

"Hey, dude!" I hollered. "Is that you?! Are you okay?!" Dang it, would I have to go back in and try to fish him out? But no. Whatever moved in response was not the boy. It wasn't even human. A wisp of emptiness reached out of the hole, like an arm. The tip of what could only be a finger skimmed along the metal shelves, which sputtered and melted. The shelves leaned from the broken support and equipment and tools rolled off, hitting the floor with a bang.

I cursed and jumped away, but the arm kept reaching, longer and longer, misted fingers stretching through dissipating remains of fallen debris. No way could I have run, even if I'd wanted to. Dragging Dinah up those stairs would put us both in immediate danger; maybe I could outrun it on my own, but she wasn't moving so neither could I. There was nothing to do but cower on the floor, hoping it would miss me. But then it changed directions, leaning down. I knelt in front of Dinah's still form, leaning back and reaching my arms out to cover her. The fingers kept coming, forcing me to stretch my neck back as far as I could. A whimper escaped my throat as I braced. For what? I had no idea. Not until the fingers wrapped around my forehead. Not until the pain came, ripping deep tears within my soul as it pulled me apart, taking what it wanted and tossing aside the rest. And then my world went black.

Chapter 4

For a moment there, everything was peaceful. Like I'd gotten my best night's sleep. Better...like I didn't even need to sleep because nothing existed that might ever stress me out. Physically or spiritually. Nothing was real but peace. Just the serenity of blackness.

Then the headache came. Salt water air and stiff ground grew sharp around me. I groaned and opened my eyes, looking straight up at a blaring sun. My hand rose to the rescue, shielding me with shade, but the sudden movement made me nauseous. I moaned my way to a sitting position and grabbed my head in my hands, as if I could stop it from threatening to explode. What happened? Where was I?

It came back in fragments. The images were so surreal I couldn't swallow them as truth. Surely I had hit my head too hard. A house with no energy. A crazy experiment in the basement. The trapped boy. The vacuum in the shape of a door. Dinah.

I blinked until I got used to the sun and looked around. There were no signs of her. Nor were there any signs of anything that happened. I wasn't even in a house anymore. I was....

On a boat?

No. It couldn't be. Yet the floor beneath me swayed with rhythm. A steel deck lined the sudden drop off. I worked myself to my feet and stumbled to the edge, smelling the metallic tinge from the wet steel. Endless water loomed from all directions. No land was in sight, only floating ice and waves. I looked to my right and saw the length of the deck. No. I wasn't on a boat. It was too big. To call it a boat would be to call the Hulk a hobbit. I was on a ship. A huge chunk of steel the length of two football fields. What the — ?

How was I on a ship?! I forgot how to breathe and forced air in and out with conscious yet raspy effort. I was on a ship. "Dinah?" I choked on my confusion. "Dinah!" She had to be here somewhere. She would know what was going on. Did our family decide to go on vacation? Did I just hit my head on my way to the cafeteria and have some whacked out dream? Or was I dreaming now? A flash image of Dinah still on the floor of that strange house stung my eyes. Oh geez, I hoped I had hit my head on the way to the cafeteria. Please let that image just be my mad imagination skills. "Mom! Dad!"

Then I heard it. The humming, so out of place against this metal trap. What was that tune? I'd heard it before. Was someone humming *Hit the Road, Jack*? I whipped around at the sound, and there was the source. A boy stood in the shadows, doing a half lean against a closed door. I could just make out his silhouette…tall, built. It looked as if he wanted it to be a casual lean, but his body was too tense. He kept turning his head, looking around like he was waiting for someone. No, he hadn't noticed me yet, which meant he wasn't searching for a face. Instead, he looked at the ship. The ocean. Like maybe he didn't recognize it either.

I stepped closer and he saw me. His face slipped into the light, shining off his messed up blond hair and eyes as blue as the ocean which had trapped us on this ship. The guy from the basement. The one we had tried to save. The reason this all happened.

It took me three steps to reach him, and less than a second to grab him by the shirt and pin him against the wall. "What's going on?" I snapped, my voice low and serious. Even I was a bit intimidated. "Where's my sister?"

His eyes widened and he held his hands up in surrender. "Whoa there, calm down."

"I'm not going to calm down until you tell me what you did to us, and what kind of sick person makes a trap like that?"

"Wait, what?"

"We were in there to help you!"

"No trap!" He shook his raised hands, as if to remind me he'd surrendered. "No evil plots on my end, I swear! Listen, I don't know what you're talking about. But…," he added when my pressure on his chest deepened, "I will help you figure it out. You just gotta let me go."

I hesitated. He seemed to be telling the truth, but I watched TV. Anything that seemed real and honest on TV only meant that a good actor could fake it. So I closed my eyes and looked around. That gap in the energies, the bubble of darkness, was gone. I found myself relieved when energies answered my call. At least here, energy acted normal. His aura shined a dominant yellow tinged with a subtle red, showing just hints of fear and shock in his system. But did he lie? I searched through the colors swirling in front of me. Layers upon layers, all different colors and tied to different emotions, but I didn't have time to study them all. I sifted through, tossing aside what wasn't relevant. He was confused, yes. Curious, yes. But I couldn't find any signs of deception. He meant what he said.

I sighed and opened my eyes. He studied me with shocked confusion, pale blue eyes staring into mine like I'd completely lost it. "Listen here," I said, more so I wouldn't look like I had completely backed down than from a need to actually threaten him. "If I find out you had anything — Any. Thing — to do with what just happened, or if my sister got hurt, I will toss you into that ocean quicker than you can say your prayers."

He swallowed. "Got it. Only mess with you if I want to swim. Could you let go now?"

I dropped my hand and stepped back. He rubbed his chest as he walked away from the wall, letting the sun hit the rest of him. He looked almost tan, with desert colored hair and a decent jaw line for a high schooler. He couldn't have been older than high school. If I had to guess, I would have said sophomore, like me...maybe a junior. He wore a plain white T-shirt and jeans...a classic look, and one that worked well on him. But it was the eyes that made his face worth the view. They were a pale blue I'd ever only seen on TV, like a whisper of the sky through clouds. I frowned and looked closer at him. If he lived in that house, so close to the school, I should have seen him in class before. Only no, I knew the first time I'd seen him was when he sat on the porch as Dinah and I drove home. Maybe he was home schooled.

"What's your name?" I asked.

Now it was his turn to frown. He went still for a moment, thinking. A change in the air told me his energies had gone tense, like the question made him anxious. "Do you know how you got here?" he asked instead of answering.

"No." I shook my head and played along. "The last thing I remember was the foggy stuff coming through the freaky metal door and attacking me."

He looked at me and raised an eyebrow. "That sounds like a cool story."

"You were there."

He frowned again. "No, I wasn't. I think I would have remembered something like that. Freaky metal doors attacking people. Don't see those every day."

I studied him for a second, but still got no tells of a liar. "Do you, by chance, happen to have a twin brother?" I asked. That would happen to me sometimes. People would mistake me for Dinah and just start chatting away about things I'd never heard of before.

"No twin brother that I'm aware of. I'm sorry, I feel like I'm missing something here. Have we met before or something?"

"Apparently not." I leaned against the wall and sank to the floor to hug my knees. The ship moved with enough speed to create a sharp breeze that bit through my thin clothes. My mind went blank. Not because there was nothing to think about, but because there was too much. I didn't know where to start. On the one hand, where was I? How did I get there? How could I get home? Where was Dinah? Was she okay? The next thought bubbled up against my will. It was my fault. I was curious. I wanted to see the strange new energy pulsing around my town. We never would have heard the screams if we'd just stayed home like she wanted. The deck of the ship seemed to nod up and down, taunting me with agreement. *Yup, it's all your fault. Mmhmm.*

I closed my eyes and leaned back, not caring that the cold of the metal seeped through my hair and into my scalp. The boy's yellow aura lit up in my mind the moment I tried to block out my visual surroundings. It came closer. Footsteps stopped to my left and, by the ruffling sound of clothing and the way his aura folded in on itself, he'd sat down next to me.

"What's your name?" I asked again.

The air went silent for a few moments. Nothing but the beat of the sea against the ship before he finally responded. "Hmm."

"What?"

"Nothing. I just thought if I waited long enough, a name would pop up." I opened my eyes and looked at him. His gaze lingered on his hands resting on his tucked in knees. He stared, as if waiting for the answer to appear in the wrinkles of his palm. "Complete blank."

"You saying you don't remember your name, or you can't think of a reason not to tell me?"

We waited in silence for a moment. "I don't remember," he finally said. He didn't frown or try for a fake smile. Instead, he just looked at me and shrugged.

"You're calm."

"So are you."

"No. I just can't decide where to start my freak out."

He "hmm"ed again. "May I ask your name?"

I opened my mouth to answer but paused. I knew my name. Of course I knew my name. I hadn't lost my memory. It was just jumbled and confused because it didn't make sense. One minute in Cheyenne, next on a ship. Kind of hard to make sense of anything, but that didn't mean I'd lost any memories. So why wasn't it coming to me? It should be instant, without thinking. Instead I felt like a deck of cards, in perfect order until that void shuffled and now I was all out of place. Come on, girl, finish the sentence. My name is….

Dinah. All I could think about was Dinah. If she woke up there, all alone with that weird vacuum thing sucking all the life from the room, she'd freak. And what if she got sucked in? How would I find her then? How could I get us home? My hand went to my necklace. I stroked the familiar curves of the penny. It was a family heirloom. Back in the day, people carried a penny around their necks in case of an emergency and they needed food or shelter. It became a symbol of love and protection. My ancestor had worn it and survived the Lusitania sinking. Now, it was just a penny. Couldn't even get a bottle of water with it. But Dinah had found it when we were going through Mom's personal ancestry collection…dozens of letters and old belongings. Dinah polished the necklace up and gave it to me. "A penny is always valuable." That's what she had said.

"Hello?" the boy asked. "You okay?"

"Penny," I said. I slipped the necklace under my shirt and looked at him. "My name is Penelope Grace."

"Nice to meet you, Pen—"

"I've decided where to focus my freak-out." I stood up and looked around the deck for the best way to start my search. Because Dinah had always been there for me. Even when Mom and Dad forgot, she remembered. I had to be there for her. We had to get back. "I'm going to figure out where we are, and then I'm finding a way home. You with me, Stranger?"

He tilted his head in disapproval of the nickname, but stood up too. "All right. Lead the way, Grace."

Chapter 5

If I wanted answers, I needed to find people, so I closed my eyes and looked. Below us were hundreds of life sources. Auras laughing and sleeping and flirting their day away. A small town lived down there, a thousand souls at least. Maybe more. But I didn't need to go down there to find life. There were people on deck, swaying and playing just out of hearing reach. I opened my eyes and took in the physical difference. We were alone and yet in a small blind spot of the deck. I stepped to the corner and peered over, and the length of the ship came into full view. A small town could live here. A couple whispered to each other as they enjoyed the seclusion of a small alcove, but behind them kids were playing jump rope while their parents read by the sunlight. I hadn't heard it before, as shocked as I had been waking up here, but now if I listened carefully, there was laughter mixed with the crash of the waves.

Every step on that ship swayed not only my body but my understanding of society. If I hadn't written a twenty as the beginning to each year on my dates, I would have sworn we were deep in another time. Perhaps this was some themed party. Mom did that at her museum sometimes…regency tea times, renaissance fairs. The people were still too far away to get concrete details, but they weren't sporting the usual jeans and T-shirt look. Not one pair of yoga pants in the mix. That alone was unusual. No, these women wore thick dresses that draped down to their ankles, with wide brimmed hats to protect against the sun.

My brain seemed to work on repeat. I wanted answers but kept getting stuck. I wanted to know where I was, if Dinah was okay, how to get back home, but instead all I could coherently think was *how is this possible?* The last I remembered, dark shadowy fingers had been coming at me, burning through metal and strangling my head. Somehow I'd gotten here.

I had to get back home. "Do you think the ship's headed to America?" I asked. "Mom's going to kill me if I call from Australia or something. There's no way I can explain my way out of this. On the bright side, maybe Dad will forget about the missing tablet."

"Huh?"

"Nothing. I'm rambling. I just need to find someone with a phone so I can call my parents and…." I made a face. "Explaining this is going to take a while. Hey, Stranger, any ideas on how to explain our current situation to our parents without either of us ending up in therapy?"

"I'm guessing 'who are you?' wouldn't win any points," he said matter-of-factly.

I glanced at him through the corner of my eye. "Can't remember your parents either? What can you remember?"

"Nada. It's a clean slate up here." He tapped his dusty blond hair. He seemed to be taking it better than me, and I couldn't decide if it was more admirable or disconcerting. On the one hand, well played, dude. But on the other, ten minutes ago we'd both been in Cheyenne, Wyoming. Now we were in the middle of the ocean. There were definitely some missing details in there somewhere. Shouldn't he be freaking out twice as much as me? At least as much? Maybe he acted so calm because he remembered less. I knew my family, what had happened, and what I'd lose if I didn't make it back home. How much could one claim to lose when there's no memory of it left? When Stranger knocked me out of the vacuum zone, he must have gotten sucked in and somehow ended up here. When the shadowy thing reached out and grabbed me, I ended up here too. But Dinah was nowhere in sight. Did that mean she was safe, or that something even worse had happened to her? And why did one of us remember while the other didn't?

The deck spread out into a wide opening, bigger than a basketball field. Despite the lazy afternoon, both men and women were dressed up like it was a party. The men wore layers of white clothing, button-up shirts, vests, and even loosened cravats, as if they wanted to be formal but still survive the sun's strength. The women wore dresses…long dresses with skirts that kissed the floor, while lace and delicate floral stitching danced along the fabrics. Most women wore their hair pinned in puffed piles above their heads.

I walked up to a group of three gentlemen and interrupted their conversation. "Excuse me, sorry to interrupt, but can anyone tell me where this ship is headed?"

"Liverpool," one of the men said with an English accent. He stood taller than the rest and looked older. There was an air of nobility in the way he held his chin which surpassed his friends.

Liverpool. Well, that was not going to be easy to explain. "Does anyone have a cell I can borrow?" They blinked at me. "No bars on the ocean, I'm guessing? Darn. Well, there has to be a phone on ship I can use to make a call, right?"

"There's a radio operator on deck," the noble-looking man said. "An inquiry office on the starboard side of the ship. You can leave a message at the desk there and they'll take it down to the operators." He gave me a polite smile and returned his attention to his friends.

I frowned and turned back to Stranger. "People today still use radios on ships? I guess that makes sense." He shrugged, which wasn't helping. I mean, sure, I could swallow radios on deck...pretty sure that was a thing. But the way the people dressed? The nice clothes, long sleeves, and so many layers of clothing they had to be a sweaty mess inside? It was just so...antique, but without the fading. Quite the dedication to the themed party in this weather. Was it everyone or just the people on deck?

"Come on." I nodded at Stranger to follow me and went to ask someone a little less dedicated to their roles.

"Grace! I thought you said you weren't feeling well and wanted to stay below deck!" A man jogged up to us, waving for attention, with slick combed back hair and a Superman steel jaw. I paused dead in my tracks. He knew my name. He knew me. He...the man slowed down. "Oh, sorry," he said. "Thought you were someone else." And he did a quick spin back to his chair.

"Who?" I asked.

He cringed and turned back with an embarrassed grin. "Ah, my friend. She looks kind of like you from a distance. Sorry, name's Preston Prichard." He held out his hand.

"Penelope Grace," I said, and shook it.

"Two Graces who look alike. That's quite the coincidence." He laughed and looked at Stranger. "And you are?"

"Confused," Stranger said, as if commenting on the weather.

I coughed. "Uh, we're lost. Can you tell us where we can make a call?"

Preston blinked at us. "You can send a telegram. Just go to the inquiry office on the—"

"Starboard side of the ship." I nodded, and tried to hide a disappointed sigh. "I remember now. Thanks."

He nodded. "You really look like Miss Grace. It's incredible." With a shake of the head, he left.

I blinked at him, my mind racing. The name was familiar. Preston Prichard. Where had I heard that before? "Stranger, does that guy seem...?"

But Stranger nodded behind me. "Is it just me or are those people staring at us?" he asked.

I turned. A group of three women was looking me up and down with faces I had become familiar with in my two years of high school. The look that said *she's seriously wearing that?* Seeing that their staring had been spotted, one of the girls gestured for us to come over. *Oh goody*, I thought, *this will be fun*. And yet, a quick scan of their auras showed no signs of malice. In fact, one of them wore an aura of clear, healthy orangey-red. Her confidence seemed to spike when she smiled at me as we walked over.

"My dear," she said, offering me a seat beside her. Her accent implied she was American. "Please clear up a note of contention between us. My friends believe your clothes were stolen and you were forced to wear your brother's clothing as you search for the thief."

"My what?" I gaped.

"We're not related," Stranger argued.

The woman didn't seem particularly interested, however, as she kept talking. "I personally believe that you are risking the wrath of social protocol in support of women's rights."

"Women's...." I glanced down. "Because my jeans are baggy? I don't think that's something we have to fight about."

The woman laughed. "It shouldn't be! So silly that women *must* wear dresses. Surely there are bigger issues in the world than the suffrage, and yet fight for it we must."

"Oh, not again." One of the other ladies groaned. "Theo, give it a rest."

"Only when we can vote," she insisted.

"Okay." Stranger's hand twitched like he wanted to raise his hand. "I'm confused again. Women don't wear pants?"

"Only women working in factories, and even then it's considered degrading," the first lady, Theo apparently, explained. "Why should working women be treated with less respect?"

"Right...." I nodded because that seemed like the only right thing to do in the situation. I kept my jaw from dropping from the rush of *uhhhh*.

"Forgive me. I've forgotten my manners in my excitement," Theo said. "I'm Theodate Pope."

Now that name *was* familiar. Historical. Theodate Pope Riddle was one of the first female architects. My mom had done a temporary exhibit about her at the museum. This wasn't just a themed party. They were in character. But my sister was MIA and my patience was wearing thin. "Okay, listen." I stood up and looked down at the women. "I get it. It's a...themed ship adventure thing. That's great, sounds super fun and all, but could someone just please be straight for a second? I need to contact my parents in Wyoming. What's the quickest way I can do that?"

"I'm afraid the only thing you can do is send a telegram—"

I waved her suggestion aside, "I know, but it's the twenty-first century. There's got to be a quicker way to tell my parents I haven't been kidnapped or...well, as far as I know I haven't been kidnapped."

The ladies looked at each other and mouthed *twenty-first century?*

Stranger leaned in and whispered in my ear. "Are you sure you got the year right?"

"Yeah. I didn't forget what year it is," I snapped back. "Sorry," I added when I remembered he probably had.

"Sweetheart." Theo leaned forward and grabbed my shoulder with soft, gloved fingers. "It's 1915."

"Like I said, I get that you are all pretending it's the past, themed adventure...I got it, okay? But I don't know how I got here, so will someone please...." My voice caught in my throat. Everything was so overwhelming that, for a moment, I struggled to keep my calm. Theo's fingers tightened in firm support on my shoulder, but it felt condescending. Beside me, Stranger tapped my elbow in comfort. His touch reminded me of the stability of the walls, something to catch me when I stumbled. I tried again. "Can someone please tell me what's going on?"

"Penny," Stranger said, "Can I talk to you in private?" He gave me a significant look as he led me away from the group. I wanted to argue, to keep leaning on the women until they admitted it was all a joke, but didn't have the strength to pull against Stranger. The ladies looked at us like we were crazy, which I thought kind of unnecessary, considering they were the ones who wouldn't break character. *Do you see any cameras around, ladies? Then maybe help a girl out every once in a while!* "Penny," Stranger whispered once we were out of hearing, "I think it might actually be 1915."

I sighed and grabbed him by the shoulders. I tried for a sarcastically sympathetic look, but he towered over me by a good three or four inches, and that look lost something in translation when I was straining up to look him in the eye. "Okay, I'm letting your last comment slide because you're having memory issues, but it's 2017. You're implying time travel exists, which is as ridiculous as…." As maybe waking up on a ship after a weird shadowy thing knocks you out in some random guy's basement? Is it any worse than that? I cursed and Stranger nodded. Now, he could pull off a decent false sympathetic look. His eyebrows furrowed together just right, but his lips were tight as he tried to hold back a smirk. "It's 1915," I whispered.

"On the bright side, looks like your parents aren't freaking out that you're gone, seeing as they haven't been born yet."

"Oh geez." A wave of instability washed over me. I turned nauseous and leaned over, hands on my knees. The air turned thin. I couldn't breathe. For a moment, I thought I was having a panic attack. I couldn't be in 1915. It was impossible. But then the air turned empty, thin and unnatural, as if something was sucking more than just the oxygen out. Just like it had at Stranger's house.

Chapter 6

"Okay, you're freaking out now." Stranger stepped closer and gave my back an awkward pat. "It's all good. We'll figure this out. Just breathe."

"I'm not...freaking out," I gasped between breaths as my nausea faded. "There's something...in the air." I almost said *in my head*. "I've felt it before." That afternoon. We were all in this mess because I'd investigated that feeling. Maybe if we found it again, it would take us back. "Follow me."

I ran down the deck. Okay, I freaking booked it down that deck like it was 1915 and I was not supposed to be there. It wasn't a short deck either...it took a while to reach the edge. My lungs screamed because of so many days of skipping out on gym, but the adrenaline kept me going. The feeling slipped from view but I refocused my abilities, sharpening my inner sight. Below me, auras showed the movements of people...blues and greens and purples glowing throughout the ship. Next to me, Stranger's aura held bright; such a dominant yellow color. The kind of yellow that reminded me of the way the sun felt against my skin on the first day of spring, when the year was still full of fresh starts and possibilities. But the emptiness had left.

Wait, no. There it was. I turned with the feeling and stepped toward it.

"Whoa." Stranger said. He grabbed my elbow. "Okay, let's pay attention to where we're going, shall we?"

I blinked and the colors faded into the physical. Two more steps and I'd have walked right into the railing. I closed the distance and leaned over the metal, searching through the depths. The sea was so still it might as well have been glass. But the emptiness, it was somewhere out there, in the ocean. Just out of my reach. I couldn't even spot the source. No hole there, no gap or leak like when the vault-like door had opened in Stranger's basement. Just splattered pulses coming from somewhere under the waves.

A thought came to me that sent a shiver up my spine. I immediately tried to dismiss it, but somehow couldn't shake the sensation. Because the emptiness energy hadn't originated in the waters. I had felt it *on* the ship, which meant it had moved. Like it had jumped into the waters to hide from me and now lurked like a cat on the prowl, waiting for the prey to turn their back, to relax before the attack. It watched me now. I knew it.

But no. It was just energy, and energy didn't have a mind of its own. It was just the result of a conscious mind's efforts. Perhaps it was residual energy from the basement and got carried onto this ship with us.

"Well," I whispered, "there goes plan B."

Stranger looked at me with furrowed eyebrows as he tried to understand. "Is this part of the freak out?"

I gave a half laugh at his expression. "Sorry, no. I thought I'd found a trail back home, but I was wrong."

"You got an idea and figured out it was wrong in that short of a time? How?" He waved his hands around. "Nothing has happened. You didn't talk to anyone or look at anything, literally because you had your eyes closed half the time. I feel like I'm missing something here."

"No. You're not. It was just a dumb idea. I tend to have those sometimes, but I worked it through in my head and realized it was lame." I tried for an innocent face, but couldn't quite remember how it worked so I looked back at the ocean. This situation was weird enough, but at least for right now, Stranger was an outcast with me. If I told him, chances were he'd react just like everyone else…play it off as a joke or treat me like I was something strange or wrong. Like Dinah and her great wall of spiritual defense just in case I decided to poke around in her secrets. Like I would do something like that.

But my lie didn't faze Stranger. A hint of a smile flickered passed his pale blue eyes. "A girl trying to convince someone she gets dumb ideas…. I'm not buying it." He folded his arms across his chest and raised an eyebrow at me. "You're keeping something to yourself."

"What could I possibly keep to myself? You were with me the entire time. You saw everything I did."

"Then you made a connection I didn't, which brings us back to me wondering what you're hiding."

I narrowed my eyes at him. "Would Sherlock just explain everything to Watson, or would he let Watson figure it out for himself?"

"No idea." He smirked, but then his face turned serious. "Listen, I don't know who I am. I don't know where or, apparently, *when* I am. But I'd like to know who I'm lost with."

I hesitated. *Maybe he is different,* I thought. *Maybe he wouldn't think it was weird.* But, just losing his memory was no reason to believe he'd lost any instinct on what people should and should not be able to do. At the end of the day, that's what my abilities were. Just something people shouldn't be able to do. "I had a feeling. I acted on impulse but was wrong. It's nothing special."

He narrowed his eyes at me for a moment, but then relaxed. A note of disappointment dinged in my core. It was always a bit of a knock in the gut when I met someone who might be able to see the real me, and then watched as they decide to accept the façade. But then again, what kind of friendship would I want with him? It was his fault I was here in the first place. His call for help had sent us down this crazy rabbit hole. I didn't owe him any explanation, and I certainly didn't need his friendship.

Behind Stranger, a young woman stepped onto the deck. She held her shawl close despite the strong sun. Her pinned-up hair swayed against the breeze, but loose strands tickled her face as she walked along the deck. Guess we weren't the only restless ones on the ship. I was about to ask Stranger what he thought we should do next when another pulse of emptiness overtook the air. It knocked the wind out of me, but I regained my composure before Stranger got suspicious again. Wow, that was a strong force. Powerful, perhaps, but enough to knock me a century into the past?

Stranger shifted his weight and nervous energy radiated from his skin. "What's up?" I asked.

He opened his mouth, but gave an embarrassed chuckle and shook his head. I widened my eyes, nodding at him, coaxing encouragement. "If I tell you something, will you promise not to think I'm crazy?" Stranger asked.

"I can manage that. What's up?"

"I keep thinking we're here for a reason. We couldn't have just been plopped down. I feel like we're here to…." He scratched his chin. "We're supposed to save someone. I can feel it in my bones."

"Save someone? No one's in danger. There's no one to rescue," I said. "Except, you know, us."

"I'm 100% certain that's why we're here." His eyes were wide and pleading, an attempt at the puppy dog look, but his jawline went tight, unmoving. Did he expect me to argue or something? Or was he arguing with himself?

"Okay," I said. "So? What does that mean? We save someone, and then whatever it was that brought us here will take us back?"

He shrugged. "Maybe?"

"Well, I mean, that sounds a tad bit idealistic, but okay. Let's give it a try. Who are we saving?"

He blinked at me. "Um…."

"Yeah." I sighed and leaned against the railing. "Square one is an Everest in itself."

He laughed. "You act like you've been in this position before."

"Square one? Spent my whole life there. Of course, these particular circumstances are new." I tapped an impatient beat on the railing with the palm of my hands, clicking along with my tongue. "Okay, so if we're supposed to save someone, don't you think there'd be a sign leading the way? A direction? Anything?"

The young lady with the shawl walked back into view. She glanced at us but looked down as soon as I returned the gaze. She looked a touch green. Would it count as heroic to give her some Dramamine? Unless….

I took a quick scan of her emotional state. Her aura seemed jittery and tight. She wasn't just seasick, she was on edge, nervous, helpless. Her insides were jumping to do something, anything just to be safe. I dug a little deeper for details. The emotions hit me like a brick, but I didn't fight them. The phrase "It's too late" kept ringing in my head, as if she had repeated it so many times it had settled on her skin. An ache the color of lifeless blood brewed below her stomach. She was afraid.

"Stranger," I said, "I don't know about any great heroics, but I think that girl over there could use some help."

Stranger turned around. "That girl? She looks fine."

"Trust me." I straightened my shirt and walked over. The lady had

43

to be in her early twenties, with ash brown hair struggling out of her pins and a long no-frills dress flickering with the ship's movement. At first she tried to ignore me, but gave me a polite smile when it became clear I was heading straight for her. Stranger kept up and didn't say a word to question my plan, for which I was grateful. I didn't have an answer. Only a feeling. But then I got close enough to see her features. Her skin was paler, but her eyes, the cheeks, the way her hair curled like a curtain around her eye—

"She looks like you," Stranger whispered.

I closed the distance with new determination. There were so many questions right now, and I had a feeling this girl was the answer to all of them. Perhaps we could help each other. "Hey," I said to the lady. "Name's Penny. What's yours?"

"Grace," she said. "I didn't mean to stare. My friend told me I had a doppelganger on board. I had to see for myself."

"Preston Prichard, am I right?" Stranger asked.

"Yes," she said. "I thought he was making it all up at first. Today's the last day before we land in Liverpool, and I don't think he liked the idea of me missing out on all the last hoorahs." She tilted her head as she looked at me. "Definitely some similarities though. Looks like he wasn't playing tricks after all." She tried for a careless giggle, and a soft waft of carefree yellow struggled to survive against the almost overwhelming blood red. Although the mixture of colors was new, I recognized the struggle to hide, to pretend the bad things weren't there. But what was there to be afraid of? The ship was sailing on a clear day. The deck was a place of laughter and celebration.

But it was 1915. World War I had started last year. Maybe not every country was involved yet, but this ship was heading to Liverpool. England already had a high death toll. German submarines patrolled the seas, armed and ready to torpedo. I glanced out at the sea. So still, reflecting the sky like glass and hiding whatever lie underneath. "Are you heading back or leaving home?" I asked.

"Going home. I live in Scotland," she said.

The conversation trailed off. Stranger gave me a curious look but I waved him aside. Dots shuddered to connect in my head, and yet I needed more info.

"How long were you gone from home?" I asked.

"Just visiting family in America. After the war broke out…." She picked at her long sleeve. "The United States hopes to avoid the war.

My family invited me for a month, but I think they hoped I'd stay for good where it was safe. But Scotland is my home."

"I've never been."

"It's beautiful."

I nodded. Ah, yes, there it was, that moment when I remembered I had no idea what I was doing. Right on time. It was math class, soccer, and pretty much everything I've ever done before all over again. I needed more to work with before I could get anywhere. I glanced at Grace to check that she wouldn't be looking my way anytime soon before I closed my eyes for a quick scan. I narrowed in on the ache near her stomach, the settled energy coursing within her spirit. Yes, red dominated the energies. Fear, not just for the journey through dangerous waters, but for what might come afterwards. Questions appeared in my mind as if her energies had embroidered them into place within the fabric of imagination. Would the war reach her home? Would it take loved ones away from her as it had already to so many? Would she be able to support herself with her dressmaking?

Ooh, there's something. The red associated with dressmaking was softer than the blood red fears of war. Like silk. Dangerous, risky, but intoxicating. It was more than just a plan, it was a dream. Something she feared would never come to be. But how could I help her there? I knew nothing about this woman's future. But if there was one thing I did understand, it was shaky confidence. Maybe a pat on the back would be enough, and then the energy would send us back home. "I have to say, that's a gorgeous dress. Where did you get it?"

"This?" She pointed at the brown. "Honey, these are my lazy clothes. I made it myself. Just something comfortable for those days when I'm not feeling well. If you like this, you should see some of my other dresses."

"I'd love to. Do you sell them?"

The red softened into a pleased blue. "I'm hoping to open a dressmaking shop back home. Do you really like them?"

"Yeah. I mean, as you can see, I have no idea what's cool to wear in 1915, but you make it look good."

She chuckled. "I've never heard anyone speak like you."

"Bet you've never seen anyone dress like me either."

"No," she agreed. "Perhaps when we land, I'll get your measurements and make you a dress so gorgeous you'll never want to wear pants again."

45

"That would be quite the dress," I admitted. Something stirred in my peripheral. Rich greens and analytical blues. Without thinking, I glanced at the source, deep below the still sea and far away, but coming closer. I frowned.

"I have a necklace just like that."

I froze, realizing I had grabbed my penny necklace in my concentration. Grace slipped her hand to her neck and pulled out a long chain. Just like mine. A penny pendant fell into view, and she held it out to compare. I obliged, my heart rushing. "Made in the same year too," I whispered.

Stranger leaned in. "Do all pennies have that notch on the top?"

"No they don't," Grace said. "This is an old family heirloom. The first one to wear it was my grandfather, who fought in the American Civil War. Guess not even a penny can escape war unscratched. He gave it to me a few years back, said it was lucky. Do you know where the notch came from on yours?"

"Same," I said, but I could hardly tear my eyes from the two identical pennies. A mirror image couldn't have created better copies. No, it was too surreal. No way my suspicions could be true. "I didn't get your full name," I said.

"Grace French."

My ancestor on my mother's side. The pennies didn't just look the same...they *were* the same. I was talking to my great-great-great-grandma. Which, under any different circumstances would have made for a pretty fantastic evening. I remembered the stories Mom had shared during those rare family dinners. Grace French was awesome. She had started her own dress making business in Scotland and lived independently until she died at the age of ninety-five. I existed because this woman had learned how to support herself, and eventually a family, through hard economic times. She'd had kids who kept pursuing their dreams, and on and on and on, until my mom became director of her own little museum and had Dines and me.

But that was not why my heart pounded, why adrenaline shocked my system. Because Grace French was only on one ship in the year of 1915. After which, she vowed never to travel by sea again for fear the same horrors might attack her.

"What day is it?" I asked.

"May seventh."

"Time?"

46

"Oh, I don't know. Two perhaps?"

The colors in the sea, the ones that steered closer with each second...now I knew what they were. Men in a submarine. On May 7, between 2:05 and 2:10, a torpedo hit. Eighteen minutes later, the entire ship was under water. Out of the 1,960 people aboard the ship, only 767 had survived. Despite daily lifeboat training, constant surveillance of the sea by crew, and enough life jackets to go around, the survival rate on this ship was 37.7%. All because a German submarine had caught sight of the great, *safe* Lusitania.

I gasped and grabbed Stranger by the sleeve of his shirt. "You were right. Everyone's in danger. This ship sinks today." His eyes widened and he opened his mouth to answer, but I didn't have time to chat. If it was "around" two now; exactly how much time did we have to warn the captain? Captain William Thomas Turner. "Where's the captain's deck?" I snapped at my great-great-great-grandma. Grace pointed and I ran.

All those history books Mom had made me read, all those evenings we had pored over our family history, and now here I was, living it, and all I had were numbers. I was running past souls about to be turned into statistics. Names, I realized too late, that I'd read from lists of victims. I'd pored over their tattered letters and obituaries. Never once had I wondered how the Lusitania could have been saved. Never before this second were those names more than just words in a book.

"Hey, you found her!" Preston jogged over with a chuckle, blocking my way. "I told you she looked like you."

"Move," I snapped.

"Whoa." He leaned back. "Is something the matter?"

"She thinks we're in danger." Grace French was out of breath from running after me. "And I know she's not wearing a corset. Please, give me a second to catch my breath."

"We don't have—"

"Don't worry," Preston said. "I spoke to the captain a few hours ago. We're out of dangerous waters."

"Well, either he's lying to keep you calm or he's wrong, because...." Something moved. A long, deathly white scar gashed through the glass-still waters. *Oh, please no.* "That's isn't a torpedo, is it?" I pleaded.

Everyone turned. Grace gasped. And yet fear hadn't settled in. Not yet. The ever-nearing scar was somehow beautiful. I wasn't the only one entranced. We all stood, like spectators in an art museum, studying the artist's swipe of paint and wondering what exactly it meant. Surely it had a different meaning than the ones we saw. One by one and then in whole groups, people went to the rails of the ship. They stood with us and wondered.

And then it disappeared beneath us and no one wondered anymore.

Chapter 7

For a merciful second, nothing happened. The torpedo disappeared. Had it missed? Had the fact that Stranger and I were on the ship somehow changed history?

But then the metal below us screamed. A geyser of water, rope, and shards of steel burst into the sky twice the height of the ship. A lifeboat shattered from the impact even before the water started its rush down. It all happened in slow motion, as if someone had taken the camera and set it on painful. Every drop of seawater immortalized itself in my memory as it towered above us. The group of kids playing jump rope stopped jumping.

The water hit the deck, soaking every passenger to the core. Debris dented the metal floor, missing us by mere feet, but not missing everyone. A wave of water rushed down at me, slamming me off my feet. I gasped as the wave subsided. "Stranger!" I sputtered, coughing.

He was leaning over the rail, chest over the edge, but his grip on the metal kept him on deck. He righted himself and jumped away, breathing in gasps, whether from the water or from fear, I couldn't tell. Both probably. "You okay?" he asked.

I nodded, then froze. "Where's Grace?" We looked around. Nothing. "Grace!" I screamed. "Grace French, answer me!"

"Help."

There she was, hardly stirring on the ground ten feet away from us, an overturned chair collapsed on her back. Stranger and I ran to her side and tossed the chair off her. "Are you okay?" I asked.

"I think so." She let Stranger help her to her feet. "Where's Preston?" Stranger and Grace called out his name, but I couldn't get my voice to work. I'd read Grace's journal entries. I knew what haunted her the most. One second her best friend was by her side. Suddenly, he was gone forever.

One minute after the explosion, and already it was too late for Preston Prichard.

A second, muted explosion echoed through the hole in the middle of the ship. The ship lurched starboard. Stranger grabbed my arm before I lost balance. For a moment, we all got a clear view of the depths that promised to consume us whole. "Life jackets," Grace whispered. "We need life jackets."

I gaped at the view. People were already streaming onto the deck from below…the ones who'd survived the initial impact, at least. Slowly, a thought fought through the muted numbness of my shocked brain. Life jackets. They were all located in the passengers' rooms. "Go back to…." I stopped. Grace was gone. "Where'd she go?" I went to the tips of my toes to see over the crowd, but she was gone.

The consequences hit like falling debris. Grace French was supposed to be in her room reading when the torpedo hit. She grabbed her life jacket in seconds. When she reached the deck, she was strapped and immediately put in a lifeboat. But because there was a girl who looked like her on the ship, because of me, she had left the safety of her room. She was far away from her life jacket. And if she died, the last four generations of my family would be erased.

"Stranger, do you see Grace French?" I asked.

He shook his head. "Please tell me you two looking the same and having the same penny is just some crazy time traveling coincidence."

"She's my great-great-great grandmother." I studied his reaction with a desperate plea. Realistically, if he wanted to survive, Stranger needed to get a life jacket and grab a seat in a lifeboat before they were all out. There was no reason why he should stay and linger behind with me, searching to undo the mistake that might cost my family their very existence. His shoulders slumped as he stared at the lifeboats. Already people were climbing in, ready to launch. "Let's make sure she gets on a boat," he said, and tore his eyes away. I could have cried in relief, but there wasn't enough time.

"Come on," I yelled. "She said she was after a life jacket. There might be some up there."

50

The walk to the crowd was strange and surreal. The combined starboard and forward list created an uphill journey on slick metal. People's voices shook from the adrenaline as they struggled to maintain social protocol despite the ever increasing urge to shove everyone out of the way and fight tooth and nail for their chances of survival. That stifled blood-red fear I'd seen in Grace now screamed from every soul we passed. The deck was crowded. A vent burst near me and I screamed, braced for another explosion or wave to attack, but instead saw a face. A man gave me a quick glance before tumbling out, coughing. There were more behind him.

The deck was crowded in minutes. Minutes. How many had passed? How many were left? Not enough. That's all I knew.

"I see her," Stranger said. He grabbed my arm so we wouldn't lose each other as he pushed his way through.

She looked stuck, not physically but mentally. Like she didn't know what to do next. She looked at us and blinked. "The life jackets are in our rooms. There's none up here."

"Then we need to go down and grab them," I said, but she shook her head.

"It's been flooded. There's no going anywhere."

"Those lifeboats aren't launching," Stranger noted. "What's keeping them?"

"The ship's going too fast," Grace said. "Even though the engines are down, it's still slowing. If the lifeboats hit the water at this speed, they'd shatter. We have to wait."

The whole ship shuddered as another explosion mangled the ship. "Boiler rooms," I remembered. "Water in the boiler rooms overheated them, created pressure. More holes."

"This was supposed to be the safe ship," Grace argued, as if the fact might reverse the attack. "People changed their plans to be on this ship. Germans can't reach us."

"That's why the Germans attacked," I said. "It was a challenge for them. And there are US citizens on the boat too, so they ticked off multiple countries. America will go to war after this."

"Oh well, that just makes it all worth it," she snapped. Strangely, I heard my own sarcasm in her tone.

"No. It doesn't," Stranger agreed. "I could have sworn we were meant to save them."

Behind Grace, a new lifeboat started to load. "There," I said. "Go.

Now. Get in the lifeboat and you should be fine." Hopefully.

"Right," Grace nodded, and started walking. "Let's go."

Stranger stepped to follow, but they both paused when I stayed still. I couldn't get my legs to move. Lifeboats were finally starting to lower. They maneuvered through the debris filled sea away from the sinking ship. Away from where Stranger and I landed after an involuntary time travel. If I got on one of those boats, maybe I wouldn't sink, but I surely would never make it home again. Not without that dark void energy's help....

I could find it. Maybe I was the only one who could. And if I could find it, maybe I could at least prevent adding two more deaths to the statistics. Maybe time was fixed, like in the more depressing time-traveling films. And maybe Stranger and I couldn't save anyone from a different era. It didn't matter now. As the ship tilted and people barked orders or jumped to the nearest lifeboat, some making the distance, others crashing into the sea below, I had one not-so-heroic thought...I would not die here. Those shadows had brought me here, and they would take me back.

"I'll be right there," I told Grace. "Go. I promise. I'll be fine."

She frowned but didn't argue. Why should she risk another second on a stranger with her cheekbones? I don't think I properly breathed until she settled into a seat. Safe. She was safe.

Stranger, on the other hand, stayed by my side. "You have a plan," he guessed.

"Not really," I admitted. "Thing is, we didn't travel by ship to get here. We time-traveled, right?"

"Right."

"So what if the only way home is still here somewhere? What if we get on a lifeboat and lose our one chance to go home?"

"Who cares about going home?" he asked. "Penny, we haven't saved anyone. People need our help."

"The ship is sinking, Stranger! What do you want us to do, super-glue it back together? We can't even get my great-great-great grandmother a life jacket. There's nothing we can do here!"

"How about keep people calm! Help them get their life jackets on. Something!"

"This ship is full to the brim with helping hands, okay? That's the problem. We'd just be in the way, and we don't belong here!"

"I can't believe you're actually suggesting we turn our back on—"

"We've got a small window to go back home, to the right time, and if we miss it, I'll never be able to help my sister! She was out cold, Stranger! The last thing I remember is trying to protect her because she wasn't moving, and now I'm not there! She could need serious medical attention, and I'm the only one who knows where she is!" My shaking fingers clawed through my hair to keep the chaos in my mind under control. Stranger didn't look convinced. There were far more people on the ship. Dinah was nothing to him. Both of our directions were just as hopeless as the other.

One of the lifeboats started to lower. A boy, maybe four years younger than me, raced to the rails of the ship and jumped over. Against the odds, he landed feet first in the boat. Others were not so successful.

"Listen, Stranger," I tried again. "It's women and children first. That's protocol in emergencies, which means that if we stay out here long enough, we'll be forced onto a lifeboat whether you like it or not. You'll take some poor kid's spot who was supposed to survive. Are you willing to take that chance?"

Stranger's stubborn face fell. But it wasn't just his gut that ached at the realization. My words hit me hard too. I hadn't thought of that before. I had just said what I needed to get Stranger to back off. But it was the sobering truth. We weren't heroes in this story. In fact, we ran the risk of being victims. Or worse, survivors. Knowing that we had taken someone else's place. I might not be able to make the past better, but I refused to make it worse.

"So what's your plan?" Stranger asked. He looked at me like he was ready to obey. Like he had this entire time. I hadn't realized it before. Either the stakes had been too low or I didn't have time to notice. But now....

Stranger wasn't just asking me what the plan was. He was asking how I would save him. I didn't have a plan. I couldn't save him. I grasped at invisible straws, hoping that the emptiness, which was out of reach before, had somehow gotten closer. Or maybe that it would come back to pick us up, to save us. After all, it had put us here. I couldn't explain my plan to Stranger. I didn't want him to know our lives depended on hope and hope alone.

"Just trust me," I said. He opened his mouth to press for more details that I didn't have, so I raised my finger to quiet him and closed my eyes.

The easy energy around the ship had hardened since the collision.

There was no time to hide the fear or joke to ease the tension. The dangers were too real. The screaming metal drowned out any hopeful inner voices. A violent red energy shook around me, the way their bodies moved on full alert. The whole ship, every passenger and employee, struggled against the ever-growing impulse to barrel through the crowd, push down the people in their way, and fight for a lifeboat. Some managed to keep control better than others.

I ignored the screaming auras and kept looking. The last time I had felt the energy, it had been at sea. Dots of red clustered the ocean as people clung to fallen debris to stay above water. I cringed as a few of the dots flickered out like starved flames.

Almost worse than the failing red as people drowned around me was a sickly lemon yellow coming from farther out at sea, where a large group of people deep underwater celebrated their victory. The Germans were shouting for joy.

There! A rip right through the energetic world, like torn canvas. Pulses of shadowy tendrils leaked through, so much slower than the incoming flood. My heart almost jumped out of my chest in surprise. It was close by! I grabbed Stranger's arm and pulled him with me as I went to the rails. I could see it…it was just overboard. All we had to do was….

Ah, right. I forgot. I didn't know how to get home, even with the energy.

Oh, Penny. Of course you know. It's as easy as peace in the dark.

The voice was hardly a whisper, too vague to be described. And it had come from within my mind. There was something familiar about it. The same way a nightmare might feel familiar the second time around.

But before I had time to question the voice, a scream shocked my eyes open. It wasn't the fact of the scream…there had been a lot of screaming the last few minutes. Rather, it was the familiarity of the voice. Grace French. Her lifeboat tilted precariously as they struggled to loosen it from the ship. Stranger and I watched in helpless horror as it capsized and my great-great-great grandmother disappeared under water.

54

Chapter 8

There were so many gone in that moment. Red auras getting pulled down by debris or the current. Stranger and I took one look at each other before we both jumped over the railing. The cool water hit me like a burst of energy. The salt stung my eyes, but I had to keep them open. To my left, a man's jacket fluttered like failing wings. The man seemed passed out and he sank fast. I grabbed his leg and pulled against the tide. He was heavy and dead weight. I struggled just to keep from going down with him, but I couldn't let go. It was one thing to stand on deck and convince myself I couldn't help, but it was quite another to have my fingers wrapped around a beating pulse.

So I tugged and I pulled, fighting through the water as my lungs begged for breath. My fingers touched the cool surface for one precious second before the waves pulled us back down. The beating pulse grew weaker from within my grip. My lungs screamed now, and I couldn't help thinking, *If I only let go, I could breathe again.*

Mercy relieved us of the wave's pull and I struggled to the surface. The salty fresh air tasted sweeter than fruit as I gasped. I yanked the unconscious man up with me, using my body as a floating device to get at least his head some air. Hands reached out and grabbed the weight from me, pulling him into a stable lifeboat. Hot tears mixed with the cold sea on my cheeks as I cried in relief. But then the hands reached for me too, heroes of the day, survivors lending a hand as they gripped the shoulders of my clothes and sought for a good enough hold to haul me up. To take the seat of someone else.

"No!" I shoved away from the ship. They hadn't expected that, to say the least, and stood there, stunned, still bent down and reaching out as I went under again.

Stranger. Where was Stranger? I got out of arm's length from the lifeboat and resurfaced, spinning around as fast as the heavy water would let me. Where had he gone? "Stranger!" I screamed. Ocean water rushed into my mouth and I coughed. "Stranger!"

Nothing.

Something brushed against my leg, a light flutter. I caught one last deep inhale before letting myself sink back down. Once again the salt stung, but I kept my eyes open. The attacker was the jump rope the little boys had been playing with earlier. I waved it aside. And then... there he was. Struggling against debris. Was he stuck?

I swam closer. No. He wasn't stuck...Grace French was. The sinking lifeboat clung to her dress as if in one last desperate act to save itself. The wood caught against the hem of her dress, pulling her down with it. Stranger tugged but to no avail. They had both been under since the jump, and neither looked well. Grace's fingers slipped from the hem of her dress, floating to her side as she started to fade. Each of Stranger's efforts seemed to have less energy than the one before.

I swam to his side and grabbed a hold of the dress. Two yanks with double the effort just barely budged the fabric. I swam down closer for a better view of the problem and saw the fish-hook shaped wood blocking our attempts. I motioned for Stranger to push down and guided the torn dress hem out and away. I pulled Grace closer and wrapped her arm around me. Stranger did the same on the other side and together we swam.

Somehow I had expected Grace to be lighter than the unconscious gentleman, but layers upon layers of her dress had turned her petite frame into an anvil. Up we swam. At one point Stranger started to fade, his arm slipping just an inch under my own. I grabbed a fistful of his sleeve and stared at the surface above us. It wasn't much further, but I wouldn't be able to go another foot alone. Despite my kicking legs and pumping arms, we slipped down. Even as my lungs struggled on whether or not to risk a breath, hopelessness burst in my chest in a need to sob.

Oh, Penny. The voice was clear as day despite the echoing water. *Why do you let these people weigh you down? The way out is in your soul. Perhaps ignored, but never gone.*

56

I ignored the voice and pinched Stranger's arm hard. A kick. Another inch up. Then another. Air washed over us and I was pleased to count three gasps for air at the surface. Grace choked and sputtered and moaned, and I had never heard such relieving signs of life. Stranger's hair dripped down the frame of his face and he blinked at the ship. "Look," he said.

The nose of the ship was all that was left. And there, at the very edge, stood a man with the best view of the tragedy before us. There had been records of this moment in dozens of the survivor's accounts. They all remembered it so clearly…the captain as he disappeared with the last bit of his ship. None of them thought he would survive, and yet he had been one of the rescued. Would be. Already a lifeboat was headed his way.

I looked around for any lifeboats with room to spare. The one that had reached out for me was now full. In my place, Theodate Pope leaned on another in exhaustion. "Over here."

Stranger pointed at a large piece of debris. Possibly a side of the ship, or maybe some flooring. We swam over and untangled ourselves around Grace. She gripped the sides of the debris and pulled herself up before moving over to give us room. But there was only room enough for two.

"After you," Stranger said.

"I'm fine," I argued. "You two went longer without air. I'm sure you're exhausted."

"I saw you drag a full grown man to a lifeboat. Alone. The amount of energy that must have taken…. I'm not being a gentleman here. Who knows when rescue will come? I'm just offering first shift."

Rescue. I sighed at the thought. Ships with enough room to go around. We wouldn't be taking anyone's place this time. We could stop swimming in this declaration of war.

And leave me out here, all alone in the middle of the ocean?

The voice was back. I glanced at Stranger, but he just nodded for me to climb up. If he heard it, he showed no signs. In all the chaos, my mind had thrown out anything that wasn't just plain survival. Now, it came back. The void energy. It was here. And if we left now, our one chance to get back home might leave too. But that wasn't the only disconcerting idea. What if it was that pitch-black energy that spoke to me now? Without a body. And no soul I'd ever seen looked like that, so how did it speak? How did it even think?

57

Wow, the voice said. *What. A. Hypocrite.* A terrible hiss shuddered down my spine, and I realized the voice had sighed.

Everything about that voice, that energy, was wrong. It had baited me, following me home until I convinced Dinah to turn around. It then led me to that basement, and stole me from my home. And now it was swaying in the waves right below us. A great magnetic pull tingled the tips of my toes. The strangest thing was a thought that popped in my head, spoken in my voice. That if I reached out and called to that energy, it would respond. Not only that, but it would open up like a great portal and send me right back where I belonged.

"Penny," Stranger said. He tilted his head at me, confused. "Where'd you just go?"

"What?" I blinked. "Yeah, just more tired than I thought, I guess."

"Help will come soon," Grace assured me.

Sometimes help destroys a future. Come on, Penny. You know what to do. The magnetic pull grew on my leg like a playful tug. *Just give it a go. Reach out that hand. Think about home.* The pressure softened as the energy let go. *Or, forget about Dinah. After all, it's a century from now, she's not technically in danger yet. Not even born yet. Surely someone will find her down there. Out cold. You always have the choice to cross your fingers and hope it'll all work out without you.*

Of course, I didn't have a choice. And really, nothing to lose. I kept Stranger in my peripheral as I let one hand slip from the debris. I didn't want him to see me. At first I let the hand just float there, swaying in the water. Perhaps a part of me didn't want to try. Something in my gut screamed that it was wrong, not just unnatural but a trap. *Danger, Penny, danger*, it repeated. And I would have listened but for Dinah. So I stretched my arm out to that void energy below us and closed my eyes.

The connection was instant, like old friends reuniting. The energy bubbled and rose in response to my call. I thought of Dinah, of home, of a stranger's mad scientist basement and a missing tablet. I didn't open my eyes until steam caressed my face. Stranger, Grace, and I looked down at the same time. The surface of the water glistened from the sun, still shining despite the loss around us. Each reflection was deepened by the circle of pitch black swirling beneath us, stealing away the greens and blues of the water. Steam escaped in a perfect rectangle around us, almost like a door.

"Ah...." Grace pointed. "Is that normal when ships sink?"

58

Stranger was already looking at me. I shrugged. "You're kidding," he said, but it wasn't a question. By the peaceful green in his aura, he was actually relieved. He glanced back down at the darkness growing beneath us before asking, "Do you think my memories will come back when we get home?"

"Worth a shot."

"Huh?" Grace asked.

"Listen, Grace." I turned to my great-great-great grandma. "You're going to be fine, okay? More than fine. You are going to start your own business as a dressmaker and become a local legend, okay? You got me?"

"What?"

I smiled. "Trust me. You're gonna be great."

"That's wonderful. Why are you talking like you're saying goodbye?" Grace rushed to say. She waved around. "There aren't exactly a lot of options out here."

"There's one," I said as the depths called me down. "Listen, that's our way out. We're going to be fine, I promise. But yeah, this is goodbye." I slipped my arm to the edge of the debris, ready to let go. "Oh, and whatever you do, don't follow us." I checked with Stranger to make sure he was still okay with this. He nodded, his face hard and tense. "If it doesn't work," I reassured him, "we just swim back up."

He moved his own grip of the debris to just the very edge. One hand fell into the water. Fingers curled around mine as he gripped my hand tight. I gave it a little squeeze in support. We would be fine, I knew it. Okay, my insides were screaming that everything was terribly wrong and please, somebody make it all stop, but I had to believe that was because of the history traumatizing me in real time. It couldn't be because of my only chance home.

"Ready?" Stranger asked.

"Ready." I nodded and we let go.

Chapter 9

I remember falling through the threshold. That moment when my feet slipped through the waters and into something without any sensation at all. No heat, no cooling breeze, just a sliver of emptiness. Then my foot landed on a solid floor. A dry floor. The rest of my body followed, the debris sprinkled sea disappearing into black as my vision went through the strange portal. A cool breeze washed against my face and I blinked as color rushed over me. Brighter than I remembered. Motion-sick greens and suffocating angry reds. Depressed blues so heavy it was a surprise the auras held their shapes. I blinked again. Then again. But the colors never faded away and were too bright for the physical realm to seep through.

I couldn't breathe, as if I were still underwater, still sinking. Air came in quick desperate gasps. I couldn't see...the emotions were too high. The floor swayed underneath me, threatening to ditch me altogether.

A sunshine yellow aura stood beside me, his hand still in mine. "Um...." His aura moved and I could only guess that he looked around. "I admit I don't remember anything, but if this is home then let's go back."

He could see. I squeezed my eyes shut until the pressure gave me a headache before trying again. Nothing but explosive color. "Stranger, I can't see." I gripped his hand tighter and grabbed his arm with my other. "It's all too raw. I can't.... I can't—"

"Whoa, calm down." Stranger grabbed my shoulders. "It's okay. You're hyperventilating. Uh...breathe."

"Oh, gee...thanks! I knew I'd...forgotten something."

He chuckled. "Your sarcasm made the trip just fine. Hey, hey, hey." He wrapped one arm around my back as the other tangled in my hair, pulling me to his chest. I held on tight as I focused on my breathing. *Just slow it down,* I thought. Then I could think of a plan. Stranger's breathing was steady. I listened to it, my ear against his lungs. The colors dimmed with each exhale. My skin tingled as if I was settling back into my body. As if, for a moment, I had been somewhere else.

The sharp greens and reds and yellows faded to grays and browns and blacks. Metal surrounded us in railings and riveted walls. Barrels held months' worth of supplies, stacked on top of each other. The only red came from the rust along the corners. The floor continued to sway.

I groaned as salt air settled in my nose. "Not another ship."

"Yeah." Stranger loosened the hug and leaned back to take a good look at me. "You don't recognize this, right?"

"Right. This is not home."

"Phew," he said. "Cannot be awesome living here."

"I wonder who does."

He was quiet for a second. Even though we technically weren't hugging anymore, he kept the edge of his fingers against my skin. Or maybe I kept my arm by him...I wasn't quite sure which.

"You better?" he asked finally.

"Yeah. Thanks." I tucked a stray hair out of my face, suddenly embarrassed. "Sorry, I just freaked out, I guess."

"You said you couldn't see. Does that happen a lot?"

"Never before." Only that wasn't exactly true, was it? The exploding colors might be new, but the vision loss had happened once before, just for a moment, back at the school. Back before I could see the void energy. Whatever was going on, it all came back to that...thing.

Just one glance at the place told me it wasn't a passenger ship. It wasn't anywhere near the size, yet could still claim the title of ship. The emptiness had been snuffed out like a fire without oxygen, but the door was the same old, rusty thing that brought us out. Just...well, I'd say empty of the emptiness, but I wasn't sure if that made any sense. The gap was gone. That answer would have to do for now.

I flexed the hand that had reached out to the void energy back there. The one that knew exactly what to do to somehow get the energy literally steaming into action as a strange portal through time. How had I done that? Was it really me, or was that voice playing with me, tricking me? Why would it do something like that? I had truly believed going through that portal would have sent us straight back home. I had hoped that there was some notion of sense to everything, even if I couldn't quite see it. But this was too much, too confusing. The voice had implied I would go home. I had trusted it, and it lied to me.

"So, do you have any idea what just happened?" Stranger half-whispered. He wasn't touching me anymore. I couldn't remember which one of us let go, but a part of me wanted to grab his hand again. I was lost, still, and old childhood mantras stuck in my brain. Stick to the buddy system. Hold hands so you don't lose each other. But I stifled the urge. Stranger's arms were up in a disbelieving half shrug/half wave at the completely foreign surroundings. "No wonder you didn't take the time to explain. I mean holy…." But his voice trailed off.

"Actually…." I bit my lip, thinking maybe there were some things he shouldn't know. "I didn't realize this would happen."

"Are you still trying to convince me you just get dumb ideas? You knew exactly where to go, how to escape, and you're right, if we'd gotten on one of those lifeboats, we'd still be stuck there. But…," he glanced around, "we were drowning."

"I know." My voice was steady, which, to be honest, I hadn't expected. I felt like crying, but couldn't quite accept the fullness of my situation. Or perhaps I was just too tired. I had been on a sinking ship just moments ago. I almost died. And now what? A quiet breeze and a setting sun? No more screams. No more tragedy. The transition was too weird. Nothing to connect the two. My brain couldn't keep up. "I honestly don't know what happened, Stranger. I just knew we had to find more—" I was about to say emptiness, but stopped myself. That had been a close call. If I said that, then I'd have to explain how I saw it. Then he'd know what I saw, what I could see. I kind of liked that he trusted me. He respected my advice.

It was naïve, really. He didn't know me. If I were him, I wouldn't blindly follow some kid who claimed to know what they were doing but refused to give any real answers. Maybe he trusted me because he'd lost his memory, like he forgot to be suspicious of people too. But I hadn't done anything wrong. I never deserved the distrust people sent my way once they realized how much I could know. "We had to find that door. Or the place it would appear, anyway. It was like the one in your basement."

"Assume I remember nothing," he said.

I explained what I remembered, how Dinah and I heard the screams, ran into the basement, saved him, and got sucked into that metal door-shaped invention. Maybe I left out some vital bits, like how the energy had pulsed from his house, how following that energy had led me to him, but the story still made sense. At least to me.

"That doesn't make any sense," Stranger said. All right, but to be fair, the confusing bits weren't my fault. "What are you trying to say I am? Some kind of mad scientist?"

I shrugged. "Maybe you just stumbled onto it. Although, it kind of seemed like you knew what the stuff was, at least."

He bent down and half sat against the rusted old railing. He looked down at the metal floor as he digested my story of his past. "So all this was my fault."

"Let's just find our way home, okay? Blame isn't going to get us anywhere. Especially when we don't know all the facts. Don't start feeling guilty just to have it turn out you're only related to a mad scientist or something." What was I doing? Less than an hour ago, I was all for blaming him. Or blaming me. Whichever.

He laughed. "I can't decide if you're great at comforting or absolutely horrible."

I shrugged. "I'm okay with either. Or both."

"So where do you think we are? How did we get here?"

"I don't know," I said as I studied the energetic fields around us. Those same agitated reds and greens came back, but no more black. Whatever had brought us here was long gone. The metal ship felt and looked like every metal ship I'd ever seen. The water was just another sea, cold and still, but solid, real. Unlike the shadows that had brought us here. Did we just use up our only chance? Was this where we'd be stuck forever?

"When we appeared here, it was like we went through that door." Stranger nodded over me. "I almost felt it close behind us."

I tapped my knuckles against the steel. "It's just a door now."

"I know I lost my memory, but I'm pretty sure doors don't work that way. I mean, this is a different ship, Penny. It's evening here. We haven't just moved into another room. We've moved through massive space, and even time. I mean...." He gaped at the floor like it was supposed to explain all our questions and was just being stubborn.

I blinked at him. "Yeah, this happened already. Kind of old news."

"Yeah, but I didn't remember it last time. To be honest, Penny, I kind of thought you were crazy. I was just going along with it."

I gave a half laugh. "Thanks, dude. I thought you trusted me."

"I didn't mean it like...well, I kind of did, I guess. It felt right, though. Instinctively I knew I didn't belong there, I just didn't actually remember. But now...." He waved at the sun tossing light our way like stuff like this happened all the time. "Doors don't do that, Penny."

"Duh."

"So what did?" I tossed him an irritated look, but he didn't seem to notice. "Maybe it's a wormhole or something."

I bit my lip. A part of me felt guilty...proof I was way too good of a person. But there wasn't much to tell. It wasn't like saying, "Oh, I saw a gap through space and it yanked us through time" would explain anything. But he put a lot of trust in me and, so far, I hadn't noticed any signs of secrets on his side. My inner lie detector never went off, no notes of deception. *Ugh, fine, I'll tell him.* I opened my mouth, paused for a moment to choose better phrasing...and just then, he decided to continue.

"Maybe we're supposed to be here, like before. We need to save someone."

"Yeah, because that plan rocked last time."

"I think maybe it did." Stranger turned to me and, seeing the question in my face, continued. "The man in the water. You saved him."

"I wonder who he was."

"Maybe that's why the portal opened and sent us someplace else. The mission was complete. You saved the guy we needed to save."

I raised a cynical eyebrow. "Really?"

"Just think about it. We land smack dab in the middle of a tragedy, one you know almost everything about, which gave us the edge we needed to be active. So you save the guy, and then a door appears and takes us somewhere else."

"But you're assuming there's someone to call the shots. Stranger, I've seen nothing to prove that. It's just random."

"As far as we can see. But the timing was too perfect, don't you think? For a door to just randomly appear?"

But it didn't appear. We almost died. And then what? I just reached out and grabbed it with my mind? Magically pulled it closer and morphed it into an escape? Could I claim that as my heroics when

I didn't even know what happened? I'd never been able to do that with energy before. No, I was desperate. I was pleading. But was it any more likely that some other power had answered?

The voice had answered, though. That horrible, thick, empty voice which whispered in my mind as if it was tangled with my own. If that was the being calling the shots, we were in a lot more trouble than Stranger believed. It had told me to reach for the energy, practically guided me through the entire ordeal, all the while making me believe it would take us home. Perhaps Stranger was right about one thing…it had plans, although I doubted they were honorable ones.

"Penny." Stranger tilted his head and gave me a contemplative look. "Do you believe there's more out there than we can see?"

Did I ever. My whole life was about trying to convince other people that what I saw was real. Or perhaps, trying to pretend I didn't see it. "Do you?" I asked.

He nodded. "I think that's why I was in that basement."

"What? Wait, do you see things? Things other people don't?"

"Oh no," he said. "I'm not crazy or anything, no worries."

Crazy. Right. Silly me. My stomach plummeted before I even realized I'd gotten my hopes up. I'd never met anyone like me before. Might have been nice to compare notes. "Then are you remembering?" I pressed on before the hurt could leak into my face.

"No, but the thought keeps popping up in my head. We're here to save someone and something's helping us. I can't tell you why, though." He went quiet and I let the silence mingle with the salted air. "Well?" Stranger asked after a moment.

"What?"

"Do you believe there's something out there and we just can't see it?"

Maybe you can't see it, I thought. "It's possible, I guess. Wait, are you saying we're just supposed to save random people until this unknown force decides to take us home?" I asked, changing the subject. I even added my irritated face. People tended to forget the conversation if they felt on the defensive. Manipulative? Sure. But successful? Why yes, if I do say so myself.

"What's wrong with helping people? At least until we can think of something better."

Well, there was that whole idea of free will, which wasn't a factor in his explanation. "Fine. Until I can think of something better, that's the plan." I waved at the deck stretching out around us. "Which way do we start?"

He paused for a moment, sticking his lips in and out as he considered. "Let's go talk to some people. That's usually a good start. This way." He pointed.

I hadn't realized I'd miss anything about the Lusitania, but as we walked along the un-mopped deck, I started to miss the shine and basic cleanliness of the passenger ship. Whatever purpose this floating mess served, it wasn't to entertain. Stranger led the way to a door, conversation leaking through the cracks. We were about to knock when the door swung open.

Five men gave a start when they saw us. I took in their uniforms, untucked khaki tunics with brass buttons, and roughed up looking boots. They each wore hats of the same khaki material with a leather strap along the width and smaller brass buttons. The men all stood straight and at attention. Too at attention. These weren't waiters or crew members on a passenger ship. They weren't calm and here to make sure everyone was safe and happy. The shock left their faces within a second, and then their hands went for the muskets at their sides.

"Whoa!" Stranger shouted as he jumped in front of me. We both raised our hands in surrender, but the guns were already aimed. One man wore over-glorified buttons and his hat laid straighter than the rest. While the other men's coats were faded to where color was a guess, his was a deep blue. The white-tipped curl of his hat reminded me of the British Army during the Revolutionary War. I labeled him the captain.

"Who are you?" he asked with a thick English accent.

"Just passing through," Stranger said, and gave them a smile. "No need for weaponry."

Two of the men put their muskets down, only to replace them with thick iron handcuffs.

"No, you don't have to—" But Stranger stopped with a wince as the man roughly cuffed his arms behind his back. I braced myself for pain as they yanked my own wrists back a touch too tightly. The man finished cuffing me and placed a hand roughly on my shoulder to keep me in place.

"How did you two escape?" the captain said.

"Um…." Stranger and I shared a look. "We didn't escape anywhere. We were just on deck and…," I started, but the captain's eyes widened and I stopped. Somehow, that was exactly the wrong thing to say.

"You were just on deck? You two are stowaways?"

"Huh?" the man holding my shoulder said. "That's the second time this week. I don't get it. Who'd choose to be a stowaway on a hulk?"

"Probably mistook it for that daisy of a thing heading to Spain," one of the guys laughed.

"Take them downstairs with the others," the captain said. "I hope you don't think we're going to share rations."

I gaped open mouthed at him and turned to Stranger just in time to see his similar expression. He shook his head in disbelief at me. What the heck was going on? Where had we landed, and how were we supposed to get off now? The man leaned my shoulder to the side and forced me to turn around. We started walking, handcuffed and confused, deeper into the ship.

"What kind of ship is this?" I asked.

"Oh, I'm pretty sure you'll figure it out soon enough," one of the guys said with a chuckle in his voice. I didn't like that chuckle. It didn't fit right with the dark hallways and flickering lights. Just moments ago I'd run across a playful, easy going deck, praying for a way out. Now the uniformed men led me through the kind of staircase meant for a horror film...long and foreboding, with unpainted metal walls and a ceiling meant to leer down at the people instead of welcome them. Nothing about this place welcomed me. The walls leaned in as if to whisper *she doesn't belong here. Crush her.* Fear forced its way up through my aura, my chakras, my entire system, but I forced it down before anyone would notice. Before it choked me. Because it was silly, my mind playing tricks on me. The only thing I needed to worry about were those handcuffs cutting off my circulation. And of course, the whole "getting out" issue. Then the staircase leveled out, and the walls separated into larger rooms. The second I saw the metal bars, thick and parallel to the walls, it hit me just where Stranger and I had landed. We were on a prison ship.

Chapter 10

The hallways of high school were always filled with angst and hormonal teenagers. When I walked through them, I hated my abilities to feel other's emotions. Then, at the Lusitania, all that panic and fear had matched mine. My terror mixed with everyone else's into a stir pot of dread. But when I stepped down into that prison ship, those stale emotions attacked me like the stench of rotten trash. All that pain and suffering and longing stifled, with nowhere to go, nothing to do but turn putrid. Hatred danced with desires for revenge, while shame dipped into despair. I felt it all. Every single one. That was the moment I realized the truth about my abilities. I didn't just have a talent no one understood. I was cursed.

"Penny, you okay?"

Only at Stranger's voice did I realize I'd stopped walking. A guard pushed me forward and I stumbled. Stranger stepped toward me to right me, but his hands snagged against his cuffs. I righted myself and gave him a smile. "I'm fine," I lied. "Quite the smell."

"Hmm," the prison guard said with a nod. "You never get used to it."

No, I thought as they continued to push us deeper through the prison cells, *I won't get used to it*. I stretched my neck from side to side as if that could lessen the rising emotions littering the air. Some of them passed by like a tainted whisper, but others were so strong they wanted to settle into my skin, like a second home. Starvation and disease stole the color from their cheeks and sucked the bone against their skin. A few prisoners lifted their heads as we passed, curious about the new faces. Some insisted on staring, unconcerned for social convention, while others were too busy battling seasickness to bother looking up.

Although none of the prison cells were brightly lit, one cell stood out in its darkness. It came up to our left and Stranger glanced away from the cell the moment we passed it. The guards didn't pay it any attention as they walked, nor did they show any visual signs of discomfort, but their auras lit up in red alert and didn't ease back until they were far away from the dark cell. Even the prisoners in adjoining cells kept to the edge. No one looked at the dark corner. No shifting eyes kept it in their peripheral. The only thing everyone did with consistency was avoid it. So I focused on it.

Like Stranger's house, the jail cell gave off no energies. Literally nothing. My heart stuttered, torn between flipping in hope and dropping in dread. On one hand, that energy represented my only hope to go home. On the other, it also was the source of so much pain in so little time. After being manipulated the first time, I highly doubted it would just guide us home the next time around, but at least there was hope to get away from here. The prison guard increased the speed as we passed so I couldn't investigate as much as I'd like, but I mentally recorded the spot and kept moving.

Finally, quite a few prison cells later, the prison guards opened a vacant cell and tossed us in. The lock clicked into place before I turned around. The prison guards started walking off, but one lingered. "Stowaways on a prison ship," he said with the shake of his head. "I don't get it. We just float around. What exactly was your plan?"

"Hey." I tried to point my finger at him but succeeded only in straining my skin against the cuffs, so I resorted to raising my eyebrows in warning. "I don't like your judging eyes. We're exactly where we're meant to be." The sailor shook his head and followed the others away. Once he was out of ear shot, I turned to Stranger. "Why are we here?"

He gave a constricted shrug. Then he blinked, looked down for a second, and smooshed his lips to the side of his face in thought. When he looked at me, his pale blue eyes sparkled with excitement, mischievousness, and uncertainty. Maybe it was how the lights flickered or the way his hair had gotten disheveled during the arrest, but dang, that expression looked good on him. "What would you say if, hypothetically, I told you I knew how to pick locks?"

I kept my face blank, just to mess with him for a moment. "Seriously?" I asked, but then I couldn't control the relieved smile. "Right now, I'd be tempted to call you my hero."

"Well, you've already given me my superhero name," he said with a wink. "Come on, help me find a loose nail or something so I can use it."

"Nah, I've got a bobby pin in my hair...keeps the strays off my neck. Of course, I can't reach it, so—"

"Maybe I can...."

Someone cleared their throat. We both turned to see a bear of a man, whose head brushed the ceiling, leaning against the bars that separated our cells. His shoulders were broad, and a crescent-shaped scar half-circled his right eye. He hadn't shaved in days, and the disgruntled hair lashed out in warning for me to keep my distance. But his aura was a tranquil green, like a spring stream, and my intuition felt he meant no harm. He rose a dinner plate-sized hand up and waved for me to come closer. "I'll get it," he offered through a thick southern American accent. Confident the bars could prevent any evil intentions, I stepped closer and turned my ponytail toward him. He lifted my hair and slipped the bobby pin out before placing it in Stranger's outreached fingers.

"Thanks," I said.

The man just grunted and went back to his hard bed to stare at the ceiling. Stranger went straight to work, straining his fingers as he wiggled the bobby pin back and forth in the lock of his cuffs. I hoped it didn't break or anything. We didn't exactly have an endless supply. There was nothing for me to do but wait, so I decided to take a look-see at the energies around this place. See if that emptiness energy still lurked in the dark cell.

I wouldn't say I forgot about all the other energies that lurked around me, or that I'd somehow gotten used to it through exposure. I don't think anyone could ever get used to so many harsh emotions, not even the people who made them. But I underestimated the power. I closed my eyes and opened up my mind to the energetic world around me, and they hit me like a skilled boxer's right hook. Murderous thoughts. Revenge. Desperation for a drink or some drugs. Longing for home or some form of peace, so intense it was accompanied with thoughts of self-harm. I couldn't focus. Everything was too sharp, too stabbing. The emptiness I searched for was too soft to find among the knives of emotions.

"Hey!" Stranger knelt beside me and searched my face with concern. How did I get on my knees? "You okay?" he asked.

My eyes were open but I couldn't get away from the forces flooding my senses. "I'm...um...."

I'll kill that woman as soon as I get free.

I never did anything I didn't have to. It's their fault. They're the ones who should be paying.

That captain needs to learn his place.

"Penny?" Stranger struggled against his cuffs and cursed. "Penny, talk to me. What's going on?!"

"I'm fine, I just...." The energies melted into my own. Who resented whom? Who needed that revenge? I was mistreated too. It was someone else's fault. Stranger's fault. I never would have entered that house if he hadn't been yelling. I never should have. If anything happened to Dinah, the same thing would happen to Stra....

I groaned through clenched teeth, trying to drown out the thoughts. Those weren't mine. I wasn't like that. Was I? Hadn't I threatened him when we first woke up on the Lusitania? Was I any better than these people? Or was I just young, not caught yet? Innocent until proven guilty and all that.

Metal fell with a toss to the floor and hands grabbed my shoulders. "Penny," Stranger repeated. "You've gone pale. Are you sick? Are you hurt? Talk to me."

"No I'm just...." My wrists shook against my cuffs. "Just get these things off me, okay?"

He scooted to my cuffs and started working. I bent my head down, eyes wide as I tried to swim through the chaos.

"Hey." It was the scarred prisoner, rattling his bars for attention. Harder this time, quicker. "Hey!" he repeated, and I looked at him. "You're fine," he said. Dark green eyes looked straight into mine like he knew, as if he could understand. Who did this guy think he was? "It's not you," he continued. "It's just other people mixing in. You gotta separate yourself from the rest of the world, okay? Don't let it mix."

"Shut up," I breathed. His voice was deep and knowing. It ticked me off.

"Create a shield," he persisted. "Anything you like, anything that makes you feel safe, and imagine wrapping it around you. It'll keep the outside world away."

71

Safe. Nothing was safe. I was lost in time, surrounded by the unknown. There was no safety in the unknown. I didn't belong here. I was not meant to save anyone. "I can't focus," I snapped. Behind me, Stranger cursed again as his fingers slipped against my cuffs.

"Okay." The scarred man licked his lips. "Everyone stay calm. She's just fine. Listen, kid, find something familiar. Something safe, and focus on it until you get your head back. Then try the shield."

I'd just said I couldn't focus, and that was his brilliant plan? Why couldn't he mind his own business anyway? But I couldn't prove him wrong until I failed, so I closed my eyes tight and searched for some goodness among the bad. It didn't take long. He already knelt so close. So much light and hope, even as he hurried to uncuff me, to help me. Red etched along his aura, but it still radiated optimism. *Everything will be okay.* That's what he chanted to cool his shaking hands. *She's calming down already.* If I ever ran into Captain America as a teenager, I imagined he and Stranger would have similar auras. Just all around a good guy.

The tight cuffs fell off my wrists and blood rushed back into my fingers. Stranger wrapped his arms around me in such a tight embrace that his sunshine energy surrounded me. The tears of someone else's pent up emotions clogged my eyes, but I was already at work on a shield. Something that made me safe. In my head, I went back to the attic at home, that feeling of safety as Dinah and I explored the artifacts of our long-lost ancestors. All that pain and terror were just stories back then, back when Dinah and I were safe. Dinah handing me the penny, which even now clung to my necklace chain. I surrounded myself with that memory.

The hatred eased away...the resentment, the fears, everything, even as I tightened the loose gaps of my mental attic, Stranger's hopes. There was nothing but me within these walls. It felt dark. Empty. But at least I wasn't overwhelmed. I opened my eyes and straightened up. It had been nice in Stranger's arms, but I was ashamed to have fallen. I'd never acted like that before, never felt anything even similar. I didn't want Stranger to think I was weak.

"You okay?" Stranger asked. His hands lingered on my elbows, like he was prepared for me to melt down again. I nodded but he didn't let go. "Are you sure?"

"I'm fine. I'm sorry. That won't happen again."

I stood up and his hands fell to his sides. He gave me an "I'm not convinced" look before getting to his feet and dusting off his pants. "What exactly did happen?" he asked.

"I'm not quite sure." I didn't know if I lied or not. I had no name for it, no proof or explanation of why only I felt those things.

"She's an empath," the scarred man said like it was another day at the office. "A strong one by the looks of it. One-of-a-kind type of power."

"What?" Stranger and I chorused.

"An empath?" I asked, tasting the word.

"What's that?" Stranger asked.

"Kind of like a telepath, I guess, but using all the senses. Not just one. You don't seem to have much training."

"No." I shook my head. "I kind of thought I was crazy."

He laughed, a quiet chuckle, which juxtaposed against his large frame. "You're in a prison ship talking to a guy who hasn't seen land in months. Don't knock crazy out of the playing field just yet." He glanced at Stranger, who stared between us with a blank face like he couldn't decide how to react. "Guessing you didn't know?"

In answer, Stranger opened his mouth, closed it, turned to me, and tried again. "You read minds?"

"No. No, not exactly. It's um…." I didn't like the way he stared at me. His aura had closed in, squeezing his body to take up less room. He felt vulnerable, on the spot, like any second I might learn something he didn't want me to learn. See something he wanted to keep hidden. "I feel energies," I said.

He nodded but his aura stayed close. Just like that, it was out. I was the freak again. All because I got a little overwhelmed and some random prisoner started sharing. Stranger picked up the bobby pin from where he'd dropped it and went to the prison cell door. "I'll try to get us out of here," he said.

I turned from him, hurt by how tight his subconscious held onto his aura, and distracted myself by interrogating the scarred man. There was something off about that man. Maybe it was just because he understood. That alone proved he wasn't normal. Besides, something he'd said clicked off an alarm in my mind. "What year is it?" I asked.

"1782, so the calendars say."

"Major League Baseball wasn't founded until 1869."

He tilted his head as if in confusion, but an "oops" grin marred his face. "So?"

"So you just said 'knock crazy out of the playing field.' You shouldn't know phrases like that yet. Who are you?"

"Richard Noble, but you can call me Ricky," he said, and slipped his hand through the bars. I hesitated. A quick scan of the aura usually told me all I needed to know about a person, but not this guy. That wall he'd taught me to create around myself? Well, he had one too. But it wasn't just a room for comfort. The guy had a defensive castle wall at least a foot thick. The only way I could read him now was to convince him to ease off the barrier.

"You're a time traveler," I said, and took his hand.

"I know people." His face smirked from humor I didn't get.

"You said you trained?"

"Meditating. Not my favorite thing, but when your wife knows the Dalai Lama, what do you do? Am I right?"

A prisoner on an 18th century British prison ship who married a girl in the Dalai Lama's inner circle? Huh. "Can you see auras too?"

"Nah, still not that good. But I understand it in theory. Only a newbie wouldn't have her shield up. So, you're untrained. But only a natural could feel all the crap floating in the air around this prison. So, you're a natural."

"Thanks for the shield advice." I glanced at Stranger, who seemed a little too focused on the lock. "Of course, you could have been a bit more subtle about it," I sighed under my breath.

Metal squeaked on its hinges. "Got it open," Stranger said. "You ready to go?"

Go where? I thought. If the guards spotted us again, we'd have to start completely over. And I didn't have another bobby pin. But then I remembered the empty cell, the darkness no one saw. Maybe it was hope. More likely it promised danger. Either way, it wasn't something to ignore. "I think I know the way."

Chapter 11

"Whoa, whoa, whoa." Ricky raised his hands like *what the heck* as we started down the hall. "I helped you."

"Um…thank you?" I said.

"Show, don't tell." He waved at his own prison door. "I didn't have to help you, you know."

I gave a helpless shrug. "I don't know what kind of person you are. What if you have evil intentions and we let you out?"

"Can't you just—?" Stranger pointed at my head and then up and down at Ricky, like scanning.

"Usually, but he's got a wall up." I was going for my ultimatum face, but instead of intimidated, Ricky seemed amused.

"It's not trust if you know everything about the people you work with," he pointed out.

"I don't make a habit of trusting strange people on prison ships. There's a lot of rage on around here. How much of it comes from you?"

"None," he said without skipping a beat, but my gut warned of a lie. I gave a cynical face. "All right, not much," he admitted. Ricky leaned away from the bars, his fingers tapping the metal as he screwed his lips to one side and thought. He narrowed his eyes at me, then sighed and shook his head. "Fine. Just don't go poking around."

Stranger glanced between us, and his gaze made me feel self-conscious, but I couldn't let that stop me. So, I closed my eyes and watched as Ricky's stone wall crumbled. I braced myself, expecting to see more of the violent anger so common on this ship. But I gasped as his aura slipped out between the cracks of the broken wall. It was a liquid, glacier water green, clean and enchanting. I reached out and tapped the aura with my mind. Senses flashed through like a quick montage of his most dominant thoughts. A family sitting around a dinner table. A craving for adventure, to learn, to explore. And a promise whispered throughout his memories. *I'll protect you, trust me.* It was someone else's voice, but a promise he'd vowed to keep. I opened my eyes and looked at Ricky, trying to connect the physical form with the aura. The scars, the mischievous glint of the eye. The wall reversed itself back up, but he left a small window, letting me see, or perhaps choosing what I saw. For once, Ricky wasn't smiling.

"If that's the kind of person you are, why the wall?" I asked.

"People have to earn my story," he said.

"So...am I picking his lock?" Stranger asked. I nodded. For a moment, he didn't move. This was the moment, I thought, when Stranger would realize I was 99% crap and refuse. Then, after a long sigh and a shake of the head, he went to work on Ricky's cell.

"There's another guy you need to release," Ricky said as soon as Stranger got to work.

Stranger flashed me an incredulous look. "For some reason, the saying 'give them an inch and they take a mile' just popped into my head."

"He's kind of right," I said to Ricky. "We'll repay you, but I'm not here to start a prison escape."

"Is that so?" Ricky raised his right eyebrow and it spilled into his scar. "Then why are you here? I get the impression you don't know." His hand absently twirled a wedding band around his ring finger. It wasn't the usual polished gold, but rather....

"Is that petrified wood?"

"Yup. Everybody should wear it. Nature is the way back to serenity." He smirked as if even he caught the cheese in that line. "And you avoided my question."

I narrowed my eyes at him. "I thought you said you couldn't see energies," I said instead of answering.

Ricky spread his lips in such a goofy grin in which, for a moment, I saw a mischievous ten year old caught in the act. "All right," he admitted, "I may know for reasons other than empathic intuition."

"Enlighten me," I pressed.

He hesitated. "Part of a deal I made a few years back." He pointed at me. "Time traveler." Then he pointed at himself. "Time traveler. I'm not here for the kicks or authenticity of what it was like to be a prisoner back in the day. An old friend of mine told me to keep an eye out for you. I'm here to help you go home."

My shock stuck in my throat. He wasn't lying. His aura didn't tighten, nor did he show any tells. Stranger flicked his gaze at me as he worked. He raised his eyes as if to ask how much of this I believed, but before I could make a face in answer, his attention returned to the lock. I'd be the first to admit I had no idea how to respond to that. A time traveler. Someone with friends in the business, making deals with criminals, and…. "How long do I jump around like this?" I half whispered. "How long until I get back to my family?"

"Sorry, promised you I wouldn't share," Ricky said with a shrug.

"Promised *me?* You know me? Future me, I mean?"

He weighed his hand back and forth. "Eh."

"Then I'm pretty sure I'd want me to know."

"Yeah, you probably would," he admitted with a chuckle. "Fine. You never made me promise, but personally I feel like you should have. That was poor planning on your part."

"This guy's not being straight with us," Stranger half whispered to me, loud enough for Ricky to hear. "I say we ditch him."

"This is a big, scary prison ship." Ricky spoke to us as if we were kids who didn't understand something obvious, as if believing him should somehow be our natural response. I let him continue, but raised an eyebrow in disbelief. "There are desperate men behind those bars, and the men with the keys don't have to answer to anyone way out here. I don't think you get where we are in time. This isn't a criminal ship. Not completely. It's also a prisoner of war ship. It's the American Revolution. Those prisoners are soldiers fighting for freedom."

"I never got that in my readings," I argued.

"Months of being starved and tortured tend to mess with a guy's aura." The sarcasm was strong in Ricky. "You get me out, I can protect you. You get my friend out, you can get your job done."

"What is the job?" Stranger asked. "What are we supposed to do here?"

"You're here to save people," Ricky said. His aura around the window tightened, and a drop of deception tinted the green coloring. I tensed up instinctively. He'd lied. "We gotta make a difference where we can." That wasn't a lie. Not exactly. Did he know I could tell and changed the wording? Or did he feel guilty and chose to use vague terminology? My guess was the latter. I thought of Stranger, who hadn't noticed the energetic shift in the room, the way Ricky and I stared each other down, the liar and the lie detector. But Stranger believed there was a purpose, that we were meant to be here. I didn't know if I believed him. Something inside me whispered that it was too sweet a story, a nice little "everything will be okay" illusion, the kind of lie people stopped telling when they grew up. But it was a nice illusion. One I'd like to believe in too.

"Do you claim to know everything?" I asked, and to my surprise, he understood exactly what I meant. He believed himself to be lying, but did he know for certain? Could it be possible that he told the truth and just didn't believe it?

Ricky smiled. "No," he admitted. "Like everyone else, I'm all opinions."

"Good," I said. Stranger unlocked the door and stepped out of the way. "Now where's this friend of yours?"

"Follow me," Ricky said as he flicked the heavy barred door out of his way.

No longer were the prisoners only mildly intrigued by the faces walking past. Now they stood up as we passed, hissing, "Hey, what about us?"

"Shhh," Ricky snapped. "You get us caught and we're all stuck here for the rest of the war. Do you want that?"

Most got quiet, but one short, red haired guy raised his chin at Ricky. "We ain't gonna keep quiet just so you can slip out."

"Then how about I tell the captain what's hiding under your floorboard and see how he reacts?" Ricky snarled. The guy glared but kept quiet. Ricky turned enough to look every imprisoned cell mate in the eye. "Anyone else want to make a scene?" They all looked down and Ricky grinned. He playfully knocked me with his shoulder and winked at Stranger. "Glad I'm here yet?"

"You're kind of creepy," Stranger said with a nod of respect. Ricky glowed with the compliment and kept walking.

I could feel the darkness in the cell even before I could see it. A thought came to me like smoke, subtle at first, and then catching in my mind like a windowless room. A craving. It didn't want to be empty. Whatever it was, it wanted in…it wanted life. It sucked in everything it could, a never ending inhale as it strained to breathe.

"Here." Ricky stopped. The dark gap was so close, waiting for the final puzzle piece to life. But Ricky didn't point at the dark cell. Instead, his finger aimed at the one next to it. Another prisoner sat on the hard floor. Tall and with twigs for limbs, he didn't seem like much of a threat. His hair was messed up, as was everyone's here, it seemed, but the ends were even. His skin seemed dainty, if such a thing was possible in a place like this, and I got the impression that, before his prison days, the guy had lived pretty well. He looked up when he saw Ricky, then did a double take at Stranger and me. "Told you they'd come," Ricky said. He held his chin higher as he spoke.

The prisoner struggled to his feet and gave us a deep bow. "I am Gilbert du Motier, Marquis de Lafayette, at your service." He spoke with a thick French accent.

Stranger didn't wait for my okay before working on the guy's lock. Ricky's lie only fed into Stranger's own belief that we traveled with purpose, which meant he no longer questioned anything. I, however, wasn't quite convinced. "Lafayette. That name sounds familiar, but I can't place it."

"A mere blip in the history books, I'm afraid." Ricky spoke too softly for the man behind bars to hear. "He was like a son to George Washington and could have been a serious asset to the Revolution but one day he just disappeared before the Revolution got a good start. One guess where he ended up." Ricky gestured at the unwelcoming surroundings. I have to wonder how the history of America would change if this man returned."

"But is that possible?" I asked. "To change history like that? What if the world changes and it's somehow even worse?"

"Butterfly effects don't have to be bad things, Penny," Ricky said. "Save this man. He's important. Just look at that soul. You can tell, I bet."

I looked at the man who watched us whisper. By the suspicious look on his face, he hadn't overheard us. Despite the murky undertones common with mistreatment on the ship, Lafayette's aura dominated a bright metallic silver. A rare but world-altering aura shade, a color that meant he was receptive to new ideas and eager to trade the old traditions for better lives.

I stepped closer and spoke loud enough for him to hear. "What do you know about us?"

"You're the ones who rescue." Lafayette closed the gap between us.

"The way Richard spoke of you, I believed you to be a fictional being. The kind of mythical hero that we need, but sadly does not exist."

"We must exist or we wouldn't be here," I joked. Stranger smiled. Ricky picked at his cuticles. Laughter echoed in the back of my head, amused and disorienting. The voice. It was back. My first thought was, *What's so funny,* but I had meant it to be rhetorical. I hadn't expected an answer.

Just laughing at the delusion of humanity. You're really quite hilarious.

And you're a liar, I accused. *You tricked me into thinking I could go home, and then you dumped us here. I'm not listening to you.*

Oh. So that's how you want to play the game, huh? Fine. I'll play, but don't accuse me when you don't like the ending. You brought this on yourself.

The threat in the voice churned my spirit. I decided to focus on something else, anything other than that nothingness whispering in my ear. That was all it was, after all. Scary or not, it was honest to goodness nothing. I didn't have to give it the time of day. At least, not right now.

Problem was the void energy in the cell churned too. Like string made of air, it twirled around the edges of the walls, an anaconda of mist swirling, twisting around the metal. I could have sworn the prison bars steamed. The emptiness was everywhere, just waiting to explode.

I closed my eyes and looked. It was easier with the shield Ricky had taught me to use. I saw everything from a distance, separated through the glass. The rage, the fears. Ricky's peace, Lafayette's longing for equality. Stranger's hope. And the nothing as it steamed through the lock. By the calm way everyone stood watching Stranger do his work, they didn't notice. They didn't see. The steam inched around his skin as he kept at the lock. It wasn't just Lafayette's cell, either. There were pockets of the steam in every cell door down the long hallway.

The click of a lock made my heart jump. Stranger straightened up and gave us a smug grin. "That's right," he said. "I'm that good."

Before I could suggest that maybe something else had unlocked that door, clicks echoed through the iron halls. Barred doors swung open in unison. Just like that, all that rage, that hatred and blame, was free.

Chapter 12

Prisoners jumped out of their cells before the doors realized they weren't supposed to swing open. I froze in my skin. A stampede was on the rise, coming straight for me.

Fingers wrapped around the collar of my shirt and shoved me back. I fell into Lafayette's cell. Ricky tossed Stranger in after me before jumping in himself and slamming the door shut. We hid along the ship wall, away from the confusion on the other side of the bars.

The escaped prisoners paid us little attention once we were out of the way. A few gave us a quick curious glance before continuing their escape. They didn't care about us, the fools who stayed in the prison cell at the offer of freedom. They didn't even care about the other prisoners running by their side. They wanted to breathe fresh air, get to solid land. They wanted their vengeance on the people who had kept them trapped. But they were smart. They lingered behind, testing their limits before taking the next step. How long would it take before they risked running up on deck and exacting their revenge?

"They're going to go after the guards," Ricky said before I could speak up. "They're going to riot. We're lucky they didn't have any warning. No time to make a plan. No plan gives us more of a chance."

"What about the cell doors?" Lafayette asked. "How did they all unlock like that?"

"There's something off on this deck," I interrupted. I looked at Ricky, who claimed to understand energies like me. "Can't you feel it?"

"All I feel are the desperate vibes coming from those prisoners,"

Ricky argued.

"Yes, they're dangerous, but this—"

"Can wait," Ricky cut me off. He gave me a look, with raised eyebrows, wide eyes, and a straight lip. The condescending look a parent might give a child for screaming in church. It stunned me silent and my cheeks went hot. I might as well be back home, telling Dad I'd lost his tablet.

But he himself said I was the natural when it came to this stuff. I deserved to have my voice heard. "There's more at stake than just some crazy prisoners. Something wrong is happening here," I said. I had to hold my ground, because if the emptiness energy could make metal steam, it could probably do something similar to human skin. And there was a surplus of it slinking out of the damaged locks. "We shouldn't focus on preventing a riot. We need to get everyone off this ship."

"We can't do that until everyone stops trying to kill each other," Ricky pointed out. "The prisoners aren't organized. They don't know the layout of the ship, so there's a chance we can get to the captain's deck before them. If that's possible, we can give them enough warning."

"These are prisoners of war," Stranger said. "Don't we want them to take over the ship?"

"We're too outnumbered, and sadly unarmed. The second a fist flies, every prisoner on this ship is done for. Besides, they're not all prisoners of war. Some are actual criminals. Bloodthirsty and with a knack for leadership. There are some pirates down here who'd just love to be captain of this ship. Lafayette, these men know your name. Can you get them to remain calm?"

"I can get my men to listen."

"Tell them not to attack, but rather to return to their cells before the officers notice, so we can have a more organized attack. Stranger, you know the way to the captain's deck, right? Go with Lafayette and help him."

"What about me?" I asked.

"Stay here with me. We'll work together." He didn't exactly sound thrilled about that prospect. Lafayette headed for the cell door, waiting for a chance to slip into the fray. Stranger and I looked at each other. We hadn't been working together for long, but somehow separating seemed like a bad idea. I was way out of my comfort zone. But I wasn't the only one out of my comfort zone, and that was, for lack of a better word, comforting. What if something happened? What if Stranger and I couldn't get back together?

But Stranger just gave me a smile and a silent promise in a nod. He and Lafayette slipped through the cell door, closed it behind them, and slithered through the confused convicts with speed and purpose. My stomach churned when I couldn't see him anymore. It was just me and Ricky now. And not the helpful, kind Ricky I'd met less than half an hour before. His energy had changed the second the prisoners escaped. I scanned his energies, but the window had disappeared from the castle walls around his aura. Stones stacked on top of each other, the kind that could last for generations, centuries, outlive cities and governments. The kind of structure that would be labeled a ruin for historical reference before it could even begin to decay. From what I had seen, he was a caring, protective sort of man. What did he have to hide, and why increase his defenses now? But there was no time to press him on the matter. We had bigger issues at hand.

"What do we do?" I asked.

"I'm going to slip into the group. Already know a lot of them by name. I can give them false information. Maybe keep a leader from rising. Help implant the idea we need to return to our cells."

"And me?" I asked. Ricky gave me a side glance but didn't say anything. "I can help," I promised. "Just give me something to do."

"I think it's best you stay down here for now," Ricky said. He didn't look me in the eye.

"Is this how you treat all your mythical heroes?"

The humor returned to Ricky's face for the quickest of seconds. "When my mythical heroes act like you, it's probably best not to trust them."

"If you think I'm untrustworthy or not useful, then you don't know me at all. I trusted you. Now trust me."

Somehow, I'd said the wrong thing. Ricky's face hardened. "Never say 'trust me' unless you mean it." His voice was low and sinister.

I tilted my head at him in question. Of course I meant it. Why else would I say it, for crying out loud? "Whatever kind of person you think I am, you're wrong."

A shout came from above us and he shook his head. "I don't have time for this." I opened my mouth to argue, but Ricky just waved a hand at me in a not-now manner that *really* made me want to take his attitude down a notch. "Stay here," Ricky said. "Stay out of trouble, and whatever you do, don't go exploring and get yourself lost, okay?" He went to the door and slipped into the crowd. Within seconds, he started whispering with the men. "How did we get free?" "I know I'd like to teach a guard or two a lesson." "Does anyone know where the armory is?"

I frowned as I listened to his retreating voice. He sounded too convincing. It reminded me that I'd met him in a prison cell. That maybe I shouldn't trust his word as truth. In other words, there was no reason why I should obey his orders. My frown softened as my rebellion spiked. *Go ahead, random dude in an old ironclad prison ship, try to boss me around. I'm a teenager with forget-happy parents. Challenge accepted.*

I spun on my heels, chin high and indignation triggered as I turned to the cell of emptiness. Okay, maybe I was being a little dramatic. A tiny part of me had to remind myself that no one saw me, no one noticed, so there was no reason to egg on that glare and tight-fisted stance. But it felt good, so I shushed my reason aside and closed my eyes.

The emptiness floated into view within my mind…a gap the size of a person, with wisps of smoke trailing out in thick strands that filled the cell and leaked out along the edges. Once I found the boundary, I stepped closer, careful not to touch the strange energetic smoke. There had to be more to it. It couldn't just be a darkness only I could see, because…well, darkness alone wasn't dangerous. Every day turned into darkness, every room when the lights went off, every person when they clung to traumatic memories. That didn't make the darkness bad. And it certainly didn't explain how the darkness could break every lock on a prison ship. Only the locks. Nothing else. Yet. Which meant that whatever was in there, whatever that darkness was, not only could it send thoughts to my mind, but it could also attack, take action of its own. Great.

In a corner of the cell, some of the darkness shifted in my mind, like a wave of a hand shooing the smoke away. A whisper of another energy suffered through the darkness…a gentle whir of electronics. I opened my eyes and looked closer, and saw a rectangle of pale blue glowing. A tablet with the screen lit up on full brightness, completely out of place in the late 18th century. The screen saver was on, a picture of two girls smiling back at me. Twins with dark hair and identical brown eyes. Dinah and me. My heart jumped to my throat. It was Dad's tablet!

I leaned down and picked it up. The moment my hand was clear, the darkness eased back into place like a falling curtain. My shocked hands made the screen shake. Before, this whole ordeal had seemed random, an unfamiliar cause and effect based on some experiment gone wrong. It had begun when Dinah and I went into Stranger's house. Now I was stuck on a Revolutionary War prison ship solely by chance. But this? This tablet had disappeared *before* I noticed any darkness around Stranger's house. And it wasn't just anyone's tablet. It was mine. Me, the only one who could see the darkness. Unless.... My eyes...something had attacked my eyes when I went to look for the tablet. *Then* I saw the darkness. My body froze as the dots connected, as if it might attack again the moment I moved. Because this wasn't random. It hadn't touched Dinah. It didn't steal her phone. Somehow, this was about me.

Something shifted in the cell...the sound of feet shuffling. But all the prisoners and guards were long gone, making their way on deck. "What are you?" I whispered. "Why did you set those prisoners free?"

Chaos. Isn't it fascinating? The voice again. It was wrong. Everything about that voice, the genderless tone, the way more accents than I'd ever heard before blurred into one unrecognizable mess of a voice. But the fear factor of that sound seemed to morph into annoyance. Of course it was the voice. The liar. Manipulating the situation for who knew what purpose. I pursed my lips together as I considered how to respond.

"What are you?" I repeated.

I am not, therefore I am not.

"Is that supposed to mean something?"

It would if you let yourself think.

"Well that's rude." I feigned offense. This...thing talked in riddles and wasted my time. Whatever dangers we faced because the strange energy had set the prisoners free, we were still at the complete mercy of the smoke. My fingers twitched, reminding me that the force had responded to my call once before. Perhaps it could again. I raised my hand and willed it to return deeper into its cell. The weakest tendrils at the edge of the cell quivered in answer, inching back, and for a moment I felt in control.

Then the energy laughed.

Nope. I backed away from it as the panic took over. *Nope! Stop pushing! Let it go already! It's not real! It's random! You're random. Anyone could have gotten into a situation like this! You're normal, Penelope Grace! You're completely normal, and none of this has anything to do with you—*

Lies, the voice whispered. *So human. So unlike you.*

"Few people know who I am. You are not one of them."

The voice chuckled. *If you'd like.*

That wasn't reassuring. "What's your plan?"

The chaos. It's cute to watch the ones who call themselves heroes. They never win, but they always try. A chuckle ended the voice's rant.

Heroes. The boys. "What have you done?"

Set them free. It's the only thing one must do to find chaos. Free just the right people. Would you like to watch them destroy each other with me?

"No." My voice cracked. Yelling came from upstairs. I wanted to run up, figure out what was going on, how I could help. But the voice was right. Ricky was right. There was nothing I could do. Up there. "What are those shadows only I can see?" I asked.

You mean the emptiness? There are no human words for it with which I am familiar. It is the opposite of life.

"So, death?"

No. Death is part of the life's cycle. Or perhaps life is a part of death's cycle. But this.... The humanoid gap of darkness waved what looked like an arm, and the shadows spun with the disruption. *Is what should never live.*

More yelling upstairs. Some banging. Were the boys winning? Were they catching the dangerous and desperate, locking them back up? Maybe I was a cynic, but Ricky's plan seemed a touch too hopeful. "How do I stop it?"

For a moment, there was no answer. I couldn't decide if the voice just hadn't heard me or if it couldn't decide how to respond. *What do you mean?* it finally asked.

"How do I save them?"

Save them? Why would you save them?

"Because they're my friends!" I think.

Friends who left you alone? Who don't see your powers? They abandoned you. They distrust you. Everyone will, eventually. Your friends, your parents. Even your sister. But I have always been at your side.

Creepy. "If you want me to trust you, help me."

You do not know what you ask. Here, let me enlighten you. Tendrils of smoke seeped through the metal bars between our cells. Metal steamed at the touch, melted away, except no metallic lava dripped down the bars. That's when I realized what the steam was. The dusted remains. The metal completely dissipated, just like back at Stranger's basement.

I staggered back before the smoke of darkness could reach me. But it kept coming. Kept forming into fingers. I booked it to the cell door and jumped out, running to the stairs and not looking back, my feet beating against the ironclad's stairs. The last time that happened, I had ended up on the Lusitania. Who knew where I'd end up next time. If I survived contact.

When I reached the door to the deck, I slowed my run and eased through, peaking around the corner to assess the situation. Escaped convicts littered the deck, but I didn't see Ricky or Stranger anywhere. Oh, wait…nope, there they were on their knees with their hands in the air, surrounded by not only angry but also armed prisoners. Where had the weapons come from? Ricky's plan must have not gone well. I set the news aside to toss in Ricky's face later.

Hmm. I smooched my lips to the side and thought. How to protect three idiots from countless and armed escaped prisoners? All right, two idiots and Stranger. I frowned at the predicament. I couldn't see the captain or any of the guards. By the banging sound and the way the door to the captain's deck rattled, they had been locked in. The door knob looked mangled, and I presumed one of the prisoners had broken it as a makeshift lock. Three prisoners stood as guards. They must have been smarter than Ricky had hoped. I'd have to ask the boys later how they got caught, but first, I'd have to save them. Singlehandedly.

Chapter 13

I couldn't fight them. I couldn't reason with them. Not now, when they already had the upper hand and there was no bribe I could offer that they'd exchange their freedom for. I could feel that clear as day in the hyped energy on deck. They were tasting fresh air for the first time in weeks, months even. They'd kill before they went down those stairs again. But they weren't completely invulnerable. They were on full alert, jumpy. Already the men were arguing. Some wanted to go back home or to their battle posts. Others wanted to get far away. They argued over whether to kill the guards or put them on a lifeboat. To listen to each other or keep true to their stubborn attitudes. I didn't like that they were armed. They must have gotten the guns from the guards, which increased the likelihood that I was the only one coming to the rescue.

One of the men, the short, redheaded, bearded thing with a big gun, and the greatest example of the Napoleon Complex I'd ever seen, paced back and forth in front of Ricky, Lafayette, and Stranger. He couldn't have been over five feet tall; I was even taller than the guy. Yet there was something in the way he walked — the gait, maybe the energy he radiated, or just the way his beard pointed off like a sharp spear — that made him so intimidating. Sure, the other men argued with him, but they didn't knock him down when he snapped. They didn't start fist fighting for control. He acted as the level head in the chaos, the one with the answers, the plans for a plan, and that made everyone else listen. He was the Ricky of the rebels. Only, he wasn't on his knees and hopefully thinking, *Oh why didn't I listen to that smart girl I left alone to defend herself in the basement?*

That's when it hit me. The basement. The inside of the ship. The cell. And whatever force smoked within that cell. If I wanted to get control of these people, I'd have to out-intimidate the leader of the pack. Spear-Beard wouldn't know what hit him. Of course, neither would I. I hesitated on the edge between the deck and the stairs. It wasn't a plan that formed in my head. More like a daydream, an if only. If only I had control of what only I could see. If only I could use that darkness to help instead of destroy. But I couldn't. I knew it like a fact, and yet….

I glanced down the stairs. I'd like to say that this moment was a turning point for me. That right then, sandwiched between a mutiny and a void, I chose to be grand. But in reality, there was nowhere to run. If I wanted to run away, I'd have to get rid of the barriers first. So I closed the door behind me and retreated back into the ship, back to the cell filled with darkness. With the weird voice.

I kept a safe six feet away from the cell, yet I could feel the distorted energy swimming in the air, the smell of hot metal, which had outlived the bars themselves. I closed my eyes and focused on the energy. Back at the Lusitania and then just for a second earlier, I had made it move to me, forced it to come closer. If I could just remember how to do it again….

I'm glad you've returned, the voice said. *Let the humans destroy themselves. We don't have to worry about them…what are you doing?*

Nothing by the looks of it. The nearest tendril of dark smoke shuddered but remained in the cell, as if the smoke just shook its head to gloat, *Nope, not happening, kid.* I tried again. The only response was a shiver down the steam's length. I lifted my hand and reached out, imagining my grasp lengthening past my physical skin and grabbing the smoke by its apparently sassy tendril. The palm of my hand tingled, awake and alert. The smoke choked and resisted the pull, but I kept my grip strong. To my surprise, the tendril grew a foot as it followed me to the stairs. In my shock, I almost lost the connection, but voices above me kept my focus true. Stranger needed help. "I'm going to need this," I told the mysterious voice, and stepped back.

Why didn't you say so in the first place? the voice said with a chuckle. I didn't like the chuckle. It sounded too friendly. As if two friends were hanging out at a sleepover, and a super self-conscious one asked the other for the restroom. We weren't friends. I was stealing this. Wasn't I?

No. The pull came too easy. I wasn't dragging it along anymore. In fact, I had to slow it down, keep it from taking me over. Adrenaline flushed my bloodstream. Big mistake. Big mistake! I couldn't control this! The smoke passed through my imagined grip, running toward my skin with hunger. I stumbled back but tripped against the stairs. My back slammed against the metal steps with a breath stealing thump. "Stop!"

The smoke stopped. I couldn't see it with my eyes open, but I felt the burn. I gritted my teeth to battle the nerve-racking instinct to keep my eyes wide in search of more danger, and squeezed them tight. The smoky emptiness had stalled not even a paper's-width from my nose. I exhaled in relief and it swirled an inch or two back. The humanoid gap stood still in the cell, head tilted as it watched. I blew the energy back another few inches and got back to my feet, ignoring the pain in my back. That might bruise later.

I tried again, slower and with a lot less force. The smoke stumbled up the stairs with me, steaming off the railings. My insides yelled at me to stop, not because I was in danger but because it felt wrong. Something about how easily it followed me back to the deck door felt like a deal gone wrong. But I hadn't made a deal. Hadn't promised anything. The voice had made no contingencies, nor was I even certain it had anything to do with the smoke's current compliance. Somewhere deep within my skin, a part of me pleaded to stop. *It isn't worth it*, she whispered. *Just run away. Don't use the darkness.* But there was no choice at all, and not just because I couldn't run away. My friend and some other random guys were in trouble and, unlike the Lusitania, I could actually do something about it. Ricky's voice echoed louder than the scared voice in my head. He didn't think I would be useful. He'd told me to stay put, stay hidden, and wait for them to save the day. So I kept walking. I dragged that smoke of emptiness up those stairs and told my inner voice to shut up, because I was useful and maybe Stranger was right. Maybe I was there to save the day.

I reached the door and held my hand up in a stop motion. The emptiness energy slowed to a stop just before reaching my fingers. I held my breath as if the escaped prisoners might hear, and eased the door open to peek through. Not much had changed. There was a layering of restlessness in the energy, but everyone still argued with words only. Well, words and exaggerated gestures, which I won't elaborate on. Stranger knelt still as a statue, watching Spear-Beard pace back and forth with tense muscles and a stone face, which worried me. He was ready for a fight. I just hoped he wouldn't start it.

Lafayette watched everyone with calculating eyes, taking everything in and waiting for his chance. But his aura was a frantic overheated red, revealing the lie in his calm. Ricky seemed restless in a much different way than the rest of the prisoners. He leaned from side to side like his knees were giving him trouble. The sun glinted off his hair and, for the first time, I noticed a salted glean to it. If my life was a story, perhaps he might have been my mentor. But as it were, he was just a fool with graying hair. Because he'd left me behind.

I slipped through the door and closed it behind me, thankful to be at an awkward angle from the sun. The shadows hid me from the men. I sank deeper into the shade as I pulled the smoke through. It was slow to obey, slipping through the cracks like sap from a tree. The guards kept beating against their locked door. The convicts kept arguing over what to do next. And Stranger looked straight at me with a smile on his face.

I put my finger to my lips to motion for him to keep quiet. He nodded and looked back to Spear-Beard, glare back in place. But the second he passed, Stranger returned his attention to me. And with a thump of the heart, I realized why. He waited for instructions. I nodded at him again and hoped he understood it meant stay where you are. He didn't move.

Then Spear-Beard flipped around and punched Stranger square in the jaw.

The force of the punch whipped Stranger's face. His hands caught himself as he fell to the side. "I said," Spear-Beard yelled, loud enough for me to hear, "Where is the girl?! Did we all make her up? Did she disappear somewhere? I said gather everyone up, and she's the only one unaccounted for!"

"There's no women on the ship!" Ricky snapped back. He turned his head just right, and I noticed a flush to his scarred eye, the beginnings of a bruise. Spear-Beard had punched him too. Ricky spit out some blood and straightened his spine. Even on his knees, he could look Spear-Beard in the eye. "This guy is crazy!" Ricky looked at the escaped prisoners scattered around the deck of the ship. "Are you guys seriously taking orders from him? I can get you to free soil, help you escape!"

"And keep the girl for yourself, is that it?" The way Spear-Beard said it, the implications of the word "keep" sent shivers down my spine. My top priority had just become *do not get caught.* "I know who you are," Spear-Beard snarled, the edges of his lip rising to show teeth like a feral dog's. "I know your game, and it's no different from mine, so don't get all high and mighty on me now! Tell me where the girl is and I'll ease some of the slack. Hell, maybe I'll even let you in. But friends don't keep secrets."

"Just because we have the same occupation doesn't make us friends. You make me sick," Ricky snarled back. He had the facial expressions down pretty well, but somehow it just wasn't as convincing. Spear-Beard had more of his heart behind the crazy, I guess.

"We need to return to America," Lafayette said. "The war needs — "

Spear-Beard aimed his musket in Lafayette's face and he stopped speaking, but his calm resilience remained. "Who are you?" Spear-Beard asked. "You look familiar. As if I've seen sketches of you on the British wanted lists. Are you one of those fools crying out for freedom on the savage land?"

"My name is Thomas." Lafayette hid his French accent well. "And, yes, I believe America to be the home of freedom, if that's what you ask. Most of the men on this ship agree."

"Ah, they might have before, but now I think a fresh meal and some dry land is all they seek. I can promise them that. You, on the other hand, promise death by musket, or from the severe weather in that godforsaken trap of a land." When Lafayette didn't react to the words, Spear-Beard chuckled. "I can see it in your face, soldier. You're just begging to spill blood for a good cause. In that at least, I can help you." He lowered the gun to Lafayette's chest.

Ricky's history lesson returned to me. Lafayette, the man who disappeared at sea. What would the world be like if he survived? Lafayette, who looked Spear-Beard in the eye and smiled. "You can kill me, but you cannot stop America."

Anger spilled over Spear-Beard's face as Lafayette refused to show fear. I didn't have half the smoky emptiness I'd need to pull this plan off. But it was time to step out of the shadows. "Hey!" I shouted, and eased into the light. Everyone turned and looked at me. The prisoners aimed their guns. Spear-Beard seemed to forget Lafayette as he looked me up and down. Stranger gaped at me in shock, but Ricky just rolled his eyes. "Heard you were looking for me," I said. My hands shook, I was sweating, and for a second I lost control of the emptiness. It started to slip back into the ship, but I mentally grabbed it again.

"Just in the nick of time," Spear-Beard said with a smile as he motioned for his men to put their guns down. "Figured you were listening in."

Oh, man, I did not feel confident in my plan anymore. There I stood, surrounded by escaped, angry, even *frustrated* prisoners, who hadn't seen a girl in who knew how long, while the only three guys who might be on my side were on their knees with bloodied faces. The bad guys were armed and dangerous. I had unpredictable energetic fields and was slightly irritable. I clenched my hands into fists and straightened my spine. Who knew I'd go out like this? "Let my men go and I'll spare you," I said in my most intimidating voice, trying to get as low as possible.

Spear-Beard blinked at me for two whole seconds before laughing. "A girl with some fire. I like that!"

"Will you like it when it burns you?" I asked. He kept smiling at me. My fists were so tight my nails stung my skin. I tried to move the energy, but it must have sensed my apprehension. I forced my fingers to spread, reached out, and pulled the energy higher, forcing enough from the basement to make an impact. Back at Stranger's basement, it had burned metal with ease. Maybe I could get it to do that again. I envisioned tossing a hand full at Spear-Beard's feet. The metal seared with a harsh hiss. Spear-Beard jumped back as the steam dissipated to reveal a hole straight through. The guns went back up, and I'll admit I smiled. It kind of felt like a compliment. "You should thank those men you beat." I stepped closer to them, and a few stepped back. "For not telling you where I was. It wasn't me they were protecting. It was you." More than a few prisoners glanced at each other with uneasy looks. Ricky smirked, and Stranger dropped his jaw at me in shock. Lafayette looked at me like he believed the mythical creature explanation. Spear-Beard just tilted his head, his beard at a forty-five degree angle.

"How did you do that?" he asked. I felt the hunger for power reach through his skin as his energy locked with curiosity.

How did I do that? I had no good answer. So I faked a smile and raised both my arms in an exaggerated attempt to scare them. "I'll offer this one time and one time only. Go back to your cells, and I won't show you how the metal felt."

93

None of the men lowered their weapons. No one surrendered back to their imprisonment. "You forget, pretty girl, that we far outnumber you," Spear-Beard said. "You have silly magic tricks and a sharp tongue. We have guns and ammunition. And a ship."

"I have something you don't." I raised one eyebrow, tilted my head to my left, and gave a sharp half smile. Never before had I used the kind of smirk I sent to Spear-Beard, but dang, it felt like a good one. I imagined the smoke twirling around the men, locking them in a trap. Then I slammed my arms down, forcing the smoke to the floor. Metal seared in a perfect circle. I lifted the smoke back up before it worked its way through the floor. Still, steam faded to reveal the inner workings of the machinery. "Still want to turn down my offer?"

The prisoners closer to the edge of the circle seemed ready to cuff themselves to their cells, but Spear-Beard glared in defiance. "I'm not one for going down easy," he said. "You're nothing but tricks and illusions. And I don't think you've got the stomach for a fight." He grinned from nasty memories and I flinched, not expecting to see those moments through my mental window. Swords and gun shots. Gold and blood. "I got an eye for fights, know when my opponent's got a good one in them. If I'm about to have some fun. And you, little girl, are all talk. It's in the eyes," he said, aiming the barrel of his gun to his temple before casually pointing it at me. "You don't have any moves left. You've shown your cards."

I closed my eyes and imagined the tendrils of smoke sneaking through the men and wrapping around their weapons. In one synchronized squeeze, every gun sliced in half, missing the men's skin by less than an inch. Everyone dropped their guns in shock, jumping away from the scrap metal. Even Spear-Beard. He gaped at me and I increased my smirk. "Seems like you're all bluff and ego."

Ricky coughed behind Spear-Beard. No one looked at him. No one seemed to notice any sound at all. All eyes were on me. But I looked down at him and caught his gaze as he mouthed *get them off the ship* and nodded toward ten lifeboats, all waiting for an emergency.

I looked back at Spear-Beard. "Offer's off the table. You're free to drift on the ocean and beg for help." I stepped to the side and motioned to the small lifeboats. *Having the upper hand is fun*, I thought. "Now!" I snapped when no one moved. "Before I make the floor beneath your feet disappear and you fall into the ocean!"

I remembered to move the smoky empty energy to the side just before a prisoner walked through. Phew. That was a close call. Figuring out what the smoke did to skin just after the bad guys surrendered would not have been a pleasant experience. The men kept their distance as they passed me. It was surreal to watch. It only took a few minutes for them to fill six of the lifeboats and prepare to take off, giving side glances filled with fear. Aimed at me. Those gruff, rebellious men sidestepping around me to the lifeboat I ordered them into. All those stifled emotions, which moments ago had overwhelmed me. I'd never considered myself a power-hungry person before, but dang…. Problem was, I didn't know what to do with the smoke now that I'd brought it out. And it didn't like taking orders, either.

Chapter 14

The boys got to their feet. Ricky and Lafayette stood over Spear-Beard, Ricky's shadow covering the now weaponless leader. "The woman said get on the lifeboat," Ricky growled in his deepest voice. I had a sneaking suspicion he *had* practiced his smirk.

"You think she'll let you take control?" Spear-Beard said with a nod at me.

"We're working together."

Mmmm, debatable.

"I get it," Spear-Beard said. "She used her freak thing to unlock the cell doors. That was her. And pretty much everyone saw you break out after you talked to her."

"Uhm," Stranger raised his hand, "that was actually me who broke him out. In case anyone was wondering."

"This break out was all your idea." Spear-Beard poked Ricky in the chest. "She's your weapon."

"All right, get in a lifeboat before I throw you out," I snapped. I wasn't anyone's anything.

Spear-Beard glanced at me before joining the others as they got their lifeboats ready. I couldn't decide if the look was more fear or murderous.

Stranger stepped beside me, his hand grazing my elbow before falling to his side. I braced for his interrogation. How had I melted the ship floor? What was I? But nothing prepared me for how his eyebrows pinched together in concern. "You don't look so good."

"Just what every girl wants to hear," I said, trying to make it sound like a joke, but I felt lightheaded. Like a rock band pounded in my head, disorienting me. I couldn't feel my legs, and black spots started in the corners of my eyes. The strange smoke got too heavy. I couldn't stop it from leaking through the door. And it didn't like being confined. It wanted to consume. Keeping it off the ship felt like weightlifting. Technically, it was nothing, a stringy gap where reality should be, yet it felt like a world, an entire reality, aching to leak into ours. "I think I might have bitten off more than I can chew."

"What was that back there?"

"I'm not exactly sure," I admitted.

"Are you doing okay?"

"Not great." I swallowed hard. My knees gave out on me and I toppled to the side. For a second, everything went black. Then Stranger's arms wrapped around me, holding me up.

"Whoa, whoa, whoa," Stranger said. He righted me and looked me in the eye. "What's happening here?"

"Ow!"

Spear-Beard jumped into his lifeboat with his arm to his chest. A runaway strain of smoke lingered where he'd once stood. It charged at the lifeboats, eating away at the rope, the only thing holding it to the ship. I yanked the smoke back under control only to have the black spots return in my sight. "Sorry," I half-hollered to them. "My bad." That only upped their fear as their eyes flickered from me to Spear-Beard. They untied the rest of the rope and flopped into the water.

"How about we get you in a chair, huh?"

I forced myself to find my legs, but they wobbled. "I've just got to find my sea legs again. Don't worry."

Ricky sifted through the gun remains, tossing aside the broken bits with a disappointed shake of the head. He glanced up mid reach and saw me watching. "Hey," he said, "I'm just checking. Don't forget we're prisoners too. I'm not dumb enough to free the guards only to have a gun on us two seconds later."

"Just as long as you weren't looking for a working one," I warned. His castle wall was still up high and thick. He tipped an invisible hat at me and turned to Lafayette. "There's more lifeboats. I say we fill one up and get you back to shore."

"I long for the day I no longer feel the floor sway under me, but the provisions would take up space. Don't you want to escape this ship as well?"

"Not currently." Ricky looked at Stranger and me. "We'll need all hands to get this lifeboat ready as quickly as possible." But without waiting to see who was coming to his aid, Ricky started rummaging through the supplies. I nodded for Stranger to go help him, smiled to let him know I was fine, and stumbled to a railing I could lean on for support before my legs gave out again. Stranger didn't seem to buy my bluff, but he must have realized I'd only get angry if he tried to argue, so he agreed.

The lifeboat was ready in minutes. Lafayette climbed on board and Ricky got ready to lower him down, but the American hero stopped him. "Are you sure about this?" Lafayette asked. "I feel strange leaving you all behind."

"Don't worry about us," Stranger said. "We've got Penny."

Lafayette gave me a quick glance. "Strange girl, that." He spoke in a low tone I most likely shouldn't have heard, and wouldn't have if the wind hadn't carried it to me.

Ricky grunted in nodding. "You've got no idea."

"I managed to keep my identity from the other prisoners," Lafayette said. "And the British have been spreading rumors of my capture since before it was real. I doubt those I care about would put any more thought in the accusations, but I plead with you to keep this adventure quiet. I don't know what would happen if news spread I was human. It is a heavy burden to be looked upon as inspiration in a war for America, but to lose that would be even worse."

Ricky nodded. "We only ever helped a Thomas. Go on now. Win a war."

The great French ally smiled like the young general he had fought to become. "I plan to."

As soon as Ricky started lowering Lafayette down, my head started to spin. Not just with the onslaught of rebellious void energy, but as if the world itself spun quicker than normal. It changed. Memories rearranged themselves in my head to fit with the new information. Never once did the history books reference Lafayette's disappearance nor his capture. The war didn't last decades. Washington never lost the man he saw as his son. Ricky swayed to the side for a moment, seeming as dizzy as me. Then he smirked at me. "America will win the war in a year. Tops." He chuckled and looked out at the sea. "The Marquis de Lafayette. Cannot believe I just met that guy." Then Ricky nudged Stranger. "Time to let the rest go."

After a quick warning to the men on the other side to back up, Ricky and Stranger started attacking the dented door with their shoulder. It took multiple tries and a comment or two on Ricky's end about how he was "too old for this kind of work," but the frame finally gave in and the door swung open. Uniformed men poured out of the room, stretching their necks and taking in the scattered remains of their weaponry.

The captain ran to the railing and threw back his head when he saw the retreating lifeboats. "Aw, they're getting away!"

My muscles started shaking from the effort of keeping the energy off all materials. The captain started arguing with his guards. Stranger tried to calm him down, which only turned the attacks on him. He blamed Stranger and me for the riot, since it happened not long after we came on board. Stranger defended both of us, but there was no evidence on either side so the yelling just went in circles. The guards started searching through their weaponry, looking for something they might be able to use. Some ran into the steering room to change the course to pick the prisoners back up, and Ricky...Ricky just stared into the sea. Waiting with narrowed eyes. For what, I didn't know. I didn't care.

If I didn't find some way to get rid of this energy I'd black out again, and who knew where it would scatter or who it would hurt? I thought about tossing it into the sea. Could the ocean drown it? Would a few drops of seawater steam into the sky, or would the void energy just spread, infecting coast to coast? I had no idea how this stuff worked, but considered the easy out. Maybe it would just be a problem for the future, another time. But my gut warned me not to let it go, not here. Not anywhere in my world. This energy was wrong, the exact opposite of all life. Letting it spread might just be the worst case scenario.

Aren't worst case scenarios the best? The voice was on deck. I struggled to turn my heavy head. The humanoid gap stepped through the open door and to me. Emptiness leaked out of it like a bad smell. *You struggle,* it said. *Why?*

Because I'm human, I thought. *I'm not meant to do stuff like this.*

The humanoid void tilted its head at me. *Are you trying to save them?* it asked.

"Please," I whispered, and my voice shook with my muscles. I

99

could feel the sweat gather at the base of my neck. "Help me."

Stranger turned and looked at me. The Void gave a chuckle and, even though there was nothing to see, I could have sworn I felt it smile. It closed the distance between us until we were a mere inch apart. A vacuum-like force radiated with control from The Void. It pulled against my very cells, threatening to tear them apart if it got any closer. I winced and leaned back, but it only leaned over me. A hand-shaped darkness almost grazed my cheek with a caress, but stopped. *You owe me*, it said, *for this favor.*

And just like that the weight disappeared. The smoky emptiness that surrounded the ship got sucked back into The Void. It stepped back and I knew, instinctively, that it looked straight at me. *I will collect*, it promised, and then it too was gone.

With it, the physical world pinched out like a candle flame against fingers. Sharp, bright colors attacked my vision, just like before, when I'd used the energy to escape the Lusitania. All around me was the energy of the world. The primal red swirls underwater as the fish went about their daily searches for food and safety. The red cheeked reds of the infuriated British captain and officers as they desperately tried to gain control of a lost situation. Stranger's dominate yellow as he worked for the peace, keeping everyone calm despite the circumstances.

Then there was Ricky. Before, his castle walls were too strong, too powerful for me to see through, but not now. His walls were still up of course, in full force, to keep me away, but with the physical world snuffed out, the energetic one was stronger than ever. His walls were no defense for my sight in that moment.

The green was still there, technically...that family-loving, protective aura Ricky had let me see, but it wasn't the dominant energy of his soul. No, it shared that title with another side, one I quickly understood why he hid. I never would have trusted him if I'd seen this. The color was murky green, like swamp water. The man half-drowned in resentment, blaming another for his own misfortune. A hero high on a pedestal had tossed him aside like rotten meat. It was this side of him that churned with excitement now. A thought echoed in my mind when I reached out to it. *Trust me*. It was a girl's voice, too distorted for me to get anything else from it. Years of festering had twisted it into a monster's chant.

Ricky must have touched his hand to the railings of the ship, because the passive colors absorbed his energies with a hunger. Ricky's spirit was possessive of the ship, leaving his signature on the metal itself. Even though it could be done subconsciously, the strength of his mark suggested a conscious ownership. Strange, considering his brief but unwelcoming stay here. Why would a man feel possessive over his own prison? A rush of red tinted through that swampy green. Adrenaline.

"Penny?" Stranger ran over to my side. The second his hand touched my arm, the severity of the energetic world dimmed to a sunset in a time lapse. The physical world flickered back to life around me. The bright reflection of the water, the rusted grey of the ship, Stranger's sharp blue eyes. I stumbled, for a moment unbalanced between the two realities. My fingers wrapped around his muscled arm for stability. "You okay?" he asked. "What was that back there?"

"Um...." I took a deep breath to slow my heartbeat down. Nope, I would need a moment or two before I could speak again. I rose a finger up for a pause and leaned over. My stomach couldn't decide if it wanted to rattle around like my heartbeat or just skip to the chase and throw up. "There was this energy. I've never felt anything like it before, but I could use it. Stranger, it felt unlike anything that could possibly be real, but...," I gulped, "who knows?" He frowned. "I know," I said as I risked standing straight. My stomach stayed put, so at least one thing went right. "It sounds—"

"Familiar."

"I was going to say crazy." I studied him and tried to get some info from his energy, but my spiritual vision was even more drained than my physical. I'd need time to rest up before I got any energetic info. But the darkness had formed around his house, stood next to him on the porch as Dinah and I had driven home. It wasn't just me the darkness had targeted, but Stranger too. "Are you remembering something?"

"Almost," Stranger said. His right arm still held onto my elbow, like I might sway off course any second, but his left hand clenched into a fist at his side only to stretch out as if to grab something vital, just out of reach. Clench. Stretch. Clench. Stretch. Then he groaned. "I can't remember anything." He aimed those adorable pale blue eyes at me in apology. "I'm sorry, Penny. I feel like I could help, like I should be able to, but every time I get close to a memory, it just gets yanked away from me again. What you said, that emptiness, that sounds familiar. It's not dark matter. Or anti matter, because both are technically matter, while this...." He gestured with his hand. "It's like the cushion between."

"Between what?"

He shook his head. "I don't know. But did you feel it, Penny? Was that what made you so unsteady? Because if so, this entire ship is in danger. We need to get off of it now. Whatever that energy touches, it destroys, and I don't know how to control it, so—"

"It's gone," I said.

He looked from me to the clear holes in the ship's main deck. "That's what you were doing. You used…. You controlled…." I noticed with a pang that his hand fell from my elbow. I didn't need empathic powers to feel him pull away.

"It was only a matter of time before things got out of hand," I justified. "They were already starting to beat you and Ricky up, and I wasn't just going to sit back and do nothing, okay? It all ended fine. No one got seriously injured."

"Of course," he said. "You saved us. Thank you." But he didn't look up from the holes, from the burnt marks in the metal.

"Excuse me." Ricky waved at Stranger and me. "You two done having a moment?" I felt my cheeks burn and flashed him a glare. He gave a wide, over exaggerated grin back. "Then could you two kindly come over here?" He gestured behind him. Stranger and I shared a confused look before obeying. The men were coming back up deck, spreading their captain's orders. *We saved the prisoners*, I thought, as I saw all the officers gather with their reports. Sure, they were lost at sea. A few dangerous convicts got away, but they could get home. Or we'd think up a plan. The captain and his officers would hopefully return to Britain to fix their ship, and everyone would be back where they belonged.

"You think you've won, don't you? But there are plenty of us in this sea," the captain said. "Surrender now and you won't be killed next time you pass a British ship. Without rations, those escapees won't make it far. We'll get them picked up in no time. You three can be rewarded for not running away. Return to your cells, where you can live out the rest of your sentence in peace."

I opened my mouth to argue that his version of "in peace" including starvation and vile mistreatment, but before I could say a word Ricky reached behind his back, lifted his shirt just a touch, and pulled out a small, olden time western gun with a long barrel and tall safety trigger. He aimed it at the captain. "I'm glad there are many of you in this sea," he said. "Then maybe you'll find someone who'll take you aboard before you starve."

Chapter 15

The captain raised his hands in surrender, but he didn't look surprised. "Knew I should have locked you up as soon as we were free."

"Well, that would have been a poor thank you, seeing as I got you out," Ricky retorted. Stranger and I rolled our eyes at the same time. He'd kind of played a minor part in the rescuing, but apparently he felt no need to share the credit. Not that I wanted any part in his current role. My memory dinged at the way he looked at the ship with a calm possession. The way his energy seemed to claim the place as his own. I cursed myself. I should have seen this coming.

"After you got everyone else out," the captain noted. "Seems to me you're behind everything. You and those two little stowaways."

"Nah, just took advantage of a bad situation. Seems that's how a person makes it in life. Which means I'm going to take this ship, so you and your men are going to have to get off."

"What?" everyone chorused. Even me.

Ricky grinned, sending wrinkles through his scar. "Come on. You didn't think old Pointy Beard there was the only pirate on the ship. My own men are already on their way. You see they've been watching this ship for days now, waiting for my signal."

"What signal?"

"The lifeboats." Ricky gestured at the disappearing shapes in the horizon. "Men paddling away in fear for their lives from a perfectly sound ship. Makes for a pretty good signal if you ask me. And now, any moment, my men will come aboard, weapons at the ready. Not that I'll need them." He gestured toward me and I looked down, unable to meet anyone's eyes. "She burned your deck once. She'll do it again. Single-handedly sent those prisoners rowing away for their lives. I'm sure you don't need a demonstration, as you can already see by the scars in the metal. She's quite talented."

I flushed but kept my mouth shut. I didn't know why I'd trusted Ricky. Why I let him take the lead, didn't call him out. He had nothing but one gun and a bluff for back-up, because whether he knew it or not, everything that made me scary had gone away with The Void. I should toss this double-crossing liar back in his cell and send this ship after the convicts. I should let these poor guards do their job and get out of the way before I messed things up any worse than I had already. Tears stung my eyes but I blinked them back down. For a moment there, I thought I had been the hero, here to save the day, when in reality, I had helped a pirate mutiny. I couldn't even rescue right. I bit my tongue and kept my eyes on the deck, choking down any screams of betrayal. Because Ricky had said he would help me get back to Dinah. He'd said he would take me home. And, to be honest, I was a bit of a coward. The thing that made me feel so unstoppable had left. I was just me again. Just a kid who saw the energies around her, the lies and the pain. The girl who knew but couldn't do anything about it.

"What are you doing?" Stranger asked. "You said we were here to rescue people, not steal a ship."

"Plans change. Besides, you *were* a hero. We distracted the prisoners, kept them from killing each other until Penny could do her thing. And now...." He readjusted his aim and stepped around the men. Sandwiching them between an escape and a gun, and with a perfect view of the burns in the metal. "Now we watch as these oh-so-compassionate prison guards make the right choice. My men will be here any moment. And once they get here, it'll be too late. I'm an honest pirate, and am giving you an option here. Live. Go fight your war. Or become victims of my men. They aren't as kind as me."

"You were a stowaway," the captain remembered. "You targeted this ship, didn't you?"

"Not me personally. This place isn't exactly my taste, but an old friend of mine gifted it to me."

"This ship will never be yours."

Ricky smiled and his scar crinkled. "It already is."

"Which ship do you belong to?" the captain asked.

Ricky smirked. "You mean before this one? The Pirates Noble," Ricky said with a flourish of a hand twist just above his eye. I got the feeling he was used to big hats.

"Never heard of you."

"I'm a good pirate. Don't let people go who would spread stories. If you know what I mean." Ricky flourished his gun in emphasis. The captain's face went white, and it was like fuel to Ricky's cockiness. His smirk widened and he swayed on the balls of his feet like he struggled not to do a happy dance. "You tell your boss, your navy, we own this part of the sea. No one comes here. No one bothers us and we don't bother you."

"So we're supposed to trust the word of a pirate?"

"Like your life depends on it," he said, and flicked the safety off.

"I'm afraid I'm going to have to decline," the captain said, and by the look on his face, he meant to continue with some rousing speech about loyalty. But then one of his men gasped. They pointed behind us and everyone leaned to see. Those who needed to turned. Everyone looked except Ricky. Ricky just smashed his lips together against the smile, like today was officially the best day ever.

Four simple but decent sized sailboats headed our way, filled to the brim with men, ratty haired and soapless by the silhouettes. All different sizes, some tall and lanky, others short and stocky. And I could have sworn I saw what looked like guns resting on the shoulders of at least half of them. Armed and animalistic.

"Last chance," Ricky said. "Go chase your prisoners. Let one or two go. You might still catch up to them. Maybe come back heroes."

"We'd die heroes here," the captain said.

"Yeah, I always thought that was a dumb tradition. Think of your families. Who will take care of them when you die heroes?"

That got the guards thinking. More than one glanced at the other. Even the captain blinked as he digested the thought.

"Sir," one of the men said. He tried to whisper, but the breeze carried his concerned tone. "I've got three daughters."

"I've got a newborn," another added.

"I don't have any. I'm not ending my legacy here," another grumbled.

The captain rubbed a gold band on his left ring finger, his jaw tight. "Fine," he said. "But you won't go far. We'll be back. With re-enforcements."

"See ya then. Ta-ta." Ricky waved his hand for them to get moving. For the second time that day, I watched as strong men squeezed into lifeboats to get away from the three of us. Heck, even I questioned whether I wanted to be around when Ricky's friends got there. Would I have been safer with the escaped prisoners?

Holy time-travel. I kept my face calm but my insides wanted to jump to the bottom of the freaking ocean. *Did I just help a pirate steal a ship?* Granted, I'd pretty much done it single-handedly, so I was still going to pat myself on the back. But holy…. There were no words. I'd just helped a pirate. Man, I felt like I should have seen that coming. His aura hadn't seemed greedy and arrrgh-like at all. Then again, I didn't know what that would look like. Never met a pirate before. If I lived through today, I'd write this down in my diary as the impossible day. Granted, for a lot of reasons, but especially this exchange. All that and only a few punches? Maybe I'd watched too much TV, but I hadn't expected Ricky's bluff to work.

Stranger stepped closer to me and tore his face away from Ricky. "So, what's the plan?"

"You two are staying with me," Ricky answered for me.

"I don't know what else to do," I whispered to Stranger.

Ricky didn't say anything as the guards and captain continued their escape. I had questions, concerns racing to escape my mind. I wanted to confront him and get some real answers, but I knew why Ricky was silent. Whatever conversation we were about to have, it needed to wait until the captain and his men were gone. The bluff needed to stay strong. So I waited. I held my tongue until the lifeboat hit the water and the guards started rowing. Ricky grinned and flicked the safety back on his gun before tucking it behind his shirt. Wait, wasn't he even going to bother explaining?

"Hey!" I snapped, and turned on Ricky. He actually jumped in surprise, which only ticked me off even more. Did he think I would just roll over on this? "What was that? I promised to help you save people, not steal a freaking ship!" He held up his hands for me to calm down, but I had held it in too long. "Was this your plan the whole time? You used me! You used all of us! We should call them back right now and tell them it's all a bluff and put you back behind bars!"

To my frustration, that big bear of a man just grinned at my rant. "A bluff, huh? Like what you did? Was that a bluff?" He gestured at

107

the scars in the deck floor.

"That was different."

"So is it gone? That creepy energy you used to scare everyone away?"

"How did you know about that?" I asked, my voice lower.

"Wild guess." He went to the railing and waved at the incoming boat. One of the men waved back, and the boat started toward us with renewed speed. My heart thumped the beat of fear. I wanted to run away before the situation came into play, because there was no way it could end well. Which seemed to be a theme lately. Before today, I'd never cared for ships one way or another, but now I hated them. I hated the way they trapped me, unable to run away, forcing me to face whatever came. Stranger pulled me behind him as the boat neared.

"Listen, Penny," Ricky said. "You might not believe this, but I'm a good guy. Trustworthy, even as I steal a ship from the British Army. This old friend of mine, she's a genius. Barely human, if she's even that, but she promised to take care of me, and I…." He hesitated, then gave a small, hesitant grin. "I trust her." He stepped over and put his hand on my shoulder, like a father might to his child. "I think she'd want me to tell you. You are what you choose to be."

"What does that mean?" I asked.

He shrugged. "Never quite knew what she went on about."

Stranger narrowed his eyes at Ricky and leaned his head back to speak to me. "Why do I get the feeling he just said a lot of nonsense in hopes you'd forgotten your question?"

Ricky smiled. "The job wasn't to free anyone. The escape, the teetering riot, the lost American hero, your great big performance, none of it had anything to do with the plan."

"Which was?" Stranger pressed.

Ricky sighed in the way one might after setting down a heavy box pressing against their back. He walked to the edge of the railing as the four boats neared. They were still too far out to see, but some of the occupants waved at Ricky. Giggling made its way through the wind. "I have a sneaking suspicion the plan was to save me."

Chapter 16

The sailboats docked at the ship. From this distance, the ruffians didn't seem so dangerous. Yeah, their hair was ratted and their faces dirty and scary-looking, but it all looked so fake close up. Already they were patting their hair down, rubbing the dirt from their cheeks, and straightening their clothes. The wildness look to them was an act, part of Ricky's bluff. They weren't even grownups, but kids of all ages. Most of them seemed to be around twelve to seventeen, but a four-year-old or two zoomed under the legs of the others, playing tag. Boys and girls, all from different parts of the world, spilled out of that boat. There had to be at least fifteen of them. And what had looked like guns from afar were actually carved sticks.

Within a few quick seconds, they'd booked it up the stairs. "Ricky!" they yelled, and attacked him with hugs. He laughed and fell over and soon was overrun. I blinked and hurried out of the way. One minute Ricky was the helpful prisoner, then the scheming pirate that kept to himself. Going from the noble guy who'd take a punch to protect a girl, to stealing a ship, to…. Papa bear?

"What the…?" Stranger's voice trailed off.

"Yeah," I said. "Where exactly did these kids come from?"

"Here and there," Ricky managed to say between tickle attacks and tackles.

One of the older kids held back, watching the younger ones attack Ricky. He wore black pants and matching black shirt to match an almost unnatural shade of black hair, as if it were the only color he appreciated. He nodded at me when our eyes met. "Ricky likes to take in orphans," he explained. "Can't resist a homeless kid. Gummy?" He pulled out a bag of gummy bears from his pants pocket.

"No thanks," I said. He shrugged and split the bag with the other kids that chimed up at the request. Did gummies exist during the Revolutionary War? I wanted to say no. So where had these kids come from? Different places, clearly, but could they be from different times too?

Only one grown up had come from the boat. Whoever they were wore a wide, clichéd pirate's hat with a worn feather along the side and long baggy clothes, so I couldn't make out any specifics of the person. But I watched as they took up the rear of the crowd and made their way up the steps. Then the stairs reached the deck and the mystery person turned toward us so I could finally see details.

Power radiated from the woman. She had a strong Indian frame and a pixie haircut. She seemed dressed to look scary, with torn, oversized pants and shirt, while her hair pointed out in all directions. Up close, her hair just looked like she'd drank one too many energy drinks. "Did we scare them all away?" she hollered over the sound of kids "tickling" Ricky.

"Yeah!" he yelled back. "Bet we got a couple of hours before we have to run for it!" He tried to get to his feet, but the two four year olds tackled his arms to pull him down again. He straightened himself up and started lifting them up like weights as they laughed.

The older kids finished saying their hellos and went exploring, leaning their heads through the railings and pointing at the scarred metal deck like it was some fun decoration. Most of them gave me a nod of recognition when they passed, but no one bothered to introduce themselves. The woman stepped through the waves of kids with a stern face as she stared Ricky down, but her lips strained too much to stay straight and Ricky laughed.

"Told ya it would work." He grinned. "Hey Penny, Stranger, come meet my wife."

She raised an eyebrow at that before realization dawned on her. She turned and gave me a dazzling, toothy smile. "Oh, is this when we meet? How exciting. I'm Zetta Noble." She held a hand out and I took it. Rough, calloused fingers tickled my skin as she shook my hand, then turned to take Stranger's.

I'm not going to lie to you, I was star-struck when I saw this woman.

110

I'd never seen her before, but she radiated power. Completely different from Ricky's big bear energy. She seemed so…complete, like she knew without a doubt exactly who she was. Without closing my eyes, I tested the energy around her. The details were fuzzy. My inner eye was still exhausted from all that energy work to scare the people away, but I saw enough. Zetta's aura was a soft rainbow, all the different parts of herself out and in the open. Never before had it been easier to read someone. I wouldn't say it was because Zetta held everything out like a banner. She didn't seem to ask for attention, nor did she push herself onto other people. She was just so free and open. She didn't hide one single part of her.

What would that feel like? To be that accepting of myself that I wouldn't have to hide it from anyone? I was still just a kid. I didn't even know all the parts of me that I hid. I knew there were other parts of me, parts I didn't look at, which I didn't want to admit were there. At least that's what teachers said when they ranted about the subconscious. What would that feel like, though? To not be afraid of the shadowy parts within myself? "You two are staying for dinner, right?" Zetta asked. "One of our boys makes an excellent paella. He's been working on it all afternoon."

"How?" I asked. "You just got here, and I'm pretty sure the British Navy didn't stock paella makings."

She smiled and tilted her head. "He's at home in the kitchen. Did Ricky not—?" She made a face and glared at Ricky. "How long have you been around those two? And have you explained anything?"

"I just…." Ricky waved at the empty captain's deck but sighed. "There hasn't been a lot of time for chatting. As you can see by the bruise I have. Just there."

She narrowed her eyes at his jawline. "I don't see anything."

"Exactly," Ricky said. "It's happened so recently that my face hasn't had time to swell. That's how busy we've been."

"Well." Zetta clapped her hands together. "I'm going to go teach the kids how to crank up this ship's speed before all of Britain comes after us. Honey…." She patted Ricky's shoulder. "Why don't you take Penny and Stranger downstairs and fill them in on everything you avoided explaining before."

"Explaining takes the fun out of everything," he said with an exaggerated eye roll. "All right, kids, follow the Pirate Noble to hear your future." He waved at us to follow and headed down the stairs below decks. I narrowed my eyes at Ricky's words and glanced at Stranger. He had the same look, and I had the feeling he thought the same thing. If someone said that at a carnival, I would not give them my money.

"Why?" I didn't want to ask it. I was glad Lafayette was safe, and was happy to hear laughter on this ship but, at the end of the day, who were these people to me? Ricky said he suspected this whole thing was about him. Well, excuse me if I didn't see the happy ending being quite worth time hopping. "Why are we traveling from one ship to the other, enduring tragedies for the sake of one man?"

"Wasn't that the mission?" Stranger asked. "That's what we were supposed to do."

"Probably," Ricky allowed. "Never could figure that part out myself."

Stranger looked at me to explain. "I don't know. I'm the one that asked," I said. "And who's this old friend of yours you keep talking about? Are they the one who calls the shots on these *plans*?"

"Ah, my good ol' friend." Ricky shook his head. "You'll meet her eventually, I'm sure. Us time travelers always run into each other."

"What else did Zetta mean when she told you to fill us in?" I asked. "She mentioned that some of your...crew, are still back at home?"

"And that they have paella?" Stranger added.

"Yeah." Ricky laughed. "My daughter's back there, keeping everyone in order."

We reached the inner deck with those now empty cells. I wouldn't exactly say that the place was creepier without the prisoners lurking in their cells, but somehow it still didn't feel safe. Upstairs, the kids joked around and their laughs haunted the inside of the ship like ghosts. We stopped at the cell of darkness, only now it just seemed like every other cell. Dirty, damp, and foul smelling, but not unnatural. The only evidence the cell had ever held anything strange came from the burnt bars, and one sliver of residual empty energy floating in the middle of the cell like a forgotten breath.

Ricky stopped and turned to me. "I need you to create another gap through time."

Chapter 17

"You want me to what?"

"Like you did to get here," Ricky said. "Listen, Penny, I know Zetta and I are calm considering we just stole a British iron clad, but we're not exactly rich on time, so I can't explain everything right now. We need the rest of our crew if we want a fighting chance of getting this heavy chunk of metal to have any decent speed. Now, when you were on the Lusitania, you got Stranger and yourself out, right?"

"Right," I said, but didn't like where he was going. It made me feel self-conscious. Stranger followed our conversation with tense interest, and I remembered how close he'd held his energies after he learned about my talents. For a moment there, during all the action, it was like he'd forgotten, but Ricky's request had brought everything back. How could I manipulate explanations back into my favor? "I don't know what I was doing. It was just adrenaline."

"I know," Ricky said. "When you did what you did, you created a door through time and space, a gap right smack through reality. Now, that door was destroyed when the ship sank, so we don't have to worry about anyone else skipping through time. For the future, though, you should see about breaking the connection before people starting accidentally jumping. Mass chaos. That sort of thing. But first, I need you to create a door for me."

"I thought you were a time traveler too. Can't you do all this already?"

"Ah." Ricky scratched the back of his neck. "I'm more of a time hitchhiker."

"You know what?" I took a step back, "I don't feel comfortable with this. Why don't you open the door or get Zetta to do it?"

"We can't create doors, Penny. Only you can."

"You said Zetta was a natural empath, like me."

"There's no one like you. I meditate a lot, and I still can't see the energies around me. I can feel them, I've become more intuitive, but I'm not as powerful as you are. No one is. Zetta's trained in chakras, auras, and meditations since she was a little girl. She's read auras since before she could speak. But the emptiness you see? That strange unnatural energy? You're the only one who can control it, who can even see it. It's like you and the energy have some strange bond. Anyway," he continued, and I realized I had folded my arms protectively across my chest. "We need one of those doors now so I can get the rest of my crew. The rest of my family."

"So what do you expect me to do?"

"Well, is there any more of that creepy void energy left?"

Did I have to answer? Yes. Because I wanted off this ship as badly as he wanted his family on it. I sighed. "Maybe."

"I need you to do what you did at the Lusitania. Only instead of a swirling mass of scariness, we need a door, something that can be locked but without losing the power of the gap. I need it to open in the 23rd century. There'll be a girl on the other side. If she's listening to her father, and she never does, she'll be meditating and tossing out mental texts so you can find her."

"I've literally never done anything like this before," I said. "You are grossly overestimating my abilities."

"Are we?" This time it was Stranger who spoke. I raised my eyebrows at him in a harsh *you're supposed to be on my side* look, but it didn't faze him. "I mean, all this is news to me, but from what I've seen, you can do just about anything."

Ahh, okay. Well, that was just adorable. I couldn't stay mad at an argument like that, and couldn't help giving Stranger a smile. Maybe he wasn't as uncomfortable as I'd assumed. "I guess I can give it a try, but I want it on record right now that I cannot guarantee the outcome of any of this."

"It's okay, I trust you," Ricky said.

Maybe it was the sincerity in Ricky's voice or the way his eyes twitched, like maybe that trust wasn't so easy, but I wanted to be trustworthy. Not only that, but I wanted to be memorable. If I saved this man, brought his daughter to him, surely he wouldn't forget me.

"Okay," I said. "And I'll do it. I promise." I closed my eyes and focused on the energy. There was less this time, and I didn't have the adrenaline rush that had helped me along at the Lusitania. I stretched back my shoulders and stood straighter, trying to imitate confidence. I moved my neck from side to side. *It's okay. I've got this.* I knew exactly what....

Who was I kidding? I didn't have a clue what I was doing. I never had. But, in general, I kind of rocked at winging it, so I lifted my hand and imagined it reaching through the bars to the residual energy. *You're a door,* I told the energy. *You open to the 23rd century. I command you to become a door.* I could have sworn I heard it snort. I gritted my teeth and stepped into the cell.

No one makes a fool out of me.

Hey! I mentally yelled. I reached up my other hand and imagined gripping that gap in reality at both sides, like clay about to be crafted. *You do what I say. I'm the boss around here.* The words flowed through my mind like liquid. True and strong. And terrifying. My own bones shivered at the sound of that voice, even if it only spoke within my mind. The energy swirled to the edge of the cell at my command. It smoothed itself against the ship's outer wall, stretching thin until it reached the shape of a door. The ship's iron wall burned as the door-shaped energy burrowed its way in. The emptiness materialized, hardening into a homemade, raft-like door...six feet of sticks tied together with string, a roughly carved piece of wood as the knob.

"I just made a door," I whispered, too low for anyone else to hear. The object was my creation, no question, and yet the impossibility of creating something out of nothing overwhelmed my logic, which shook like an overworked wheel about to burst off its axle. My brain wanted to back off, take this slower, not go any further until I understood what was happening. I glanced at Ricky like *I just made a freaking door,* but he didn't seem at all surprised. In fact, the guy had his head tilted as if critiquing the craftsmanship of my design. Stranger gave a more appropriate response. He gaped open mouthed while squinting his eyes as if trying to work out an impossible equation. His expression validated my own confusion.

"What now?" I asked.

"There should be a gap in time and space behind that door," Ricky said. "I need you to reach out with your mind and create a mental link with my daughter. A solid link will ensure you open the door at the right moment. Then, we just go through."

I closed the distance between me and the new door and placed my hand against its cool material. If I hadn't known its origins, I never would have been able to tell that it came from nothing. How was this possible? Keeping my eyes closed, I sensed through the door, at the energies swimming on the other side. Nothing, and everything at the same time. Possibilities danced with the implausible. Having no idea what the 23rd century might look like, I couldn't make a mental search for it. Instead, I thought about Ricky's daughter. Oh, wait, I knew nothing about her, either. This was a great plan, people.

"Your daughter," I said, keeping my attention on the dancing possibilities in front of me. "Do you have some idea of what she could be thinking? What she's like? I need something to search for."

Ricky whistled. "Honestly didn't think we'd get this far." His voice was low. I got the feeling he spoke to Stranger, didn't mean for me to hear, but it wasn't exactly reassuring either way. When he spoke again, it was louder. "Her name is Shreya Noble. She's sweet, has great heart.... Doesn't believe in time travel, thinks I'm loony." He gave a mischievous smirk. "Bet me fifty bucks that I can't prove it."

"A lot of people don't believe in time travel," I pointed out. "I need something unique to her."

"She'll be helping one of my crew make paella. You know that saying 'she wouldn't hurt a fly'? It's usually just an expression, but Shreya's taken it to a whole new level. She treasures the lives of all kinds, from whale to gnat, and asks permission from her garden before she harvests. Not a great fan of humans though. Every word out of her mouth is sarcasm. Although, maybe that's just to me. Yup, that's Shreya."

"That could work." I returned my attention to the door. Shreya Noble, paella, and a borderline superpower level of love for annoying stuff like gnats. Shreya. Paella. Loves gnats. The song hit me first, a sort of lullaby. Soft and half forgotten, the hum in the back of someone's head. Then the rich saffron filled my senses, making my mouth water. *Mmm, when was the last time I ate?* That smelled good. The aura was almost a neon pink, so strong it dominated my senses, making that rich saffron about as powerful as table salt. This person loved more than anyone I'd ever met. Like it was a way of life for the person. But the soul still went through life with a raw sense of idealism and confusion. This soul was young, still guarded. Her love hesitated even as it swirled around her, as if sharing it might hurt more than it gave. I sensed that insincerity came out as severe sarcasm.

"I think I might have found her." I kept my eyes closed as I spoke. A smile of incredulousness etched across my face.

"Bring her home." I could hear the smile in Ricky's voice.

"Think she'll be excited to see her new house?" Stranger asked. "I can't pretend to understand girls, but I'm pretty sure prison ships don't exactly inhabit their dream homes."

"There are worse homes in the world than an *ex*-prison ship," was Ricky's final reply on the subject. The next step came as easy to me as breathing, like a dance my muscles had memorized long ago. I strengthened the connection between me and the aura and pulled it closer. Then I reached out and turned the door knob.

It opened to a kitchen. Not the American suburban kitchen. There was a homemade stove made out of scraps of metal and open wires. Three guys of various ethnicities cut vegetables and ground fresh spices on tables of different heights. One had a makeshift leg of wood tied together with rope. The three boys were arguing over how a song began.

"It starts with Loo Loo Loo Loo, you mouth breather."

"That doesn't even make any sense!"

"No, he's right, that's how the melody starts."

"Shreya, how does *I'll Take You Dreaming* start?"

They all turned to the teenage girl stirring a pot on a stove. But in doing so, they caught sight of me, holding a door open to another world. Needless to say, all three mouths dropped. The teenage girl, who I assumed was Shreya, had her back to us.

"Listen," she said, "I realize I'm amazing, but you really need to stop gaping."

The boys seemed too stunned to continue. I thought about saying something like *Welcome, travelers, to a land in another time!* Or maybe *got any extras of that paella?* But, truth be told, I kind of wanted to see how long it would take for Ricky the Pirate's daughter to turn around.

"What?" Shreya asked. She glanced over her shoulder and saw me. I waved. Her eyes went to Ricky behind me. Her face stayed neutral as she went to the door frame and peeked through. I stepped aside to give her a clear view of the unclean prison cells and shady lighting. Then

117

she looked at me. "What year?" she asked.

"1780, I believe. Haven't been here long," I admitted.

She tried to keep her face neutral, but I noticed a slight cringe. She went to the stove, unplugged it from a shady looking wall plug, handed the pot to one of the boys as they slowly blinked out of shock, and lifted it up with some heat safe grip handles on the side. She carried the makeshift stove into the ship. The girl was actually going to walk that thing right past us until Ricky cleared his throat. He held his hand out expectantly. Shreya set the stove down and groaned, as all teenagers know how, as she reached into her pocket and tossed a wad of wrinkly multicolored cash at Ricky. "Just because you proved time travel is possible doesn't make *any* of the other stories real," she said. She glanced pointedly at the stove. "You can carry that upstairs. I'm going to find Mom."

Ricky counted the money as Shreya headed up the stairs. The boys carried the rest of the supplies in and followed suit toward the deck.

"Wow," Stranger said. "For someone who doesn't believe in time travel, she took the news pretty well."

"Eh, she should know better than to bet against me." Ricky counted the money.

"It's the 1700s," I pointed out as I nodded at the cash. "I don't know when that money came from, but I doubt it's valid here."

Ricky tossed the wad at me. "Monopoly money," he said. "Think I'd take actual money from my own daughter?"

"You just stole a ship," Stranger said.

Ricky laughed deep from his chest. "Oh man, you two are hilarious."

I shook my head, but chuckled. "Trusting you gives me whiplash," I teased.

"Learned from the best." His face was still laughing, but his soul had sobered slightly at the sentence. He'd talked a lot about an old friend in the short time I knew him, someone who helped him time travel, told him the big plans, the why of everything we did. Maybe someone he didn't completely trust.

What kind of old friend was this? How did they do what I could do? Were there more like me? Empathic naturals who could control the darkness too? If everything Ricky said was true, this person understood time travel. Created the plans. Might be an interesting dinner if I could find that person, the one with all the answers.

But why search for answers when I could go home? Ricky had taught me how to control the time jumps. I wouldn't have to run blindly and hope for the best, getting more and more lost in the process. I could just find Dinah, take a step, and be home.

I went back to the door, checked that the kitchen was empty, and closed it. The connection snapped, and that moment in time zoomed back into the darkness until it was gone. I searched for Dinah's analytical blue, the curl of bangs she hid behind, the way she went into a stranger's home, answering the call for help.

Nothing.

A rush of panic clogged my chest. Why was there nothing? Where was she? The memory of her crumpled form in the corner of that basement, the darkness reaching out....

No. I tried.... Just no. I tried again. Nothing. One more time. Okay, last try.

"What?" Stranger's snap knocked me out of my tunnel vision. "Why can't we stay here?"

"The British Army is going to be on our tails sooner than later. I need you two off the ship."

"Are you kidding me? Your kid crew can stay, but not us? We just—"

"Okay." My voice sounded far away. I moved, but couldn't quite feel my legs. "Okay, we'll leave. You said you could help us go home. Just...." I waved at the door. My hand was heavy. "Walk me through it. Get us home."

Ricky sighed, and his aura deflated. His shoulders slumped. "You can't go home. It's gone."

Chapter 18

My blood went cold. My heart stuttered, and for a moment, no thoughts dared exist in my mind. Because if I kept breathing, if I thought…if it was true….

"No," I said. "You said you were the one who helped me get home." My voice was higher than normal. Tension started between my eyes as I insisted I didn't need to cry.

"It's just that…." Ricky grimaced when he looked at me. I hoped he felt guilty. But he steeled his face and tried again, without any trace of regret. "It's not that simple." He even gave a small chuckle. "Never is, right?" I glared at him and the forced humor faded. "I will help, Penny. I'll do everything I can, but you can't just walk through."

"What aren't you telling me?" I accused.

"It's too unstable," he said with a shrug. "The explosion from the experiment messed everything up."

My gut dinged, intuition tapping for attention. *There's more to this story.* "And?"

"And what? It's out of reach this way. You can't make a connection." He folded his arms around his chest, blinked a few too many times. "Making a mental link between this moment and that basement would be akin to surfing through an avalanche."

"And your oh-so-precious 'old friend' doesn't have any advice either, I suppose? Who is this person? I want to meet them."

"In due time, I'm sure."

"Ah, a vague answer. You rock at those. Did you know that? I'm not going anywhere until you tell us where this friend of yours is."

"Penny." Stranger spoke low, his eyes still on Ricky. "He said we have to go. Back when you were meditating, he...he's kicking us out."

"So, not only are you a liar, but you're also a poor host to the people you owe your life to." I spread my arms out in a sarcastic shrug. "I guess I should have expected as much from a pirate."

"I'd love to barbeque on the deck with you 'til the Revolution is over, and then go check out the New America if that's what you wanted to do, but this is a vital moment in my life. I just got a new ship and I'm a wanted man."

"So?"

"The future is...." Ricky paused as he considered what word to use next. "It's like marble. Hard and beautiful and consistent. No one touches a slab of marble and expects it to change. But you...." He waved at me and I leaned back. "You're the only chisel in town. You're already changing history. Lafayette's back into play. The war's been shortened significantly. The entire history of America changed because you were here. Futures melt under your grip."

"Melt?" Stranger said. "Shouldn't you say she chisels futures or something?"

"I thought you wanted me to save him?!"

"I did. It was a good change. But my future is a slab of marble too, and I like the jagged ends of it. I want them to stay the way they are. But when you're around...." Ricky shook his head. "No rules apply and, frankly, it scares the faith out of me."

"At least you have faith," I said. "Fine. I'm not going to linger when I'm not wanted, but answer me one thing first. Dinah. I couldn't feel her at all. But she's okay, right? It's just the unstable connection blocking the mental link."

Ricky blinked and looked away. His tranquil green aura swam in a sympathetic blue. "I'm sure she's fine." A lie.

The tears stung. I had to look up for a second to keep them from falling. "But you're all opinions, right? You don't know for sure."

"I know some things," he admitted. The sympathy leaked from his aura into his facial expressions. He tilted his head, almost in apology. Did the ship sway because of the waves, or was it me that moved?

"Shut up," I snapped. A fresh wave of anger gave me renewed strength. "There's no proof you know anything about my life, okay?

121

For all I know, you're making everything up. I don't trust you, and I'm done listening to you."

"You're the sister of Dinah Grace," Ricky said. "You go to Central High in Cheyenne, Wyoming. All your life you've lived maybe ten blocks from Stranger, but the two of you never met because he was homeschooled." Beside me, Stranger tensed. Ricky had never said anything about knowing Stranger before. But any facts about him were ones I couldn't prove. Ricky could be making them up. He *had* to be. "Dinah and you are twin sisters and incredibly close, but she's never quite gotten used to the idea that you can read energies, and that bothers you. It hurts you," Ricky said. "Because it means she doesn't truly accept you. You can call me a lot of things, Penny, but you must always trust me."

"You've already proven that you can read energies," I said. "You could have just gotten that from my chakras while we've been talking." And then the thought came to me, like a slap in the face. "You don't get to say whether or not I get to go home. You don't know anything about time traveling or that empty gap in energy or...." I wanted to say he didn't know anything about me, but he was right. Dinah had never trusted me, even though I had never done anything wrong. Sometimes I knew things she didn't tell me, things she didn't want to tell me, but could that be my fault? I didn't mean to see it. I never did. Even Stranger's energies were tight, closed off, ever since he found out. It couldn't be my fault I was unnatural.

"I know you, Penny," Ricky insisted. "I've seen you fight to protect me, and I know how hard you try. Even better, I know you can change the future. I'm free because of what only you can do. I have my family with me because of it. And I'm sorry if I've made you question me. That wasn't my intention. Good and bad, Penny, you make a world of difference. But you can't go to Cheyenne. Not through those doors."

His aura gave no tells of lying. His face held steady and apologetic. I hadn't realized how much hope I'd built up with my anger until I realized I believed him. Salted tears stung my eyes. I wanted to keep yelling at him, to demand he keep his end of the bargain, but I knew it would be pointless. So I sniffed and turned away to regain my composure. But he couldn't know the truth about Dinah. In that, at least, I could comfort myself.

"Can you go into more detail?" Stranger asked. I had the feeling he stepped in to give me a moment.

"It's complicated, and I don't get the science of it," Ricky admitted. "I've never been in a century where scientists understood it. All they agreed on was that that weird energy, the void energy, as Penny calls it, wasn't matter and shouldn't exist, by all scientific laws we believe in. But I know you were working on it in your basement. The legends all begin when you got it in your mind that time travel was possible. I personally think you had help. Someone who underestimated the power of the energetic fields you were working with. It got out of hand. Penny felt the pulses as the non-energy seeped out, and then...well, here we all are."

"What else do you know about me?"

"Not much."

"But why time travel?"

"Dude," Ricky said. "It's time travel. Why the heck not?"

"But, so when you say explosion you mean when the energy escaped?"

Ricky nodded. "Pretty much."

"And because it's so unstable, she can't weasel her way through the times?"

"Pretty much. It's hard enough when both times are stable and there's someone on the other side to connect with. But an unstable time with no one calling out for you? Impossible."

"But Dinah's there." I couldn't help saying it. I wiped away a drop of rogue coolness from the tears and turned back to face them. "She's alone and I just disappeared. She'd be searching for me."

But Ricky didn't seem moved. "She was out, right? Knocked cold. By the time she wakes up, the energy would have already escaped."

"So?"

"So...." Ricky tilted his head. His eyes widened like he could convey his meaning without speaking. Like he didn't want to be the one to say it. But I didn't see a problem. Didn't want to see it. "You saw what happened on deck," he finally said. "When that energy touches any type of material."

"She's not dead," I snapped. "That's just not possible. I know she's alive."

"How?" Ricky asked.

"Because—" My voice caught in my throat. "Because I would know. She's my sister. I would just know."

To my surprise, Ricky nodded. "It's always a shock to learn that the sun still rises after a tragedy."

"It's not a shock. It hasn't happened!" I whipped around and snapped at him. "You said I'm the only one who can change time, right? That means nothing you've told me has to be a part of my reality. I'm going home. I'm going to save my sister, and if it's the last thing I do, I will stop that explosion from happening."

I didn't expect Ricky to smile, but his lips still twitched upward. Only it was a sad smile. "You know what? I almost believe you. If you'll wait a moment, I'll get some paella to go for you."

"I just want to go," I said. I didn't care where. I just wanted out of there, away from the people who thought they knew my future. Who spoke with so much confidence that I would fail, that I would change and not for the better.

"Actually," Stranger said. "I literally can't remember the last time I ate. I wouldn't mind some take out."

Ricky nodded. "I'll be right back."

I wiped at the corner of my eye before another tear could fall. I didn't even know where to begin freaking out. Again. When had life become so overwhelming? Just that afternoon, I had been mad because my mom forgot to pick me up from school.

Mom. My stomach churned. I hadn't even thought about my parents in all this. If what Ricky said was true, heaven forbid, then that meant my parents had just lost both their kids. In one moment. One that was entirely my fault. If I hadn't been curious, hadn't insisted we turned around, if I hadn't been so mad at Mom for something as common as an absentminded memory, or been so worried that Dad would freak out over something as meaningless as a lost tablet, none of this would have happened. I could have gone straight home, and investigated this energy smarter. Or better yet, forgotten it entirely. Then Mom and Dad wouldn't have lost two kids in one minute. How would they handle it? I'd heard stories of parents who never quite moved on, who considered themselves forever broken because of the loss of a child. To lose them all in one go? If I couldn't prevent that tragedy, then what was the point of time travel?

"You okay, Penny?" Stranger asked.

I forced my head to nod but studied the deck. Looking up took too much energy. If I looked at him I'd have to put on my mask, and that would only be more exhausting. So I kept my eyes on the dusty floor. That's when I saw it...my dad's tablet. Still sitting on the corner

124

of the cell just barely in my eyesight. Like it had been left with purpose. Because it had. The Void had stolen it from me, but not to prove that it had been watching me. To prove that it could travel to 2017. I had just asked the wrong source how to get home.

Chapter 19

Stranger didn't say anything while we waited for Ricky. I couldn't make any attempts at conversation. I bent down and picked up the tablet, wiped the dust off, and tucked it inside my jacket before Stranger or anyone else could see it. I'd get it home before Dad even knew it had gone missing.

"I'm sorry," Stranger finally said. "I should've agreed just to go."

"No, you're right. We need food." I turned around and forced my heavy cheeks into a smile.

"Feel like I haven't eaten in days," he said.

"You looked like you'd been rocking nothing but Mountain Dew when we got in the basement."

He frowned when I mentioned the basement, but didn't say anything. "Do you believe Ricky?" he asked instead.

I hesitated, but forced myself to shake my head. Ricky couldn't be right. The price was too high. "No. The only thing he's proven is that he's a manipulative pirate. I say the sooner we get away, the better."

"Probably," he agreed. "But where are we supposed to go?"

"I don't care." I tried not to snap, but I was tired and trying hard not to let the waves of desperation resurface. Usually people didn't bother asking for my advice. I felt like I should have been grateful that he did, but it only reminded me how little I knew. "Forwards in time, backwards...I'm okay with anywhere but here." I gave him a fake smile. "Got any favorite times in history you'd like to check out?"

"I'm sure I do, but I don't remember them."

He returned my fake smile with one equally emotionless, and I noted how strange our situation was. Two kids stepping through empty space to end up in another time and place. One with memories, the other without. Neither interested in the prospects. I didn't remember Stranger hitting his head when he tried to save me from the blackness. Where had his memories gone?

"What about you?" he asked. "Any favorite spots?"

"Never thought about it," I admitted. "History was always my mom's thing. She and Dinah *really* bonded over it." Then I smiled in earnest as a memory popped up. "You know where they'd love to go? The Globe Theater. Back when Shakespeare was alive. The school is playing one of his comedies, so she's geeking out about it right now. Was," I corrected. "Or will be?" Stranger shrugged in answer to my attempt at proper grammar.

"You should make her a shirt." We turned around to see Ricky's wife, Zetta, with two brown bags. "It could say 'My sister went back in time and all I got was this lousy T-shirt.' You know, just to gloat." She handed us the bags. "Here's your to-go lunches. You two might want to get on your way soon. British backup is coming. We can see them on the horizon."

"Do you need our help?" Stranger asked.

"No." Zetta smiled at him in thanks. Then she glanced at me and the smile loosened into seriousness. "An old friend of ours —"

"Said you got away, but I'm chisel to marble," I said with a sigh. "Ricky explained."

Zetta looked at us with doubtful confusion. "It seems he explained in the only way he knows how. Vaguely, and with many interpretations." She had to bend down to look me in the eye, but when she put her hand on my shoulder, it reminded me of my mom's hugs. What if I never saw my mom again? "This family considers you an invaluable asset, Penelope Grace. Don't forget that. Your ability to change the future gives us hope. But, it also destroys any guarantee a prophecy might give. Forgive us for shortening your stay, and please know, you're always welcome to return. I would be honored if our home was your safe haven." She put a hand on Stranger's shoulder too. "Our doors are always open to both of you."

"Thank you," Stranger said. I tried to agree but got too choked up.

"Where will you two travel next?"

"I don't know," I admitted.

She smiled. "Time travels in diverse paces with diverse persons. You two better get going."

I turned to the closed door. I thought about trying to pick a place, but wasn't in the mood to be decisive. So I just opened the door. Muddy roads and a dusty sunset. Land. About time. I glanced back at Zetta one last time. The woman with the rainbow aura, the one who completely knew herself. It was possible I'd never see anyone from that ship ever again. I needed to know just one thing. "How are you so...you?"

"I'm sure you'll figure it out," she said, then cringed. "Sounded like Ricky there." Then she smiled and waved goodbye.

I gave Zetta a nod goodbye and stepped off the ship. Stranger followed close at my heels and shut the door behind him. Thankfully the streets were empty, so no one noticed as two time travelers stepped through the front door of a closed bakery. "We need to break the connection," he reminded me. "Before someone else steps through onto the ship."

I looked around for some sort of tool, but nothing nearby was stronger than the sturdy wood in front of me. Nothing, that is, except the literal nothingness on the other side. I reached through with my mind and grabbed a clump of emptiness and smeared it into the hinges. The metal broke and the door leaned to the side. Behind it, the emptiness washed away like an unclogged sink.

Stranger pushed it open just a tad and nodded at me. "Nothing but chairs and tables. The connection's gone."

"Then I say let's eat." I walked over to a street bench and sat down. There were no street lamps or cars on the road. No electricity or gas. Just a sign on a wall telling me we were on Malden Lane.

"I wonder where we are," Stranger said as he sat down next to me.

I wanted to be curious too, but felt numb. Ricky's words, his warnings, or whatever they were, lingered in my stomach like bad sushi. Dinah had to be okay. I had tried to save her before, covered her with my own body. I couldn't help thinking that if I had let that shadowy hand grab her, she'd be the one time traveling right now instead of knocked cold in the midst of an explosion. If anyone deserved to be a time traveler, it would be her. The tablet poked my ribs from under my jacket. I could make a deal with The Void, save Dinah, and then let her take the lead.

I unfolded my brown bag and let the spiced seafood scented steam

128

hit my face. My stomach growled in anticipation as I pulled out a small plastic food container and a plastic fork. The food tasted delicious. Saffron-tinted scallops and sausage in rice…pure heaven. We ate in silence. Complete silence. The whole town was empty.

Only once I finished my paella did I look around for signs of life. Every once in a while a surly businessman would step out of his building to glare at the empty streets, and then slam the door shut behind him. A few looked at us and offered a discount on fresh fish or spices from India, but once they realized we had no money, they left us alone. I asked one what year it was.

"1613," he said, and went back into his shop.

Huh, I thought. *Why not, I guess.*

"Quiet town," I said. "So many businesses on this street, you'd think there'd be more people."

"Maybe it's not the right time," Stranger said. "Rush hour might be later." I glanced at him and noted the blue tints around his aura. Blue could mean a lot of things—all colors could—but this blue was definitely the shade referenced in depressing songs.

"What's up with you?" I asked.

He didn't look up from his own plastic container, empty but for some saucy remains at the bottom. He swirled designs through them with his fork before he answered. "Why didn't you tell me you can read energies?"

"Just never came up," I lied. I figured explaining that I didn't want him to freak out would mean having to explain my past and, in a word, ugh. But I couldn't help asking, "Does that change anything?"

He took a moment to answer, which I thought was an answer in itself. "I don't know," he finally admitted. "I know it shouldn't because I don't have anything to hide, but at the same time it feels like it's changed."

I nodded. At least he was being honest. "That's the tricky thing about emotions. It's like…kind of like a torpedo, I guess. Most people only see the snake of foam on the ocean surface. Sometimes it's pretty, other times scary, but always small, seemingly insignificant compared to the greatness of the ocean or the physical realm. But you only see the conscious or your memories, your ideas, your surface emotions. It's the subconscious that powers everything. That's the torpedo. Most of the time, people have no idea what's going on beneath the ocean. Or maybe they're too scared to admit there might be a weapon underneath."

129

"Can you see the subconscious?" he asked. "Even if the person isn't aware?"

I shrugged. "Maybe? I never studied the limitations of my abilities. They tend to put people on edge. As you can imagine." I tried to make it a joke, but couldn't raise my eyes to see his expression.

Stranger nudged me with his shoulder. "You seem to know what you're talking about."

"'Seem' being the key word. I read books and blogs about it. Makes sense." I shrugged. "There's not a lot out there about what I can do."

"If you had to guess yes or no, could you?"

I smooshed my lip to the side as I thought. "If I was in a deep meditation, really into the whole emotional side of things, no distractions, yeah, maybe. Everything about a person is right in their spirit, nothing's completely forgotten."

"Then...." His head tilted to the side and he looked up, those pale blue eyes scared enough to ask, "Could you bring my memories back?"

"I...." I had no idea. I mean, sure, I could pick up that the girl sitting behind me in class was freaking out because her boyfriend was not texting her back. I could guess what days were best to ask my teachers for an extension. But to pull a guy's entire memories back into place? That wasn't just looking...that was *fixing*. "Stranger, I don't know what's causing your memory loss. If it's something physical, I don't know if I can—"

"I'm not asking for a guarantee here. Will you try?"

I wanted to say yes, of course. Why hadn't I thought about it before? But that was the thing about the subconscious. It didn't explain why my stomach went queasy at the thought of agreeing. It didn't care if I felt morally obligated to help my new friend out and maintain his trust. It just told me to run, to refuse, and to tell him never to think like that again.

"Of course." I forced the words out and gave a small prayer of thanks that he couldn't read energies himself, or he'd notice how much I freaked out over what he asked.

He smiled and relaxed. "Thank you," he said. "Maybe if I can remember how I created the experiment in the first place, we can figure out how to get home."

"Of course, yeah, that makes a lot of sense...."

I stopped myself before my sentence turned into full babbling fool mode. Why? Why would I freak out? Using The Void's energy felt less wrong than this. The idea that I might owe The Void for taking back the energy l felt less wrong than this. Stranger was a good guy. Period. Even the pirate and his daughter agreed on that. I settled on a reason I could swallow. Because right now, Stranger was a good guy. What if that was just because he had a blank slate? What if when he became himself again he'd become someone who wouldn't trust me? Someone who didn't care about my opinion, or my sister? What if the only reason he trusted me and my abilities now was because he didn't know what to hide from me?

"When do you want to do this?" I asked.

"Well…." He looked around. "Is this place quiet enough, or do you want to find someplace else?"

"I'm not sure how long it would take. Or when rush hour starts on this street. Maybe we should find someplace more private."

Stuffing our newfound out-of-time plastic containers in our pockets, we headed away from the store-filled streets until we found a river bank. The streets went right up along it, squeezing the natural flow of water as if the city would rather nudge it out altogether. We followed the length of the river to not get lost and kept searching for a more private place.

It felt strange going on a scavenger hunt for a place to read Stranger's energy. Too casual. Like we were looking for a decent ice cream parlor. He just asked me to help him find himself, which meant I would have to go searching through his emotions, even his memories. The personal stuff people kept to themselves. He might not like what he was letting me get into. I followed him with full hesitation. This was a trap. I couldn't say no without being pretty much the worst friend ever, but because I'd said yes, I'd learn things he'd never told me. The chances of me learning more than he'd want were so big it was more likely than…. I sighed. More likely than going home at this point.

Eventually the city eased into a countryside. Trees sprouted out like a wall separating the city from the country. The river spread out, free from the streets' chokehold. Grass and tiny flowers welcomed the wet soil. We slipped away from the streets and moved deeper into the rocky prairie. Boulders speckled the muddy green. One longer boulder could substitute as a bench. Stranger pointed it out to me and we headed that way. Stranger wrapped his legs around the stone and sat facing me as I settled in on the other side. The sun kissed the horizon as the river's song softened the city noise from the distance. "So," Stranger asked, "how does this work?"

"You're asking me?" I said with a raised eyebrow. "This ability didn't come with a manual."

"It's just your superpower, huh?" Stranger smiled. The way those pale blue eyes set their attention on me, like I was something special, made me forget, just for a moment, every time my talents had turned people away.

"I never thought of it like that," I admitted. Almost made all those moments when I felt different somehow more epic, like in the movies. If only they could truly be so romanticized. "Ready?" I asked.

When he nodded, I closed my eyes and reached my attention out toward Stranger. The first thing that answered was his optimism. That sunshine yellow of hope. But that was just the first layer. The ideas people wanted to project to the world, how they wanted to be seen. So I pushed past it.

The pain started as a whisper, but as I swam deeper the volume rose until it became a scream. Guttural and horrified. And...silent. A swallowed scream forced to rot within one's soul. I had never felt this pain personally. It was the type I knew only by proxy when I passed certain people in the halls of school. Or that one time I'd connected with the house that used to be happy. Stranger's house. Grief. Stranger had lost someone close to him, and not long ago. I would be surprised if it had been more than a year.

But that wasn't why he'd lost his memories, so I pushed onward. I focused on the energy around his mind, where he held his spiritual identity. All energies came to me in colors, but his head seemed shrouded in shadows. That horrible empty energy that had caused all this strife. It was there, darkening everything I tried to read. A darkness choking the light from Stranger's soul.

Chapter 20

Shadows choked Stranger's mind like a stifling blanket, covering every inch until none of his natural inner light could escape. Why were they there? Why had the shadows attacked his memory? It wasn't a question I could answer. But maybe I could remove the shadows. Mentally, I reached out to toss that shadowy blanket away from Stranger's mind. The moment I tapped the energy, colors burst into my head, tangling into each other until it formed a memory. Not mine, but Stranger's.

He was in his basement, but none of the mad scientist décor crowded the room. It was a workout room. Blue mats padded the floor and a punching bag stood where the metallic door would later appear. Stranger sat against the wall, his knees tucked up against his chest as he stared at the punching bag. His eyes were red but dry, like he'd maxed out on crying before the pain behind his eyes could dissipate. He let his head hit the wall behind him as he looked to the ceiling with a clenched jaw.

Because of my connection to his memory, I felt and thought what he felt and thought during this moment. And this definitely wasn't the Stranger I knew. No hopeful yellow in the aura. No trust or faith or search for heroic purpose to life. Just a kid drowning. He looked like he hadn't showered in days. His hair was messed up, overgrown, and by the looks of the wrinkled black shirt he wore, he'd slept in his clothes.

He glanced at a closed door in front of him. Dad's office. There was a cabinet there. With bourbon in it. Dad had used it for celebrations before...but now it needed to be replenished more and more often.

Stranger knew it didn't work, saw the evidence on a weekly basis, but still, he was tempted to try for himself. Anything to stop the catch in his chest with every breath.

But Stranger didn't want a placebo to numb the pain only to have it come back, and this time with a hangover. He wanted answers. He wanted to go back in time and stop it from happening. He knew exactly what he would do. It was the only daydream powerful enough to take his attention anymore. What he would have done differently. How he could have saved the day.

The light changed in the room. Instead of the steady flow of colors around him, the whole room started to dance in waves, like just above asphalt on a hot day, only this was the entire room and without the added heat. Stranger eased to his feet, feeling the unnatural tinge to the room for the first time. But I was already familiar with The Void's presence. *Such desperation,* The Void spoke. I was surprised when Stranger's eyes widened. Did he hear the voice? How? But no. He'd seen how the light changed and was on alert because of that alone. I tried to reach past his memory to get the truth, but that was all there was, his memory. I could only guess on how The Void manipulated the light to make it move so wrong. Only, I thought I knew why. It wanted Stranger to know he wasn't alone. The Void continued talking and my body tensed, feeling how it circled him like prey through the memory. Its voice was muffled, as though it spoke through many layers. I smelled it through the dimensions, the absence of any and all fragrances, as if someone had cleaned a room and then aired it out with a filtered air supply. Only stronger. *What do you want, boy?*

Unseen hands sifted through Stranger's memories. It felt wrong, violating. Was this what it felt like to have someone go through your energies? Was this what I did to people? Only no one I read gave signs of awareness, while Stranger's head started throbbing. He staggered back and held his head with his hands, but The Void continued its invasion. Past the surface energies, through the memories and the consciousness. The Void went straight for the subconscious. And chuckled. *Oh, you humans reach for so little. I can give that to you, boy, and I'm always willing to make a good bargain. But every domino must be set into perfect position before they can all fall. Hmm, you're not a natural with mechanics, but I can fix that. Here, boy, have a thought.*

Stranger's aura lit up back to that happy yellow, the color the house used to be before the grief. It wasn't as bright or as pure, though.

More like a muddy yellow, sifting through the weeks of numbed shock. Because, what if he could go back in time? What if he could save the day? Stranger ran into his dad's office and grabbed some paper. He wrote down plans and graphs and equations. He logged onto the computer and looked up facts, possibilities, and theories. *It has to be possible,* Stranger thought with renewed gusto. It was the only way. He had to go back.

The memory faded and my mind returned to the moment. I kept my eyes closed to shake off Stranger's residual emotions from my system so I could struggle with my own conflicted feelings. There was the cold hard proof. The moment itself. Stranger had done what he did on purpose. It wasn't some accidental crack in the universe. This really was all his fault. Only, none of it was at the same time. The Void had slipped into his mind, placed thoughts into his subconscious, led him the entire way. Stranger hadn't known what would come of it. He couldn't have known what would happen.

A part of me couldn't swallow that calming thought, though. The moment when Dinah and I drove past his house popped into my head. Something about the way he and what must have been The Void sat there, watching us as we drove. Had it been a trap after all? All I saw was the moment that started it, but The Void messed with his head many more times after that. Did Stranger know what he was doing when he screamed for help? Had he weighed the outcome and decided we were worth the sacrifice?

I wanted to scream at him until I got the truth. Dinah could be dead because of him. The Void had manipulated his subconscious, but Stranger had chosen to go through with it. He'd chosen this! Only my anger would fall on empty ears if I snapped to the soul in front of me. This guy had no idea. So I squelched my urge to scream. I'd get more information first. Then I'd decide what to do. "Stranger?" I asked. I kept my eyes closed because I couldn't look at him just then. "Did you get any memories?"

"No. Did you see something?" he asked.

Strange, how I could see what he couldn't remember. Maybe that darkness in his mind acted as a wall between him and his past. If that shadowy blanket over his mind was what kept him separate from his memories, I'd have to try again to remove it. I closed my eyes once more and tried to pull the shadows away from him.

Another image played out before my eyes—just a flash—from

when Dinah and I had gone downstairs. The Void was there too...I saw him this time. Not because Stranger saw him, but because it was closer, stronger, less muffled by whatever had held it back for so long. Stuck behind some unseen force separating the nothing from our reality. And yet it stood with strength and confidence. That strange smoke spilled out into the room, sucking in everything it could touch. Then, with the wrong spark at the wrong time, the barrier between the two worlds shattered in a spectacle no one saw.

The Void stepped through and took a deep, hungry breath, and the vacuum that resulted started to suck in everything. Stranger saw me struggling against the vacuum. *This isn't right*, he thought. *This shouldn't destroy.* He rushed between me and The Void's outreached power. The Void pulled him into the darkness that spilled out the door, only The Void didn't just toss him aside through time. It held him by the face. The imagery blackened out in my vision, but I could still feel it. The way it cradled his head with an anaconda's embrace. *I'm sorry*, it said. *But I need this fresh start. You're the only one who knows how to close the gap. Or, I should say, knew.* The energy released Stranger, and his memories snuffed out like a candle's flame.

I gasped for air but kept my cool. I was hyper aware of Stranger's tense form in front of me, waiting for answers. So The Void had betrayed him. Taken his memories on purpose. It said it needed a fresh start. What could that possibly mean? I hesitated before checking for another memory. That one had been so mixed. Parts of it had been Stranger's, yes...the desperation, the strangled soul fighting in vain against The Void's hold. But other parts, seeing the barrier between the realities shatter, the way he breathed in the new chaos, was all from The Void's point of view. Residual, yes, but powerful nonetheless.

I tugged again at the shadowy remains of Stranger's mind, hoping that a memory might pop up that could help me dislodge the emptiness. Just enough that we could get back to Dinah, stabilize that tear in time. The words echoed in my head again. *I need a fresh start. I need a fresh start. I need this fresh start.* Only, this time the words didn't come from outside of me, from Stranger's memories, but from within myself. As if my own spirit were chanting the words. *I'm sorry, but I need a fresh start.* The more I pushed and tugged at the shadows, the more I struggled to get it to move, the louder the chant became, as if The Void had somehow snuck some of its energy into me as well, and fought against me from within.

I couldn't get it to move. After what seemed like hours of tugging and pulling, it hadn't even shivered against my strain. It might as well be marble for all I could move it. After a while, I opened my eyes with a sigh, calling it quits.

"What did you find?" Stranger asked.

What should I tell him? That all this was his fault? We were in this mess because he refused to grieve for a loved one, and instead resorted to shady deals with monsters in the dark. A part of me wanted to be furious. So he'd made a deal with the wrong guy...fine, I got why he was there. But me? Why did I have to get sucked into all this? Why did Dinah's life have to be on the line? But I couldn't show him my anger. And not just because my rants would have been wasted on an unrepentant recipient. Rather, because I knew what I'd be willing to do to make sure my sister was still alive and okay. Anything. Perhaps even no questions asked. I didn't know who he'd lost, but I did understand his desperation. Wasn't I comforting myself that I could make a deal with The Void just moments ago? The tablet felt hot against my shirt... tainted, if I went through with my plan.

Stranger seemed so blissfully unaware of the grief lurking around in his energy. I hated to be the one who burst that bubble. But we both knew what we were getting into when we'd chosen to do this. Stranger agreed that he would rather know. Maybe it was less understanding and more selfishness that led me to edit what I saw. I liked traveling with an optimist. I didn't want to guilt trip that out of him until we had to confront the facts. "You lost someone," I said. "I think you built the experiment so you could go back in time and save them."

He gave a sharp inhale, but after a moment, nodded. "That feels right." He rubbed the back of his neck and shook his head. "You know what sucks? I've felt empty since this whole thing started. But it was more than just losing my memories. I...." He looked to the sky and blinked in rapid succession. I didn't have to read his energy to know he swallowed that scream of grief back down. I wanted to grab him, pull him into a hug, squeeze that pain out, and let him know he didn't have to hold it in, no one did. But instead I looked down at my hands and waited for him to continue. "I knew." He combed his fingers through his hair. "I knew I needed to save someone. And I know it's important to me, but.... For the life of me, I can't remember who." He looked at me. "Do you know what it feels like to be willing to die for someone you don't remember? To not understand why you're in so much pain?"

I shook my head. "No. I don't."

But he just smiled through the redness in his eyes. "Of course you do. You've been torn away from your home and you don't understand why."

"It's different."

"Maybe," he allowed. "But it's still pain. Listen, for what it's worth, I'm sorry for my part in this whole thing. If that experiment was really mine, then I royally messed the world up."

I cringed. That's what I had wanted to prevent by not snapping at him myself. Him blaming himself. Perhaps, deep down, beneath what he knew, he was aware of his choice in the deal. Might as well let him know someone else could share the blame. "It wasn't just you," I finally said.

"What?"

"There's something in your mind, some kind of darkness. It's choking your identity, and I think it's what's blocking your memories. The thing is, you were working…well, this thing appeared to you and said it could help. You two kind of made a deal. It would help you learn how to time travel only after you…." Stranger's eyes widened as his mind made the jump before I could find the words. His breathing came in quick swallows. I wished I could give good news. "You released it."

"Released it? From where? What kind of thing is it?"

"I don't know. I call it The Void, because that's what it feels like. But when Dinah and I heard your scream, that was when you were releasing it. Stranger, I think it stole your memories on purpose."

He went silent for what seemed like a long time. "It doesn't want me to remember," he repeated. "It wouldn't even let me save my someone? Why? What would be that cruel?"

"I don't know, but if that void *really* wanted out, it would need you to be desperate, to be willing to do anything to save whoever you lost. If you went back in time and saved them, wouldn't that create a paradox? Then the experiment would never exist and The Void would never be free. Maybe that's what you needed to forget. If you think about it, it kind of makes sense. It couldn't take you back in time. Then it would lose its chance. And that would explain why it took all your memories, not just the last year or so. Whoever you lost might have been in them."

His eyes narrowed at me. "Are you sympathizing with it?"

"What? No! Of course not. I just…. Stranger, the more we

understand, the closer we get to going home. And if we can outthink this thing, then maybe we can save your loved one as well as go home. Be heroes on our way to dinner. Come on, you gotta admit that sounds good."

"A little too good," Stranger said. "No, I think it's about time we saw this for what it is. A lost cause. I trusted something I shouldn't have, and now we're lost in time. That void thing isn't going to help us, and Ricky said it himself…our time is closed off. I'm sorry, Penny. I…." He shrugged. "I'm sorry I messed everything up."

"None of this is your fault. That thing preyed on you. On both of us."

"What do you mean?"

I hadn't meant to say that, and bit my lip at my stupid tongue. But it was too late. I couldn't backtrack, especially after Stranger had let me see so much. He himself didn't know what he shared. "I'm sort of in The Void's debt. Back at the pirate ship. The emptiness energy was too much…I couldn't control it. The Void came in and took it away from me, but it said that I owed it for the favor and it would collect."

Stranger's jaw line tensed. "I dug us in deep, didn't I?"

"Stranger, stop blaming yourself. Something took advantage of our desperation."

"Not everyone tries to create a time machine when they lose someone. Or makes a deal with something they don't understand because of an impossible hope. No, this is my fault in every way. It's okay to admit that."

I didn't like how this conversation was going. I was the jaded one. Stranger was the one with the sunshine aura, the hope and optimism radiating off of him. That wasn't something easy to lose…not to me. "We might not be able to go home today, or tomorrow even, and I might not be able to get your memories back yet, but, Stranger…." I smiled. "No matter where or when we are, there will always be someone to save. We can be heroes. I promise."

"Penny, you don't have to try to make me feel better."

But I had already stood up. "My mind's made up. You created those cracks in reality so you could save someone. So let's save them. Let's save hundreds, one at a time…maybe just with a hug, but we can save them. Trust me, Stranger. This is a good thing you've done. A blessing. Even a superpower. What do you say? You with me?"

Stranger sighed but gave me a soft smile. He was a lot of things, but a fool wasn't one of them. So he knew what I was doing. He understood that this was all pretend, an invitation for a pseudo adventure to get our minds cleared and back on track before we made another move home. No matter what happened, by agreeing with me, he would make the deal to turn whatever happened to us into a hero's tale.

He swung his leg from around the stone and hopped to his feet. "I'm with you," he said.

Chapter 21

Rush hour must have begun in town while we were away. The streets had become crowded with simply dressed men and women going from A to B with purpose. Tan clothed and sunburned, everyone seemed to know everyone as they smiled and chitchatted with every passing friend.

Lines started outside of bakeries, while the chatter grew to a constant noise. Stranger walked beside me and played along, nodding in greeting to those who met his gaze and pretending he belonged there. There was so much I still didn't know about Stranger. Our little meditation seemed to have brought in more questions than answers. But did those questions bother me? Yes. Of course they did. And yes, I was right to be worried that seeing Stranger's memories might make him less perfect than he seemed in the beginning. He wasn't perfect anymore. He was real. I liked the real version better. He wasn't just some comic book hero out to save the world. There was someone out there in particular he wanted to save. Someone he was willing to make dumb deals for, make mistakes for, like I was willing to make deals for Dinah. I identified more with the real Stranger. This one made mistakes, even unheroic ones like me. The other one made me feel kind of guilty for not being better.

Still, I wished I was more like the comic book hero. I wished I could say my abilities were superpowers and that I was special, but something about them made me feel wrong. Perhaps it was the unease with how other people reacted to them. Perhaps it was just a self-esteem issue, and if I took a leaf out of Zetta's empowering book, this would all be over. And yet there seemed to be more to it than that. How could my powers be good if even Zetta needed me to leave the ship before they could feel safe? I couldn't quite shake that image of Stranger and The Void out on the porch, watching Dinah and me drive home. Why watch me leave? Why trick me into coming back? If I could just understand what The Void wanted from me, why only I could see it, then perhaps I could feel better about my role in this crazy adventure.

"Thank you," Stranger said, disrupting my inner self-pity rant. "For what you said back there."

"Don't mention it," I said, and made a point of making my voice sound modest, with a higher tone and an ah-shucks hand wave. "You've already done the same for me."

"Yeah, but I also apparently tore you away from your family, so...."

"True," I said.

He looked at me in shock, but then laughed when he saw my smirk. "So what does that make us? Even, or are you ahead?"

"You should always assume I'm ahead," I answered playfully. "Just to be safe."

"I'll remember that," he said. Then he turned his attention to the people passing us by. "So, what are we looking for?"

I couldn't help it. I had to laugh at that. "You ask that every time."

"Wonder how long it will take for us to figure it out." And I swear to you he winked at me. "I meant, what kind of heroic deeds are we thinking of here?"

"Let's start with obtainable and go from there."

As if to answer our question, a small child's voice called out. "Hey friends!" The sudden shout made me jump. A kid, no older than ten, slipped between Stranger and me like we were the three musketeers. He was short, with curly dark hair ready to bounce into action and quick green eyes heightened by his run. "Play along," he hissed, and then smiled as he wrapped his tiny arms around our waists and pulled us closer. "Walk with me and be merry," he said between clenched teeth as he pushed us forward.

Stranger gave me a forced smile. "Are we being kidnapped by a ten year old?" he asked.

"I think so. What's going on, kid?"

"Just avoiding some fusty friends of mine." The kid ducked his head as a wave of people passed.

"Are you in trouble?" Stranger glanced at me, and I knew what he was thinking. Was it going to be that easy?

"No," the kid said, but my inner lie detector went off. "Just some annoying neighborhood lads."

"Bullies?"

"Uh...sure." The boy arched his neck over his shoulder. "Phew." He sighed and dropped his hold on our waists. "He's gone. Thanks!" And then he ran off.

Stranger stopped in his tracks, watching the kid disappear in the crowd. "Well, that was anticlimactic."

"Sort of a letdown after the Lusitania and then a prison break," I agreed.

"Maybe you were right the first time. There's no purpose to this. We just fall into different times."

"No," I said, and I wasn't lying to keep him hopeful. The kid *had* lied. He was in trouble. Someone must have been chasing him and he thought he had gotten away. "Which way did the kid go again?"

"Over there. Into that round building."

Stranger pointed and, for the first time, I took a good look at something other than the people. The building was huge, round, and made of wood. "No way," I whispered, as memories of Mom and Dinah's historical rants popped up in my mind. "It can't be."

"What?"

"The Globe Theater." I stepped back to get a better look. "This is Shakespeare's theater. Dinah would have loved this."

"Didn't you say something about Shakespeare before we left Ricky's ship?"

"The link between the two sides of the door must have logged into my subconscious." I shook my head in bewilderment. "Is there anything that stuff can't do?"

"It just time travels, right?"

"And burns metal, reads minds, and sets traps."

"Right. And creates debts."

That managed to dampen the awe-factor of our situation. Who knew when it could collect, what it would ask for, and, if we refused, what it would do to us? But right now, we were standing outside of Shakespeare's freaking Globe Theater. "We must be in London. Stranger, this is epic. I mean, the Globe Theater."

143

"Please tell me there's no massive tragedies inside that building."

"Well, I mean, Shakespeare was famous for his tragedies. Romeo and Juliet. Hamlet. But other than the scripted ones, no, I don't think so."

"That's good." Stranger smiled. "Obtainable heroics first, right?"

If the outside of the theater was jaw-dropping, it was nothing compared to the inside. The stadium was filled to the brim with a waiting audience. Around the stage there was nothing but dirt and no seats, yet even more people stuffed themselves in, shuffling through for a decent view. By the looks of the differing clothes, the upper class got seats while the lower class had to stand. None seemed to mind, though, as they whispered and giggled in excitement about what was to come. I took in everything, from the perfumed flowers lining the stage to the jewel-like dresses of the upper class.

"Do you see the kid?" Stranger asked.

"No. Not that we could see someone that short in this crowd. Wait...." I leaned onto my tip toes to get a better view. A man, dressed in his best clothes, his hair brushed back, knelt on the edge of the stage, speaking to some crew members. His fingers twirled a quill in skilled circles as they argued over some papers. It couldn't be.... I grabbed Stranger's sleeve. "Does that guy look like the writer to you?"

"Who? Ah...." Stranger shrugged. "Sure."

"Stranger, I think that's —"

"Shakespeare!" a woman from the audience yelled across the stage. The man glanced up and gave her an exhausted smile.

My fingers tightened around Stranger's arm. "Hey, the kid's probably hiding in the crowd. We should go closer to the stage so we can get a better —"

"Found him." Stranger started off in the other direction.

"But...." I pointed at the stage where Shakespeare himself dangled his legs off the edge. Stranger looked back and waved for me to follow. I growled under my breath. "Dines will kill me if I don't meet Shakespeare."

"Yeah, uh-huh," Stranger teased as I caught up. "You only want to meet him for her. You're too cool to like Shakespeare."

"Oh yeah, I totally am." I reached him and gave him a smirk before taking the lead. "But we should make sure and meet him after all this heroic stuff either way."

The kid's bushy hair disappeared through a back door. We

managed to sift through the pushing crowd. Stranger looked to me and at my nod, he pushed the door open.

"Oi!" the kid screamed. He stood in front of a mirror, an unzipped dress hanging off his shoulders as he struggled to catch a falling blonde wig. "This is for actors only! Get out!"

"Um…." Stranger glanced at me.

I had to blink a lot to overcome the shock. I hadn't expected that. "You're an actor?" I asked.

The kid rolled his eyes. "No, I come hither to try on the robes ere a play starts."

I hit Stranger's arm and hissed. "They really talk like that. I thought Shakespeare made it all up."

"Why are you playing a girl?" Stranger asked.

"Who else would play the female parts?" The kid looked at us like we were crazy. "An actual girl?" At that, he laughed.

I opened my mouth to say yes, that's definitely an option, before another one of Dinah's rants popped into my head. *They used to believe women couldn't act. So they had boys play the parts until their voices deepened.*

"Grant you mercy for clearing up common sense." The kid sighed. It was almost a whine. I tried not to grin at the formal 17th century English. "And yet, I must prepare. I'm in the first scene."

"What's playing?" I asked.

"*As You Like It,*" the kid said. "Not his greatest, but they cannot all be masterpieces."

"*As You Like It,*" I whispered. "That's the play Dinah was preparing for. Just a local high school play. Wait, what was it that Zetta said to us right before we left?" I asked Stranger.

He made a face like how-was-he-supposed-to-remember, but then he snapped his fingers. "You mean that weird thing about time? What was it? People travel at different speeds through time?"

"Time travels in diverse paces with diverse persons."

"That's a line from the play," the kid said.

"That sneak," I said. "She knew the doors could work through the subconscious. She sent us here!"

"Why?" Stranger asked. Then we both looked at the kid.

He took a step back and lifted a finger. "Wait up. You two are crazy."

"Who were you running from?" Stranger asked.

"No one. 'Twas a prank."

145

"Some prank," I said. "What kind of trouble are you in?"

"I have admirers I can't get free of in mine dressing room."

"Seriously."

"I am serious. You two are interrupting my preparation. I have lines to review, make up to put on. It's a whole process. Just get thee hence."

"We're here to help. If you'd just tell us what you're running from."

"I'm not running from anything! Can't thee take a joke?"

"That wasn't a joke, and we're not going anywhere until—" But Stranger put his hand on my arm, signaling for me to stop.

"Okay," he said. "We're out of here." He gave me a significant look and started to back up to the door.

A wave of frustration built up in my chest. Didn't he realize that we were here for a reason? That Zetta had sent us? That the kid was important, vital somehow? We just needed to keep pushing. We could get the information out and save him. A little scare now was nothing compared to—

The door closed behind us and I yanked my arm out of Stranger's grip. "What was that, Stranger? We were right. You were right. We're supposed to help him."

"We were scaring him," Stranger said. His voice was steady, firm, and he looked down at me like he wouldn't back off, no matter how much I argued. Like I was what the kid needed protection from.

I leaned back and stared him down. "You mean I was scaring him."

"You weren't exactly showing great bedside manner. Come on, Penny, usually you're the one who understands people. The kid was freaked. How did you not catch onto that?"

"I...." His words were an ice cold splash of reality. Maybe Stranger wasn't the only one who wanted to find purpose in what had happened to us. Perhaps I didn't want to see how scared the kid was because it would mean I would have to back down. And I couldn't turn away, not again. "Can you honestly tell me that this is all just a coincidence?"

"Maybe it is," Stranger said. "Dinah learned those lines in 2017. They're not exactly uncommon to quote."

"It's not Terminator's 'I'll be back' either. Most people wouldn't know that particular line."

"So? She quoted Shakespeare. That explains why we're here. But that doesn't mean we were sent here. It kind of means the opposite." He blinked, and then those pale blue eyes looked away.

146

It took me a moment to digest what he meant. This went past losing hope. Hope was yesterday's sunset. This guy was…realistic. "Two adventures ago you wanted to be a hero," I said. "Can a person change that fast?"

He sighed. "Listen, I'm tired, and I know you are too. Who knows the last time we slept? It's gotta be over twenty hours at least. We're working on adrenaline alone. I say we take a break."

"What about the kid?" I asked.

Stranger shrugged. "What can I say? Maybe he really was pranking us, Penny. Maybe we just want to see victims so we can play hero. He didn't run in here to hide from anyone. He's an actor. He was probably just late."

"Then why grab us in the street like that?" I countered. "If he was late, he wouldn't play around."

"Fine. Then he saw another actor or a set designer or, heck, even Shakespeare himself, and thought he'd get in trouble if he was caught. He wanted a chance to sneak in. Everything you said before, Penny, I'm still all in. I still want to be a hero and I still want to go home, but let's not make trouble just so we can play our parts, okay?"

I opened my mouth but couldn't think up an argument. Maybe Stranger was right. Maybe I just needed some sleep and a fresh outlook. A moment to think clearly. Reassess the situation. I had gone a touch crazy on the kid. So I just nodded without a word.

"Come on. I'll get us some seats. Let's enjoy the play and then get some sleep, okay?" Stranger smiled. "I'm sure someone will need our help in the morning." I let Stranger lead me to the back of the globe theater. He grabbed us some seats and sat me down before sitting down himself.

The play started without a hitch. The kid didn't show up until the second scene, but I chalked his lie up to getting freaked out by the crazy time-traveling teenager. He wasn't bad either. Never stumbled on his lines, and actually pulled off the tones like he knew what he was talking about. I'd be the first to admit that Shakespeare sounded like Greek to me, but the kid seemed to understand it like…okay, like he lived in the time. I shouldn't have been surprised, but seeing a ten-year-old quote Shakespeare was impressive to modern-day me. And to a completely full audience at that. The entire Globe Theater was full to the brim with judgmental but laughing people of all classes.

That was why, when he choked on his lines halfway through the play, I knew something was wrong.

Chapter 22

The kid's face went paler than his makeup. He stood in the middle of the stage, eyes on the crowd, a bouquet of prop flowers leaning out of his grip. His young aura flashed red with the impulse to run and never stop. This wasn't the fear of losing one's allowance or breaking Mom's favorite vase. It was the blood red swirling around his body, coaxing him to survive as the kid feared for his life. The other actors waited on his cue before the play could continue. One coughed, and the kid sprang back into action. Banter, banter, joke, and wise comment. The show went on as if he'd never choked. But he had. I edged to my feet, trying to see who the kid could have been looking at, but no one stood out.

"Hey!" someone hissed behind me. "Sit down!"

I made a face but went back to my seat. "Stranger, did you see that?" I looked over at him, but he was asleep. Deep asleep too, with his head leaning on his propped arm and a half open mouth. He heaved a deep sigh, almost a snore. How could he be tired when there was still so much to do? I thought about waking him up, but the kid was already back on top, acting out his lines like he was born to do this. Stranger might not believe me. He might think I was still trying to make mountains out of anthills. Maybe I was. Anyone would choke if they got a full view of the crowd. Stage fright could hit in the middle of a play too, I guessed. But auras had never steered me wrong before.

I kept my eye on the kid just in case though, noting every time he glanced into the crowd. He said his lines and continued to use the stage's length to his advantage, but his acting was off and the other actors noticed. He stumbled too many times for me to believe it was all in my head. The kid was clearly scared. That counted as something I could interfere in. When the kid finished his scene, he lingered on the stage a moment longer than he should, as if it was the only safe place. I could almost see each jolt of his leg as he forced himself off stage.

I nudged Stranger awake. "Come on," I said.

"Huh?" He stumbled to his feet and looked around. "Dang," he said. "For a second I thought I was home. Waking up is the worst."

"Did you remember anything?" I asked as the audience sneered at us for standing up in the middle of a play.

"The dream felt like home, but it's gone now. Hey, where are we going?" he asked when I grabbed his arm and started through the crowd again.

"I'm just checking something," I said.

"Penny...," Stranger warned. "We said we'd back away from the kid, remember?"

"I can go by myself if you're just going to argue," I snapped. I forced the wave of frustration down. Things would be so much easier if people just followed me without question. "Just trust me, okay? I'm not going to do anything crazy. I just want to check on him."

"Fine, we'll go check on him. But I'm not letting you go by yourself. I'm pretty sure the buddy system applies to time travelers of all ages."

I couldn't argue with that, and we kept walking. We reached the backstage door much quicker this time. For the sake of not getting off at the wrong start, I knocked. The door swung open like we were expected. The kid took one look at us before he sighed in relief and stepped out of the way. None of the other actors seemed to notice our interference as they fixed their makeup and looked over lines.

The kid grabbed our arms and led us to a more secluded corner. "Did you mean it?" he asked. "When you said you came hither for my aid?"

"Of course," Stranger and I chorused.

"Even if I have no money?"

"We never asked for money," Stranger said. He looked offended.

"The tricky ones never do," the kid said. He squeezed his lips together in thought as he looked us up and down. "Very well. My name's Rich." He held his hand out for us to shake. He was officially the oldest ten year old I'd ever seen.

Stranger shook his hand. "I'm Stranger. This is Penny. What's your problem?"

"'Tis my father," he finally admitted, but I noticed his aura flare up. This boy knew how to lie. I decided to play along before confronting him, and nodded my head in false sympathy. "First, I should point out that acting is a highly respectable trade. There's nothing wrong with wanting to be the next Doctor Faustus, am I right?"

"Right," Stranger said, like he had no idea what Rich was saying.

"Right." Rich nodded. "But Father wants me to take up the family business. So I told him, straight to his face, I said 'Father, I'm going to apprentice with a blacksmith in another town.' Only I came here and started acting, which was quite clever because he doesn't like the arts and especially not Shakespeare. Father thinks the writer is crude and too political, but I love this stuff. Sure, he likes to make up words, but the art of plays is…," the kid shrugged, "one of the few things at which I excel.

"The problem is that my father, who never once in his life went to a play, currently resides near the front row. If he knew my face in that short time, he'd already be knocking at the door. 'Tis only a matter of time, and once he does…." Rich looked at us with those pleading green eyes. "I'll not act again. He'll send me off to apprentice with my uncles. Fishing." The kid shuddered. "I don't care for fishing."

"What are we supposed to do?" Stranger asked.

"Get him out of the theater," Rich whispered. "He's one of the queen's men. If you say there's a fight on the other side of town, he'll be obligated to check it out. By the time he realizes there's nothing there, the play will be done."

Stranger narrowed his eyes. "Surely there's a better idea."

"Not one that lets me keep my job," Rich argued.

"I have to agree with Stranger," I said. "What's stopping your dad from coming to visit the next showing?"

Rich shrugged. "I shall tell him, but I need time. I don't want my father to find out like this."

He played the sympathy, righteous intentions card. Cliché but effective. Especially around people who wouldn't be around to see you fulfill your end of the bargain. Stranger started to look convinced. Even I wanted to believe him. But not one word out of Rich's mouth even hinted at sincerity. We were dealing with a manipulator. I had half a mind to tell him if he wasn't going to be straight, I'd leave him alone to deal with his own mess and just walk out. But the only thing Rich never lied about, according to that frantic red in his aura, was the fact that he did need help. For whatever reason, he wanted his dad out of the audience. And he was a lot more afraid than a kid who might have to fish for a living.

"All right." I said. "We'll get him out of the audience. Just tell us which one he is."

"He's standing by the stage. Blond hair, kind of longer and curly, but not in a natural way, more like he doesn't know what a brush is. Methinks he wore a reddish brown jacket. Name's Samuel Lombard."

"Okay," I said. "We'll find him." I glanced at Stranger, implying it was time to go. Stranger looked conflicted to say the least.

"Wait." Rich stopped us. "Are you two serious?"

"No," I said, and rolled my eyes. "This is how we prank people. Of course we're serious."

Rich blinked up at us. His eyes widened like he saw something he hadn't before. In the corner of my eye, I noticed how that look made Stranger stand up taller. I would have rather hid from it. Yet it was rewarding to see Rich's shoulders lower in a subtle sigh of relief. His muscles relaxed, and I could have sworn I saw a tear threaten to fall from in his left eye. The thick red in his energies softened with just a sliver of hopeful yellow to break it up. "Thank you," he said. "You don't know what this means to me."

"No," I agreed. "But when we come back, the three of us are going to have a little chat." I gave him a significant look and slipped out of the dressing room.

"Are we doing this?" Stranger asked as soon as the door closed.

"Why wouldn't we?" I countered as I searched the crowd for the man Rich had described.

"You mean the kid didn't seem shady to you?" Stranger asked.

"Oh, he's all kinds of shady, but that doesn't mean he doesn't still need help."

"Yeah, but is getting rid of his dad the answer?"

"I don't think it's his dad. There." I found the guy standing so close to the stage he could reach out and touch it. He hadn't moved from his spot, but he didn't pay attention to the stage anymore. Instead he stared at the back, where the actors had disappeared, with a concentrated look on his face. Frustrated too, like he was one connection away from being ticked to no end. Our job was to keep him from making that connection.

Just by looking at the guy, I knew he was trouble. It wasn't the greasy hair or how he looked like he had no idea what personal hygiene was. It wasn't the worn clothing or the slight alcoholic stench that wafted in when we moved closer. It was his energy. The stifled way it moved around his body. Just by looking at him, I felt a wave of misguided anger, fingers pointed at everyone around him. Eyes narrowed at the world, labeling it as guilty and imagining punishments unfit for the crimes. He'd blame a singing bird for getting in his way. A moment wasted for a lifelong failure.

Or a kid for his bad mood.

But anger is a secondary emotion. A response to something much deeper, usually much more painful. For a moment, I stared at him and considered reading past the intuitive first glance, but stopped myself. Would that be a violation of privacy? Did I have any right to look without permission? Or were those rights worth violating for the potential safety of a ten year old?

"So what's the plan?" Stranger asked.

His voice knocked me out of the man's emotional headlock and made me smile. Because Stranger knew who I was now, at least what I could do, and he still asked my opinion. He still trusted me. It was the first time I actually felt like an equal part of a team. I didn't even get that with Dinah…but then again, who does with their sister, right? "The first thing we need to do is get that guy away from Rich. He's definitely not Rich's father, but there's enough anger there to warrant the kid's fear. Remember how relieved Rich looked when he realized we were actually going to try?"

"Yeah." Stranger's eyes narrowed at the guy as he started to get the idea. His jaw line tensed and his fingers rolled into a tight fist. His aura felt less like sunshine and more like a boulder. Earthy, strong, and impossible to budge. "Follow me," he said, and worked his way through the crowd.

I followed from behind, staring at him in amazement. Everything about him, the way he walked with steady steps, or how he politely but firmly moved people out of our way, was really, really attractive.

"Excuse me." He grabbed the guy's shoulder and turned him around. "Are you one of the queen's men?"

"Yes. What of it?"

"My friend and I got word a crime is about to go down. If we hurry we can stop it."

"Where?" The man stood up straighter and looked down at us.

"Down by the river. Follow us." And Stranger took a step toward the door.

Only, the man didn't move to the rescue. He just turned back around and looked at the stage. "That scum," he hissed, and turned back to Stranger. "You two have been played. Tell me where that kid is right now and I won't arrest you for aiding a criminal."

"Who are you talking about?" Stranger asked, but his face remained solid, daring.

"The manipulative drain on society. About yea tall, curly hair. Let me guess, he told you I was a drunk uncle…no, a disappointed father."

Well, we were caught rather quickly, I thought. And so far, anger and blame aside, he hadn't lied. It wasn't hard to swallow the idea that Rich was a criminal. And the queen's men these days were the closest thing they had for cops. I assumed that's what the feud was about.

Stranger didn't hesitate before answering. "He's long gone now anyway. Just asked us to distract you while he slipped out."

The man's eyes narrowed at him, trying to decide if Stranger was playing him or not. "No, the boy's still here." The man grinned at Stranger like he'd cracked the code. He shoved past Stranger to the backstage.

For a second there I thought Stranger would punch him. His fists tightened and his neck went flush. But then he did something even more surprising. Something almost creepy and completely awesome. He laughed. The audience stopped and looked at him. Although some had annoyed faces for the interruption, most people just looked curious as they sensed drama. Even the actors paused.

"Wow, that kid really knows your cards," Stranger chuckled. "That whole thing played out exactly like he said it would."

The man stopped dead in his tracks and forced himself to turn. "What?" he snapped through clenched teeth.

"Nothing." Stranger grinned. "Go on. Check the backstage. Heck, lock the doors and check everyone one by one just in case it's him in a disguise. You're only giving him a better head start."

"Have you any idea what that peat has done?"

"I'm guessing bruising your ego was one."

The man grabbed Stranger by the collar so fast it made me jump, but Stranger kept grinning. "We can take this outside if you want,"

Stranger offered.

Samuel seemed to be in a personal crisis. From what I could read from his aura, he wanted to hit Stranger for taunting him. Stranger was right. The guy did have an ego prone to bruising. But he also knew Stranger was messing with him and, if Stranger was right and the kid was on the run, he'd be wasting precious time if he paid any more attention to Stranger.

"What has he done?" I spoke to keep Samuel's attention.

He didn't let go of Stranger, but turned and looked me up and down before answering. "He's a thief who sneaks into decent people's homes and steals their jewelry. Not only that, but he's an escaped orphan who prefers to live on the streets rather than whither he can be kept separate from decent society."

"Let me guess," I said. "The life span isn't high for the orphans where you'd like to send him."

"Better chance than he deserves. The peat is already a criminal. Imagine what he'd be capable of as an adult."

"So basically, as soon as you catch the kid, his days are numbered." Stranger flicked Samuel's loosened grip off his clothes. I stepped closer and stared the man down. "What do you think would kill him first? The disease or poor treatment?"

But Samuel just stood straighter to better look down at us. "It's not like the boy deserves valorous treatment. He once stole a jewel from the queen herself. From this theater. A rare piece of petrified wood from the Americas. Why come, if not for that?"

"But the punishment doesn't fit the...."

My words faded from my mouth. A cold breeze rattled underneath my skin. Empty and hungry. I looked away from the boy and the cop, searching the theater for what shouldn't be there. As the emptiness cut through the energies of the room, I only had one thought. *Not again.*

Chapter 23

"Penny?" Stranger asked. I blinked back to the argument at hand to find both men staring at me. Samuel looked at me like not only was I wasting his time, but I was certifiable. Well, there was definitely an argument for that. "Penny," Stranger repeated, "are you all right?"

"Yeah." I turned back to Samuel and opened my mouth to continue, but an actor interrupted us.

"If you'd please take this outside, we'd like to continue the play."

"This is the queen's business," Samuel spat. He turned on us. "Get out of my way ere I arrest both of you, and you can battle the odds with your friend." He sidestepped past us and rushed toward the backstage door. Only the crowd was thick and, despite their efforts to not get on his bad side and get arrested too, there was only so much room a crowd could make at a time. "Get out of my way!" Samuel snapped.

"Should have stayed at home," one of the audience sighed.

Stranger hurried through the crowd and grabbed Samuel by the collar. Samuel swung around and almost punched Stranger in the jaw, but Stranger ducked down. The audience worked harder to give them room. They made a wide circle, watching like it was the play they'd paid to see. I was surprised at how well Stranger could hold his own in a fight with one of the queen's army. But he'd fare better with help.

I stepped forward to stop them, or maybe help, but another wave hit me from behind. It wasn't just intuition either...more like something breathing down my neck, blowing in my ear. Taunting. I wanted to look around again, to find the shadow and force it out of the room before it could do any damage. But the evening sun had long ago disappeared. The only light came from torches hung on the walls, which cast deep, unreliable shadows.

I hurried to the fight and grabbed Samuel's shoulder. "Stop it!" I snapped, but he shoved me back. Stranger grabbed at his coat again. This time, Samuel slipped out of his jacket and ran toward the backstage door. "No!" I yelled, and ran after him, but it was too late. I ran into the room only to find three shocked actors, and Rich already in Samuel's headlock.

"I've got thee now." Samuel grinned at us. "As for the two of you, if you don't surrender now, I'll send my men after thee."

"Let's not be hasty." Stranger held his hands up, but his aura twisted in blue as he worked for a plan out of this.

"Where's the jewel, boy?"

"What jewel?" Rich stuttered.

"Don't play with me!" Samuel's shout made me jump, but Rich just squished his lips in disappointment.

"In my personal drawer."

Samuel went to the desk Rich pointed at and rummaged through his stuff. He pulled out a bracelet with a square piece of petrified wood in the middle of accenting diamonds. "You kept it here?"

"I'm homeless," Rich pointed out. "Where else was I supposed to keep it?"

"Rich," I sighed.

How were we supposed to stop him now? But the emptiness blew in my ear again, like a call for attention. I could have sworn I heard a whisper. *Let's see how far you'll fight for the humans.* It was The Void. *And remember, time changes when we're around.* Then a wave of heat wrapped around me before moving off to my side. I turned with the heat as it left the dressing room, and stepped out just in time to see one of the torches flutter up with a strange twirl. It stuttered to the left. Again. Longer this time, like the flames were reaching…for the curtains. *No,* I thought. *This isn't supposed to happen.* The original Globe Theater was still running in my time. History said nothing about a fire here. But, then again, what were history facts to me now?

The fire leaped for the dry curtains and caught the fabric with a hungry roar. It turned straight for the walls like dominoes. "Fire!" I screamed. "Everyone get out! There's a fire!"

157

"What?" Samuel snapped. Then he smelled the smoke. He cursed and let go of Rich. Hurrying passed us, Samuel shouted orders at the audience as all chaos broke loose, shepherding them toward the exits.

The theater lit up like kindling. Everything from the seats to the stage was fuel for the growing demon. *It's okay,* I thought. *There was no tragedy here. This was not like the Lusitania.* Then a beam collapsed right in front of the exits, and I remembered Ricky's warning. *History changes when you're around.* Did he mean because of things I did or just because I was there? Screams battled against the growing cackling of flames and settled deep in my heart. These screams were my fault.

Fire blocked every door. Every exit. Men from the audience worked to get the fallen beam away from the door, but made poor progress. Already the fire covered half a wall, heating up the blocked theater.

"What do we do?" Stranger asked. "I thought you said no one died in here!"

"I...." No. This was no time for a freak out. If my mind went blank now we'd all burn, and I couldn't let that happen. No one died here in history, which meant no one would today. I closed my eyes and got a quick scan of the room. "Get everyone by the stage."

"That's opposite the exits and closer to the fire," Rich pointed out, but Stranger was already at work.

"Over here!" he hollered. "Gather over here! Everyone stay calm!" He tapped Samuel's shoulder and whispered something to him. The man gave me a dirty look, but nodded and helped Stranger herd them our way. Problem was, most people noticed the proximity to the flames and refused.

I pointed a finger at Rich. "You're manipulative, right? Go help them."

"Ho! I resent...." He paused. "No, actually, I like that. We've found a way out! Stand closer and prepare for freedom, my admirers!"

Now all I had to do was create a door out of literally nothing while standing mere feet from an ever growing flame. *Let's do this.*

I had to fight against every instinct in order to get closer to the spill of emptiness just hanging in the air. I didn't know how The Void had gotten there, or why it would leave a puddle of shadows to cause chaos in this theater. Nor could I see The Void anywhere around me. But I knew the empty energy was there because of me. The Void could have been anywhere or nowhere. Heck, for all I knew, it could be everywhere. But I felt its humor stirring with the frightened, trapped

158

people, and creating a strange cocktail of emotions in the air around me. A burning tea of tears and laughter.

I reached for the shadowy mess and looked it straight in the eye. It was exactly the same height as me…definitely left on purpose for me to handle. My entire right side ached with the increasing heat. Tears fell down my face for no other reason than to throw the stinging smoke from my eyes. I coughed an inhale and closed my eyes. I needed an escape. Fresh air. I needed a door to take me right outside. Same time, same place, just the other side of the burning walls. Nothing more. I reached out in search for a metal knob. Nothing.

A wave of panic surged in my throat, choking my thoughts just as the smoke choked my breaths. *Just try harder. Focus more. You've done this before, Penny. This doesn't have to be like the Lusitania. It's not about just saving yourself. You have to save more. You have to save Stranger. You promised to save Rich, and you have the chance to save everyone. They don't need anything special. Just a door!*

There! Cold metal brushed against my fingertips. My eyes popped open despite the smoke and I smiled. *I did it.* I yanked the door open and a cool evening breeze spilled into the sizzled air. "Hurry!" I held the door open as wide as I could and waved my other arm for people to run through. They didn't need to be encouraged. Two, three people would squeeze through the door at a time, their clothes just escaping the nearby fire. A few actors covered Shakespeare himself from the sparks as they rushed him to safety. I watched as he used his arms to shield his face from the heat, and thought *I just burned William Shakespeare. Maybe I won't tell Dinah this story after all.*

The fire jumped to another wall, to the seats, and across the theater, closing us in, but it didn't matter. We just needed to get everyone out in time. I just needed to hold the door open.

That's when embers fell on me. I gasped and brushed them off before my clothes could catch fire. Then I looked up. The ceiling. The fire towered above us, and the crackling wood wouldn't hold it for much longer. "Hurry," I chanted. "Hurry. Hurry. Hurry!" The crowd had thinned, but would it be enough? Would they get out in time? I kept my eyes up, toward the smoke and danger. It wouldn't hold much longer. One cluster of beams in particular cracked and lost support. The shift in weight made them crack again, and more sparks flew down on us. I shielded my face from the attack but couldn't help looking back up. One more crack and it would come straight down. On the door.

I looked back at the crowd, at who was left. Only eight people now, struggling not to push the others out of the way as they rushed through. I admired their self-control. If I was running, I doubted I could hold back. Rich was still with us, holding the rear of the group with Stranger, while Samuel held a young girl in his arms. Her leg had been burned too much to use. Samuel met my eye and I saw his inner struggle, which made me sorry we'd argued before. He didn't want to leave kids behind. But he had another kid's life in his arms. I nodded to show I understood and he rushed out, leaving just Rich and us.

But the ceiling had other plans. I heard the last, deafening crack and knew my time was up. I had to protect the door. If it broke, so would their escape. I reached out for some more of that void energy. Only a stutter answered my call. I'd used up most of it creating the door. But maybe I could use what was left to deflect the falling beam, just a little bit. Just enough to save the door. Only one problem…there was only one other place the beam could go. Right on top of me. I squeezed my eyes shut and gathered all the energy I could into one solid punch. My skin shook to run, but I clenched my teeth together and focused on the cool breeze sifting through the open door. I could protect that.

"No!"

Two bodies slammed into me and I went flying back onto dry but singed wood. Fire crashed where I had been standing. Flames grasping in hunger for the meal they'd almost had. But that was not what churned my stomach. I hadn't had enough time, hadn't gotten the chance to throw my energetic punch. The beam had fallen and torn my makeshift door into splinters. On my left, Stranger struggled to his feet, coughing. He stifled some smoking sparks off his clothes and looked past me in horror, because he hadn't been the only one to scream no. He wasn't the only one who had tackled me. To my right, Rich groaned and rolled onto his back. He struggled to sit up and looked at the chaotic light as it danced around us. "I knew I wouldn't live long," he said. "Never thought I'd go down like this."

Stranger touched my arm. His fingers brushed against my raw skin and I flinched, but looked at him. "Can you make another door?" he asked.

I closed my eyes and searched for the darkness as the burning orange from the flames blared through my eyelids. It was gone. Whether I'd used it all up making the last door or the collapse had torn it to pieces, it was useless to us now. The last time, the problem had been too much nothing, nowhere for it to go. If only I'd known how easily it could shatter. Tears shocked my overheated cheeks as I shook my head. "No," I half-sobbed. "It's gone. I can't...I can't get us out of here."

"Get down," Stranger said. "Away from the smoke." Calloused fingers grabbed the back of my neck as he encouraged me to lay back down, closer to the freshest air available, tainted but clearer than even a foot above. I grabbed Rich closer and lay down, with Stranger covering my back. The ten-year-old's body shook from coughing, his clothes wet with desperate sweat. Behind me, with his arms wrapped around me, Stranger struggled to breathe. The air burned my throat as, all around me, the fire cackled like an evil laugh. It stole not only our escape, but our oxygen. If we didn't burn in here, we'd suffocate. And all I could think was how this was done on purpose. The Void had chosen to burn this place down. As if it was all a test and I'd die before I could understand the score. The reason. Or before I could make that piece of nothing understand the dangers of playing games with people's lives.

I tried to reach out mentally to see if it was around, watching us like some twisted psychopath. But the effort made my blood beat against my head. I needed more air. Even just half a breath, just to return a touch of oxygen, then I could go on. But there was none left. Sparks flew over us once again as more wood overheated and fell into ashes, like it was spitting on us. Taunting us. This was how we would die.

But that didn't make any sense. Why taunt us, put us in its debt, just to abandon us in a fire? Usually the voice got sharper the more danger I was in, as if waiting until I was open to suggestions. But now I was truly desperate and my head was silent. When usually the problem was a surplus of void energy, here we would die needing it. Perhaps it had abandoned us purely for irony's sake. To make us die begging for the thing we despised. And yet, what if there was another reason?

Rich stopped coughing. His body went limp, and from his fingers that stolen bracelet slipped into the ash. The square gem of petrified wood glinted off the light from the embers as if unaffected by the chaos. It rolled away, falling between the cracks in the wooden floor. Stranger's body relaxed with an eerie silence. "Stranger?" The whimper in my voice surprised me. I wanted to reach out and shake both of the boys, tell them they had to keep awake, that I could get them out. But black dots drowned the fire in my eyes. I felt jostled from behind, like something pushed us, but couldn't see past the black dots. Stranger gave half a groan but I couldn't get my face up, couldn't get my body to cooperate. I struggled against my numbing senses until I lost even myself.

Chapter 24

"Dad! DAD!! We need help down here!"

"What's going on?"

"Grab Dad and get the first aid kit!"

"Is that—?"

"Go, you moron!" Fingers pressed against my tender neck and a sigh brushed my skin at the discovery of a pulse. "What happened to you three?" I wanted to open my eyes, to take in my new surroundings. *Is this Heaven or Hell?* I thought. But the exhaustion, my singed remains, came with me to the other side, and I fell back into unconsciousness.

The peace that followed could never be found another way. Nothing bothered me there. No fears. No pain. No smoky memories. No desperation or feelings of failure. Nor any desires to return to the love and family I'd lost. It was a sleep not even my subconscious could interrupt. Like swimming in a pool of empty space.

But everyone must wake up. My first breath of consciousness was smoke-tinged and dry. I coughed and opened my eyes to a severe headache and multiple burns along my body. Metal surrounded me, and the only thing I could think was, *well, at least that won't burn quite as fast*. Despite the cold metal, the room felt homey. Family pictures hung on the walls and patterned rugs silenced the room's tendency to echo. But I couldn't place the time era of the room. An iPod was connected to a device I'd never seen before. An old, antique typewriter stood ready to record the owner's thoughts and whims.

I was in a bed. A single bed, which smelled of cinnamon and hot spices. I rested on top of the heavy gold and red duvet while a light sheet covered my body. Thank goodness too, since the weight of the duvet would have been too heavy on my burns. My T-shirt and jeans had changed to an Indian salwar and kameez, dyed purple and gold. On the side table next to the bed rested my dad's tablet. The thing looked half melted, with bubbled plastic along the sides and a caved in screen. It was nothing but trash anymore. Better I tell Dad I lost it than return that bubbly mess home.

But what was I doing here? How did I get here? I forced myself to sit up and take a better look around. A pile of blankets rested against a chair to my left, and a desk supported the weight of half a dozen journals and photos. Beside them was an old fifties-looking telephone. An aged Winnie the Pooh teddy bear leaned against a Russian Cheburaska doll. There was only one way in and out of the room, a door-shaped gap in the metal, but as far as I could see, there were no hinges or frame. Instead, a curtain stood in for privacy. It waved with the gentle stir of the room. I recognized that motion. That machine-run slice through waves. I was on a ship. Again.

"You've got to be kidding me." My voice croaked through my dry throat when I spoke. Something stirred at the sound of my voice, and I realized that the pile of blankets was not, in fact, vacant.

The blanket fell and Shreya blinked her nap away. "Hey," she said, sleep still thick in her voice. "You're finally awake."

"Where am I?"

"The prison ship." She pulled her hair-tie out and smoothed rogue flyaways back into a braid. "This is my room, actually, so you're welcome." She yawned.

"Where's Stranger and Rich?"

"Rich? Oh you mean the boy? They're fine. Fast asleep, and unaware they also stole someone's beds, as far as I'm aware. Mom's keeping an eye on them. How are you feeling?"

"Confused. And thirsty," I admitted.

"I bet you're dehydrated. Here." She leaned down and grabbed a glass of water from the floor. "There used to be ice in here, but it's been waiting for you to wake up for a while." I took it from her and drank it down in one breath. The cool water stung against my raw throat, but never before had water tasted so good. "Do you remember what happened?" Shreya asked as she took the empty glass from me.

I shook my head. "The last thing I remember was the fire and blacking out."

Shreya grimaced. "That couldn't have been fun. I'm sorry that happened to you."

She looked away, and I remembered what her mom had said before we left the prison ship. "I think your mom sent us there." It had only been a guess before, but the way she looked up cinched it.

"You needed to save the day," she said. Her face was deadpan and serious, but there was a note of remorse in her aura.

"Did I?" I snapped. Shreya wasn't shocked at all that her mother had sent two kids into danger, and remorse wouldn't heal the burns. This family was insane. Did they all know that we would get trapped there? That we would almost die? "That fire didn't have anything to do with natural causes! It was there because I was there! Because The Void was there! So you can't just sit back and tell me it was part of some grand plan, okay? It never should have happened!"

"Maybe not." Shreya stood up and walked over to her desk. She picked up the fifties telephone and dialed in a number. "But it still needed to happen," she said over her shoulder to me before speaking into the phone. "Hey, Dad, she's awake and ticked. … Yeah, I'm gonna let you answer the questions." She paused for a moment to listen. "She's gonna wanna relax. Talk about trauma. I don't think—" The other speaker must have interrupted, because she huffed and listened some more. Then she turned to look at me. "Hey, you wanna stay here and relax or check on the boys?"

"Check on the boys."

She grimaced and returned to the phone. "Fine, you win. We'll meet you over there." She hung up the phone and came over to my bedside. I pushed the sheet off my legs, but the movement caused a rush of pain and I flinched. "Yeah, moving is going to stink for a while. None of the burns are too bad, but there's a lot of them."

"Yeah," I agreed as I inched my feet to the floor. "Lots of sparks." I glanced at my arms. The skin was red and raw, but only rarely did the burns blister. Problem was, that still meant I had blistered burns along the length of my arms, and by the feel of it, my legs and neck too. Shreya came over and helped me to my feet. "So are you going to explain anything or what?" I asked as we started walking.

"Dad wants to."

"But how did we get here?"

Shreya's jaw tensed. For a second, she looked sad. "I found you.

Downstairs in the rec room, where the prison cells used to be. You were just all...laying there. Like you were dead." And her voice cracked. "Freaked me out. I thought.... But you were all breathing. It's a miracle."

"I'd say. It doesn't make any sense." Nor did my surroundings now. Shreya said we were on the prison ship, but this? This wasn't anything like what I remembered. It was...a home, with pictures of Ricky and the family posing in front of iconic tourist places hanging on the walls. The Eiffel Tower, the Great Sphinx, even some places I didn't recognize. They must have really worked on this place to make it so comfortable. Why live on a prison ship, though? It was beyond me. But the bigger question was, how had the three of us gotten here? "Do you have any ideas?" I asked Shreya. "I mean, we couldn't have just popped up on your ship randomly."

She shrugged. "I was born in 2218, and now live in an 18th century prison ship that my dad stole. Making sense would be pretty unusual for this family."

"I'm beginning to see that. But that doesn't mean someone teleporting into your rec room is just a normal Tuesday. Right?"

"Well, nothing about you is just a normal Tuesday, is it?" Shreya chuckled. "Frankly, I'm not asking questions. I'm just glad it happened. It would have been horrible if you three died in there."

"You talk like you know me," I pointed out.

"I know the stories." She stopped outside another curtained door-sized hole in the hallway and pulled the blue curtain to the side. There were four beds in the bedroom, but only two were occupied. Rich looked like he was dreaming of great plays and epic lines. His costume dress and make up had disappeared, and instead he wore striped pajamas. His eyebrows were a bit singed and there were a couple of blisters on his cheek, but he looked okay. Thank everything that was good, Rich was okay. I may not have been the one who saved him, but he was saved. And whoever did it, whatever it was that caused our rescue, I'd like to kiss their cheek.

Stranger didn't look quite as unscathed. A bandage covered his shoulder, along with the blistered skin none of us could escape. His regular clothes had been replaced with a fresh white T-shirt and jeans. He looked like a sleeping James Dean...maybe a bit cuter. I leaned against his mattress and brushed my fingers against the bandage.

Shreya's mom, Zetta, stood at the other side of the room mixing up some sweet smelling concoction, but she stopped when she saw me. "Obviously we don't know what happened," Zetta said. "But when you three appeared in the rec room, there was some debris sticking out of his shoulder. Went about two inches in, but luckily didn't hit anything vital. I know a thing or two about combat first aid, so I fixed him up. I've also given him some meds so he'll sleep longer and heal a touch faster."

"Thank you," I said. Zetta smiled and returned to her mixing.

Shreya hesitated before speaking up. "Thing is, that shoulder was covering your heart. That same injury would have been a lot worse on your chest than his shoulder."

"He saved my life," I interpreted. I reached down and grabbed his hand. His fingers were cool to the touch, but warm enough to show life.

Shreya stepped over to Rich's bed and checked his vitals. She glanced at me, at my hand, and away again. "So how long have you two been traveling together?"

"Not even a day," I said, and slipped my hand away.

"Hmm." She nodded. "Bet it's been longer than a day. There's no way to count the hours, and even you slept for a long time. The adrenaline and inconstant sunlight might make it seem like it's been less than a day, when in reality, it could have been thirty-six, maybe even forty-eight hours straight. All time travelers should be careful of exhaustion."

"And?" I asked. "What else are you saying?"

She smiled and glanced up at me through her eyelashes. "And I'm saying you two look cute together."

"Like I said. We barely know each other."

"No one knows anyone." We all jumped when Ricky stepped into the room. He had to bend down and step in sideways to get through the door space. "Doesn't stop us from trying. It's good to see you awake, Penelope Grace."

"Good to know you still can't enter a room like a normal person." Zetta gestured at her shirt. Whatever mixture she'd been working on had spilt down her front at his surprise entrance. Ricky grinned in success. "Come on, Shreya, help me go pick more huckleberries."

"Huckleberries? On a ship?" I asked.

"No," Shreya said matter-of-factly. "Montana Glacier Mountains in the late summer."

"Don't forget the bear spray," Zetta said to her daughter. She got on her tiptoes and kissed Ricky on the cheek. "We'll be back in a few."

"What are we doing here?" I asked as soon as Zetta and Shreya had left. "How did we get here?" With every question I stepped closer to Ricky, standing up to his massive height and broad shoulders. He raised an eyebrow but seemed otherwise unintimidated. "Why did Zetta send us to the Globe Theater?"

At that last question, Ricky nodded at the ten year old. "Because you needed to save me."

"What?" That time my voice went deep in disbelief. "That's you?"

Ricky the Pirate bent down into a deep, theatrical bow. "At your service."

"But how does that sweet, albeit super manipulative kid become... you? What happened?"

Ricky laughed. "You happened. The Grace that changed my life. Good and bad."

"I'm guessing the fire was bad." I shook my head. "I'm sorry."

"As you can see, I'm fine," he said, pointing at the bed.

"But I'm not the one who got us out. I don't know what got us out."

"Don't you?" Ricky raised an eyebrow at me again. "Come on, Penny. What's the only thing powerful enough?"

"The Void," I realized. "Why would The Void save us?"

"It was a test. To see how far you'd go to protect the people around you. Well played, by the way." He nudged my shoulder with a playful smile.

"But it didn't save us. I searched. The only signs of the Void were the residual mess that started the fire. The Void itself wasn't even there."

"No." He nodded. "It probably wasn't in the beginning."

"What do you know about The Void?" I asked. "What does it want with me?"

Ricky sat down in a chair next to...himself...and leaned back, stretching as if reaching for a plausible answer. "I've always been a simple man, Penny. The questions I ask are, where's my next meal? Is my family safe? I don't ask the big questions. I usually don't have time."

I made a face in disbelief. "If that kid is you, that means you're a full on grown up with a family and everything, and ever since you were ten, you've known about The Void. And you're trying to convince me you've never stayed up at night, wondering what it wanted?"

He shrugged. "Maybe it's bored, or it's the source of all evil. That sounds like a plausible story, right?" He picked at the sleeve of his coat. "Or maybe it's more like us than anyone wants to admit. Maybe it just wants a family, some kind of bond, and you're the only one who can hear it."

"If that sentence was supposed to be uplifting, you have some more work to do," I pointed out. "I don't want creepy what-ifs. I want answers. Surely there's something you can tell me."

"I can tell you my story. In fact, I insist. I love the life I have here, but almost every significant part of it stems from the hands of—no offense—an incredibly unreliable teenage girl. So I'm going to tell you my story and you're going to make sure that it plays out exactly like I describe it."

Chapter 25

"I was born in the 1600s, as you already figured out." Ricky motioned for me to sit down. I took the seat by Stranger, curious to finally get some answers. "My parents died when I was seven and I had no other family, so the government back then wanted to stick me in some orphanage. The problem was that it smelled and there were a lot of sick kids, and, to be honest, I couldn't stand to be there. It took me two months to figure out how to escape, and I lived on the streets for three years. I stole food and precious jewelry to sell for money. I did what I had to do to survive." He smiled. "Zetta called me her Aladdin when we were dating, because I basically lived like him as a kid. Except I had no monkey, of course."

"Or genie," I added, but he just looked at me, the scar along his eye crinkling with humor.

"I wouldn't be so sure about that. When I was ten and in the middle of one of the biggest acting career days of my insignificant life, and potentially my last day of freedom, these two teenagers walked into my life with a promise to help me out. So I lied through my teeth to convince them I was worth saving. I didn't know about your lie detector thingie back then, of course. You did more than help me out with some cop. You freed me from the only path my life could have taken in that place. You saved me."

"The Void saved you," I reminded him.

"The Void is even more manipulative than I am. I wouldn't trust it if I were you, Penny." His voice got serious fast. "Don't let it get in your head, make you start questioning fiction from reality."

"Is that what it tries to do?" I asked. "Mess with my head?"

"So I've heard. I wasn't with you at the time."

I glanced at the kid just as he breathed a deep, peaceful breath. "What happens to you next? After the fire?"

"I wish I could say we traveled for years, exploring the world and just living without having to answer to anyone. But you ditch me pretty early on, actually."

"What? Why would I do that?"

But he continued without answering. "I was angry. For years. I'd even say that I hated you for what you did." Ricky leaned closer and looked me square in the eye. "You ditched me in the middle of the 23rd century. Away from everything I'd ever known or understood. I depended on you, put my faith in you, and you slammed the door in my face. And Penny, I need you to promise me that you'll do it again."

I leaned away from him as my gut twisted. "I can't think of one reason why I would ever just ditch some helpless kid—"

"I know." Ricky rubbed the back of his neck. "Geez, this whole thing is crazy. Time travel makes a headache out of reality. I used to dream of any and all possible explanations that justified what you did to me. I idealized you two the moment you came to my rescue. You were these perfect heroes. And then, out of the blue, it was like I became nothing to you anymore. And it hurt. Like I was back in that fire again. But alone. It wasn't until just recently that I realized how thankful I am that you ditched me. I met Zetta in the 23rd century. I started my family there. And I think you left me because I asked you to."

"So you want me to abandon you?"

"I'm begging you," he said, and he looked dead serious. "I'm going to fight. I'm going to take cheap shots, and I'm going to hold a wicked grudge over you for years. But I still need you to do this for me. Please."

I leaned back in my chair and looked at the kid. *No*, I thought. *I promised Rich I'd help him*. I wouldn't turn my back on something like that. Plus, I didn't like the idea that he would be out in the world, hating me. I knew I didn't know the kid well, but no one likes the idea their actions could cause someone to hate them for years.

"I've seen you try to save the world, Penny," Ricky continued. "Day by day and one tragedy at a time. I have watched you bear the weight of a thousand lost souls, to beat yourself up that you couldn't save enough or that you should have done better. I know you're doing it right now because you're not the one that got us out of that fire. I'm telling you that I understand who you are and who you will become. And I forgive you for what you will do to me." He grabbed my shoulder and I leaned away from him. "Penny, I need your mistakes. I make a great life out of them. So please, promise me that when you three go to the 23rd century, you will leave me behind."

"There's got to be another way," I argued.

"Not one that guarantees this life, and I wouldn't trade it for the world. I know." He grinned. "I've been offered that exchange before. I just want this, Penny. I need it. It's my happily ever after." I only had to look in his eyes to understand how much he believed his story. But what if it could be better? They were pirates on the run, living trapped on a ship. If I didn't abandon him, if his childhood was easier, his adulthood could be better. But the longer it took me to respond, the more concerned his eyebrows got, so I forced myself to nod. He sighed in relief. "Thank you. You're a good friend." He stood up and stretched his back.

"Can I at least tell Rich why I leave him behind?"

"No," Ricky said as his back gave a giant pop. "It's kind of vital that I hate you for a while. Zetta gets it in her head that meditation would help me, and let's just say one thing leads to another."

"Great." I rolled my eyes and flopped my back against the chair. "You know, talking to you is never comforting."

"Well in that case, I feel like I should add that Stranger had no idea about your sudden decision to ditch me. I remember the look on his face when you reached out to slam the door. Total shock. Can't fake it, and that's coming from an actor. He tried to stop you. I never hated Stranger, and that's just as important, because I did need to get back into time traveling. I needed someone on your team that I could trust. He can't know."

Ricky had no idea what he asked of me. Every time that I had left, I'd left it worse. The Globe Theater was a bust. I was a part of a ship heist on the prison ship, and I wasn't able to prevent the tragedy of the Lusitania. And here Ricky stood, telling me it would happen again... I'd leave another era in disgrace. Abandon even more people. Only this time it wouldn't be an impulsive mistake. It would be a premeditated plan. "Any more terrible ideas?" I all but snapped.

"Since you like to find sad people, there's a little girl there who's scared. I remember you comforting her. You'll need a screwdriver, so I have one waiting by the door for you to take with you."

"Will The Void be there?"

"Now, Penny, I'm not even going to tell myself all the good stuff." He smiled with a nod at the sleeping boy. "Just remember, kiddo, I'm leaving out all the hardcore details. Everything's so much worse than this." He chuckled. "Oh, how the future sucks? Let me count the ways. I'll go grab you some food." And then he was gone, disappearing through a curtain of blue. I shook my head at the incredible situation, but couldn't convince myself there was any humor in it. Everything was just a tad too inconvenient. All Stranger and I wanted was some obtainable rescue. Something simple in our wheelhouse that could up our confidence. Now the kid we set our minds on to save was burnt and out of his time. Sure, Ricky said that he'd grow up fine and love his family, which was great and all. But right now, Rich was only a wake-up away from having his entire reality torn to shreds.

And what was the point of The Void's little fiasco at the Globe Theater? Was it really just a test? To see how I'd handle that situation? What did it want from me? Was it training me? Trying to see if I'd make a good hero or something? If so, why not focus its attention on Stranger? The boy who actually wanted to save the day? But then again, Stranger couldn't see it or sense its energies like I could. Perhaps The Void wasn't interested so much in potential or desire as much as abilities. Ricky's suggestion knotted my stomach, that maybe The Void just wanted a friend…or worse, a *family*. I had already reached out to it when I needed help. Was that its plan? Either way, I didn't like it. But perhaps I could use that to my advantage. At least see what the cost was before I agreed to any sort of deal.

Although I couldn't swallow that it had just left us to burn in that fire as long as it had. Not that it wouldn't want to see us hurt, but it never even taunted us, never got in my head and made me doubt myself. It didn't even talk. So what kept it away?

I stewed in self-doubt and half hoped dreams until Rich stirred in his bed and opened his eyes. "Hey," I said as he took in his surroundings with increasing concern. "You're okay. Everything's fine."

"Where am I?" he asked.

I explained the situation, that we were on a friend's ship and had been rescued from the fire by magic. I didn't go too far into detail, as it would only get more confusing. Nor did I tell the kid his future self had stolen the ship. There was only so much crazy a person could swallow in one conversation. Rich started looking at me like I had lost it about two words into the story, but there was no real way to ignore the evidence around us, including the constant whir of newly installed engines, another fifties telephone, and what looked like a well-loved gaming computer.

"That's…." Ricky sat up and rubbed the back of his neck as he took it all in. "Unbelievable."

"Yeah," I agreed. "But there it is just the same."

"Are you trying to make me believe I'm two hundred years in the future?"

"About two hundred years in my past."

He looked me up and down with renewed admiration. "Thou art from the future? Way in the future? What's it like?"

"It's a lot different, that's for sure. You'll get to see for yourself."

His eyes popped open so wide I thought they'd fall out. "Are you telling me I can travel in time now, like you? I can go anywhere? I don't have to go back to my own time?"

Oops. I shouldn't have said that. "Is that something you want?"

"Do you jest?" The boy laughed. "Who wouldn't want that?"

"No one sane." Ricky stepped through the curtain. He carried a large plate of fish and veggies and a tall iced glass of water, along with a pitcher for refills. He handed the food to me.

"Do you always listen in on a conversation before entering?" I asked.

He chuckled. "Guilty. It makes for cooler entrances. Pirates must always make a dramatic entrance."

If little Rich had looked at me in awe, it was nothing compared to how he looked at his future self. "You're a pirate?" he gasped.

Ricky seemed pretty proud of himself. "It's the only way I could swallow living on a ship."

"Do you fish?" Rich asked, and his nose squished up in disgust.

"Heck no," Ricky said with a shake of his head. "I don't do fishing. So you wanna take a look around? We'll get you hydrated on the way. Unless you're still not feeling well — "

"No way am I sitting in this dull chamber when I'm on a pirate ship. Goodbye, Penny."

I waved at the boy as he jumped off the bed and out the door. Ricky winked at me and followed himself out, ready and eager to brag. Then I was alone, with nothing to distract me but Stranger's light breathing and my own questions. Only there were too many to focus on. The only thing I could agree on was that my future was a lot more complicated than just a kid falling through time. There was something else going on, someone else calling the shots. The Void had taken a special interest in me. I was used to falling into the background, settling in the shade of Dinah's brilliance. Sure, I had wished I got noticed more, but from people like Mom and Dad, the fun girls at school...not from some mysterious humanoid creeper who'd been following me around and put me in life and death situations just to see how I'd handle them.

At least I wasn't alone. The Void had paid special attention to Stranger first. And after it was through with him, it tore his life away and betrayed him in one fell swoop. Great. Something to look forward to. I ate my food in pouty silence, free to glare into my lemony fish with all the frustration I could muster without having to put on a face for anyone. I stabbed into my squash and chewed with a vengeance. Stupid Void. But then a sobering thought entered my mind and made the pouting step aside for a round of horror. What would it toss at us next?

I leaned back in my chair and stared at the wall in front of me. What else could it want to know? To prove? When would it show its face and talk to me without all these manipulative games? How long would it play with us like a cat batting at a moth? I bit at the inside of my cheek and glared. My eyes landed on yet another family photo, shaking in beat with the ever-moving ship. Ricky had his arm around Zetta and Shreya while a whole bunch of kids posed in various funny faces around a half-carved David statue. They all looked so safe and happy. I'd never had any picture perfect moments like that with my family. My parents were the manila envelopes to Ricky's crazy birthday cards. But I missed my manila envelopes. They didn't have to be crazy or perfect. They didn't need to go to every game or treat me like some princess. They were my family, and I had to see them again. Perhaps I wouldn't have missed them so much if I just knew I could see them someday.

"Penny?"

Stranger's voice froze my paranoia turned self-pity. He tried to sit up, but cringed at the movement. "Careful," I said, and helped him lay back down. "You got hurt. Don't want to rip your stitches." I explained

175

the situation once again, but this time left out Ricky's demands.

"The Void?" Stranger grimaced at the thought. "Again?"

"That's the only plausible explanation." I poured some water into a glass for Stranger and handed it to him. He cringed as his injured shoulder stretched with the movement, but drank it. "I'm sorry," I said.

"For what?"

"For everything. The whole fire mess and your shoulder."

"It's no big deal," he said.

"It kind of is. According to Shreya, if your shoulder hadn't been there, the debris would have gone into my chest. I'm lucky to have you around."

"It wasn't luck." Stranger set the glass down and rested his head back on the pillow.

"What do you mean?" I asked.

"I was about to black out," he said, and he looked straight at me, those pale blue eyes staring into mine without blinking. "I could feel you doing the same, the way your muscles just surrendered to the heat, and I thought this is it. This is the end. But then you said my name and it kind of woke me up." He blinked and glanced away, massaging his jawline. "I saw the debris about to fall. I just…. Anyway, it was the pain that made me black out."

"Stranger," I said, and reached out to touch the tips of his hand. "Thank you. You saved my life. Twice."

He glanced at my hand. "No need for thanks."

"You're the hero of the team." I smiled and started to pull my hand away.

His hand flipped around and grabbed my fingers, stopping me. I held still, my heart in my chest. "It wasn't heroic," he said. "The world needs you." Then his fingers pulled mine closer and intertwined them together. My hand felt right in his, safe. A subtle heat rose through my wrist and up my arm. "I need you. You calm the chaos," he added.

Silence filled the room. I didn't know what to say. I couldn't even remember how to speak. My eyes stared at our intertwining fingers, amazed by how well they fit together. But a whisper tainted my thoughts. *Of course he needs you. You're the only door home.*

Only that wouldn't explain why he grabbed my hand. Or why I couldn't speak. I tried, but fear held me in a choke hold, because I had a tendency of messing everything up, and if I spoke, I could ruin this moment.

176

But silence was the wrong answer. Stranger's fingers loosened and he pulled away. "Besides," he chuckled, "I can't take credit for tackling you away from the door. I'm pretty sure Rich got to you first. Boy's brave. He'd make a good addition to the team."

He pulled away even on a spiritual level. I'd still managed to ruin the moment. He must have thought I turned him down, didn't want his hand in mine. And now he offered a subject change. I couldn't take it. Not if I wanted anything to happen between us. I needed to turn the conversation back. Or maybe just grab his hand again. Yes, that's what I would do. If I was brave.

But Stranger had turned the conversation onto Rich, which reminded me of Ricky's demands. To betray a ten year old. Only I knew that, if I obeyed Ricky, I'd be betraying two people. Stranger trusted me to save the day, or at least to try my hardest. And so far, I'd fooled him into thinking I could keep my end of the bargain. The moment I slammed the door between us and Rich, Stranger would see me for what I was. Not a hero. Just a girl who couldn't do anything right. When that happened, I'd rather lose a friend than anything more than a friend.

"Too bad this isn't *The Avengers*," I said, and leaned back in my chair "We're trying to go home, remember? I don't know if Rich would feel at ease in the 21st century." I glanced at the photo glaring at me on the bedside table. "I don't know anything right now."

"You know who does."

I looked back at Stranger, and realized by his sober expression exactly who he had in mind. "The Void." I nodded in agreement. "We might have to do something about that."

"What we need is some way to trap or corner it, and make it talk instead of just knocking us around. Do you think we can manage that?"

I shook my head without hesitation. "I'm powerless compared to that thing. I have no idea what I'm doing when it comes to energy manipulation. I almost killed everyone when I tried to scare away the escaped convicts with the emptiness energy. Besides, I don't even know what would trap it. What's its weakness? Does it have one? Or does it just float around, shedding chaos like dandruff?"

The corners of Stranger's lips tightened to hold back a smile. "Like…dandruff?"

"Don't judge my ranting." I glared at him, but couldn't hold back my own smile. Not for any reason in particular. In fact, there were a lot of reasons not to smile, but it felt comforting to know that he could. Like maybe it wasn't that terrible, or that I might not have completely ruined the moment with my hesitation after all. "There was something about the Globe Theater fire though, something different. I don't know what, but I think something kept it away, or else we wouldn't have stayed so long in that fire."

"You're sure about that? You really think it cares?"

"No. Not cares. That's the wrong word. But something stopped him, I think, and if we find out what that was, we might be able to coax it out. Figure out what it wants."

"I don't want to know," Stranger admitted. "But you're right. We need some way to fight against this thing."

I didn't answer. We couldn't figure out what The Void wanted. We didn't have enough information. And I thought it wanted us to be this clueless. Desperate. That was the word. Because what if The Void wasn't testing me? What if it was manipulating me instead? Making me realize that our lives depended on its mercy? It wanted me to know I wasn't the one saving the day.

But if we were in its complete control, how would I ever figure out what its weakness was? How could I trust anything? No, I couldn't just keep traveling and hoping that we might stumble over some doorway home. The Void would never be done. It had saved us for a reason... *taken* us for a reason. But I had no desire to be a part of its twisted plan. I had to find out what kept it away from the fire for so long. It was my only way home.

Even as a surge of adrenaline coursed through my veins in agreement to the potential fight, a stomach churning thought brought me back to reality. Because The Void really did have complete control. How could I find its weakness when it watched every step I took? No, I couldn't depend on some magical weapon to save the day. If I didn't know what its weakness was soon, I'd just have to confront it anyway. No way would I become that thing's puppet. Armed with hope or not, I had to keep fighting.

"What are you thinking?" Stranger asked. "Good idea or bad?"

I gave him a forced smile. "Good."

Chapter 26

I didn't tell Stranger. Anyone with a rational thought would smell the crazy on my plan. But crazy or not, it was our only option. Really, it was just speeding up the process. We'd almost died in the Globe Theater. Stranger had stitches because of that *adventure,* and we were lucky. What if next time, luck wasn't on our side? What if the next tragedy The Void plopped us into got one of us killed? Or a whole theater full of innocent people? I wasn't going to play The Void's little mind games anymore. I'd give Rich his happy ending—it was the least I could do after tearing him away from his home time—but after that, this ended.

Maybe Ricky's manipulation was starting to rub off on me. Or maybe I was always this way. Because I didn't think twice before egging Stranger on while forming my own silent truth. I would contact The Void. It had followed us throughout time and space, so I knew it would be there. All I had to do was reach out and confront it. Demand to know what it wanted with us, and what kind of "debt" it intended us to pay. That much I told Stranger. He was desperate enough to fool himself into thinking it was a good plan. But I didn't tell him that I would do it with or without an upper hand. I had to go home. I needed to see Dinah, alive and breathing and ticked at me for insisting we leave our home to investigate that stupid energy. Let her give me the silent treatment for years or yell at me every time we talked. I just needed to know she was okay.

"Penny?" Stranger asked after a moment of silence. "What do you think it wants? If it's as powerful as it seems, what could it want from us?"

"I don't know. But you don't have to worry, because I'll fix it."

"You mean we." His jaw tensed and a glare simmered behind his cold stare. "We'll fix it."

"Of course. We," I corrected. The Void's voice echoed in my mind. What it had said to Stranger right before it tossed him aside. It needed a fresh start. I wouldn't mind one of those. One where I wasn't singled out like this. One where I wasn't about to ditch little Rich right in front of Stranger when I had so long to tell him everything, to make him understand.

"Do you need any food?" I asked.

"I'm actually not hungry for once. And I'm sure you want to get back on the road."

"What? Stranger, no, you need to rest. You've got stitches."

Stranger tossed the sheet off his legs and got to his feet. "I've got stitches on my shoulder. Not my foot. The longer we sit, the longer we have to wait."

And the longer before I had to fulfill my promise to Ricky. Or confront The Void. "We can wait here. This place seems calm, and they're hospitable."

"Yeah, and pirates." Stranger grabbed his jacket and shrugged it on, letting his sleeve drape over his shoulder instead of stretching his stitches. "Come on. Let's head out."

I dragged myself onto my feet and started for the door. "Let's go find Rich."

"Why?"

"What do you mean why?"

"Penny, this place is literally Rich's home. Which means that his future self can just drop him off where he belongs, prepare him for the future. When it comes to time travel, that's the dream."

"I don't think it's a good idea for Rich and Ricky to be together too long. Might mess with time, create a paradox."

"Doesn't seem to be an issue so far."

"Maybe it just needs time to build before the whole paradoxical destruction begins," I bluffed. "There's a whole genre of literature explaining why leaving Rich with Ricky is a bad idea."

"Are you sure, though? You do know there's a difference between literature and reality, right?"

"Of course I do," I snapped.

Stranger shrugged. "So far nothing's happened, but if you feel that strongly about it, all right. If he wants to come along, he can. But we can't just drag him with us, putting him in danger. Is that what you're implying?"

"I thought you said he'd make a good addition to the team."

"Yeah, but…." Stranger shook his head and shrugged, only to grimace at the pull of stitches. "I don't like the idea of him getting involved with The Void."

"Me either. There's no reason for it. But why not give him an adventure or two, you know? He's maybe the one person in the world who'd enjoy time traveling. There's no one holding him back. And if he decides he doesn't want to travel, he can choose any type of home he wants."

"That's true. Okay, let's go find him." Stranger pulled the curtain back and walked through the door. I paused for a moment before following. I wondered if I had laid the lies on a bit too thick there. Might have made it more difficult. *Ugh*, I thought. *Just get this thing over with already.*

"Hey, he's awake!" Ricky hollered when Stranger and I stepped onto the deck. Much like the inside of the ship, the deck had completely transformed from the prison ship I remembered. Tiki lights lined the railing, while hammocks and beach chairs speckled the floor. Kids weaved around and under the hammocks, giggling while they shot each other with water guns. Ricky dodged a stream of water as he came our way. Rich stuck to Ricky's hip like they were glued together. The boy smiled at Stranger and me, his lips so spread out that each corner almost tickled his ears.

"Can you believe this place?" Rich asked. "I never thought life on the sea could be this comfortable."

"Practically unbelievable," I agreed. "Ricky, are you still in the 1700s? How did you get a hold of all this stuff?"

"The door you made last time you were here. It's still open. As long as our family stays zen and in control of our personal energies, we can manipulate the door to open in different times. But only with my permission, of course." He rattled some keys from his pocket. "Rule one on this ship…never time travel alone, and make sure there's someone here to call you home. Just so you know," Ricky added, and he looked at me in complete seriousness, "there's someone here at all times, on call for door connecting. So, the door's always open for you. If you ever need a place to crash or just to feel at home, we're here."

"Thank you," I said. "And, thank you for everything you've done."

"That's what we're here for." Ricky winked.

"We don't want to be any more of a burden," Stranger said, and offered Ricky his good hand to shake. "So we'll be on our way."

Ricky nodded like he'd seen that coming, which, since Rich was right there taking it all in, Ricky had technically seen it all before. "Come on, I'll show you to the door."

We started walking. I hadn't noticed Rich wasn't walking with us until I heard his voice a few steps behind us. "What about me?" he asked. His voice seemed small, overwhelmed. "What happens to me now?"

Ricky glanced at me but stayed silent, waiting for me to take over. It was unfair. Ricky was the one who knew what best to say, so why did I have to talk? I turned to the kid and knelt down to better look him in the eye. "What do you want, Richie?"

He hesitated and looked around the deck. I was so close to him, I could sense his energies. He wanted to remember every little detail of the place so he'd always remember a home like this was possible. But something stirred within his spirit, an echo in his aura, but deep within his chakras. At age ten, Rich had already lived years on the run. He didn't like the idea of being trapped by water with nowhere to run.

"Richie, life with Stranger and me right now is dangerous. It's possible that fire never would have happened if we hadn't been there, and more mishaps like that might happen."

"Why?" Rich asked.

"I guess you could say we're cursed. There's something after us, and I don't know how to stop it. If you come with us, you might be in danger too."

That got the kid's attention. He looked at me and a smirk whispered in his eyes. "If you're trying to convince me to go with you, well played."

Ricky laughed. "That a-boy." He winked at me and headed down the stairs.

Stranger's eyebrows furrowed together in confusion. "Was that supposed to be convincing?"

I shrugged. "That guy's crazy. No matter the age."

"Well, at least he can't claim we never warned him," he said, and followed Ricky down the stairs, where the adventure would continue.

This little haven could only last a moment, and yet I wanted to hide here until magically, the only door on the ship would take me home. I leaned my head back and puffed some agitation into the sky, only to have a wave of fear take its place when I heard Zetta and Shreya laugh on the other side of the deck. They were sipping a drink from coconut cups and watching the kids play. Some of the older kids tackled the younger ones to the ground. A few settled into hammocks and starting reading water-splattered novels. This was what was at stake. This was what Ricky had asked me to protect. It wasn't about a little boy who wanted adventure. It was about a family who needed a chance. I didn't have to be afraid. They were easy orders. All I had to do was obey them, keep to the story. I could do this.

I walked down the steps, following the boys' shadows, and repeated that line to myself. I could do this. This family would not disappear because of me.

The door was right where I'd left it, but it was the only thing that remained the same. The cell bars had been completely taken out and replaced with a foosball table, some classic arcade games, and an Xbox Kinect. From the pile of soot near the Pac-Man game, about the width of three huddling kids, I'd say this was where Shreya had found us.

"We can never get anyone to clean," Ricky chuckled.

"The Void brought us here," I said.

"Yeah. I thought we already covered that."

But I hadn't put together what it meant. The Void brought us here to the exact time and place where Ricky chose this life, instead of wishing for another. Where Ricky would ask me to keep his lifeline in proper order. If The Void hadn't taken us here, Ricky's life would never have become this. Which meant only one thing. Ricky and this life were vital to whatever The Void was planning. Did that make this family a good thing? Or bad? Was it possible that something as loving as this family could be part of an evil plan?

"So where are we headed?" Stranger asked.

I glanced away from the soot and caught Ricky's eye. He nodded and I took a deep breath to prepare myself for the next adventure. Only this wasn't like the others. I wasn't going in completely blind with no idea what to do. I had a mission. I had purpose. And I knew exactly what the world would lose if I messed up. Because it didn't matter if The Void had a hand in the creation of this family. They still deserved to exist. "So what do I look for?" I asked Ricky. "To open both ends of the door."

"Just think of the time you want to go."

Okay, 23rd century. But wouldn't that leave some room for error? "So, just...wherever?" I looked at Ricky, waiting for him to give a tad more detail without revealing our plan to Stranger or little Rich.

"Wherever you want to go." Ricky nodded. He seemed completely oblivious. "Ah, give me a hug before you head out, eh? Don't forget your favorite pirate." He pulled Rich into a tight bear hug and gave his curly hair a noogie before letting go. He gave Stranger a gentler hug, patting his back with one careful arm. "Heal up fast, bucko. Don't forget to keep that one safe," he added with a nod at me. Stranger laughed and Ricky stepped to me. "Penny," he said, and leaned in. His embrace was the embodiment of a bear hug. His large arms completely covered me, and I felt surrounded by absolute safety. Then he whispered in my ear. "Think of dust, the smell of fireworks, and glacier water. And petrified wood. A lot of it. This place will be in the western United States. Don't forget that girl, the lonely one." He slipped something small and cold into my hand. The screwdriver he told me I'd need. "Keep it close. Don't lose it." He gave me one last squeeze and let go.

I walked to the only door on the ship and closed my eyes. There was nothing on the other side. No room, no wall. Just a giant gap of nothing. I imagined what Ricky had suggested, even though there had to be more than one place in the 23rd century with those sensory details all put together. Any Fourth of July, right? Well, I'd try it before I pointed out I'd need a better description. Dust. Fireworks. America. Dust. Fireworks. America. Glacier water. Loneliness. 23rd century.

Only one place called back to me. Such simple things combined together to form absolute uniqueness. I reached out to it, mentally tying the two doors together, and opened the door. It seemed to open up into a hallway. Just a normal hallway...a cream walls and fake flowers on the side table type of hallway. I glanced back at Ricky. This had been a mistake. I'd done something wrong, right?

Ricky gave me a quick nod. "Good luck," he said. "Have fun, and don't worry about me."

Chapter 27

The 23rd century was not what I'd expected. No one wore shiny Spandex or had crazy hair. The houses weren't in circles, and not one flying car zoomed overhead, much to my disappointment. This was not the awe-inspiring future I had seen on TV. This was...dry.

After I cracked the hinges of the door and the darkness faded away, the three of us walked out of an abandoned office building that hadn't seen love in years. The paint peeled off like dry skin. Any valuables had been looted long ago. It was evening again. The sun had begun its daily flirt with the horizon; the third sunset I'd noticed in my time travels. Only this sunset was blurry, as a steady blanket of dust blew between us and the sunlight. This was definitely not a city. More like a small western town. I half expected John Wayne to turn the corner. The place seemed eerily quiet, without the cliché western duel song playing in the background.

"This is the future?" Rich asked.

"Where are we?" Stranger asked.

"Where are the people?"

"Maybe it's like in the 1600s," Stranger suggested. "It's not rush hour or something."

"I know this silence." Rich grinned. "Follow me." He ran down the street.

"Rich!" I snapped, and ran after him. Stranger groaned and jogged with me, along the cracked concrete and past the closed street shops. A few cars lined the streets. They looked slicker than the ones in my day, with a half arc top so soft there was almost no curve at all. But the windows were broken, the wheels were missing, and there were random gaps under the opened hoods where engines should be. Every once in a while a chunk of petrified tree trunk stood out in the middle of the broken asphalt, although why anyone would put that there, I had no clue. I wanted to slow down so I could search for the scared girl Ricky had mentioned, but Rich ran too fast for me to focus.

As we ran, I spotted two guys a couple of blocks away. They wore tan dusters with deep pockets, and knives were strapped to their hips. They walked in a rushed yet trained line. Neither seemed to notice us as they snuck through the shadows.

"Creepy," I said. Stranger nodded in agreement. I kept running after the kid. *Never mind*, I thought, *this place isn't anywhere near John Wayne worthy.*

Rich stopped running a few blocks in front of us. He turned to the corner and gave one clap of celebration. "Ha! Told you I knew what was going on!" He pointed around the corner. Stranger and I caught up and glanced down the street. Fewer buildings populated the edges, and concrete fizzled out into a dirt road.

A decent walk away stood a three story house. Every window was open. Both the front and side doors invited air and guests to enter. A couple of dozen adults laughed and sipped from metal camping cups, while a simmering fire struggled for life inside a double wall of rocks. They wore loose shirts and baggy pants made from thinner fabric than cotton. Dirt marked their faces and skin. Those with longer hair had it pulled back in slick buns, like no one had bathed in years. Yet, they cared about their looks. Every once in a while one person would reach out and dust some dirt off their friend's face. This seemed normal, and was a caring gesture.

"A town party," Rich said. "I love those. Although this is a smaller town than London."

"Are you sure this is the future?" Stranger asked. I nodded.

Rich shivered. "What happened?"

"I don't know," I admitted. "Maybe it's just some normal, small desert town." But the casually mutilated cars and the ill maintained roads made me think this wasn't the western USA I remembered. If this was the norm, something horrible must have happened in the history of my tomorrow.

"If it's a party, there's food," Rich said, and took a step towards the house. His foot hit against a loose rock and it tumbled down the street.

Hot red flared in the energies of the party. The men closest to us, the ones who might have heard the sound, tightened up. Their easygoing auras jumped into survival mode. Their shoulders tensed, their necks sharpened up, and their hands went to guns strapped to their sides.

I grabbed Rich by the collar and yanked him behind a building, pulling Stranger with me by his good arm, before the men could turn and see us.

"What was that all about?" Rich asked.

"I don't think that party is open to new faces," I said. "We're going to have to be careful."

"How would you know that?" Rich asked.

"I'm good at reading people." I leaned my head against the store wall.

"I vote we leave," Stranger said.

"Me too," Rich agreed. "This lodging is a bit rough for my taste. You can't steal from the rich if everyone's dry. Know what I mean?"

"Or you could try not stealing," Stranger said. "Just as a suggestion." Rich gave a snort of derision.

Ricky wanted me to ditch Rich here? Seriously? No. I must have gotten the place wrong. This couldn't be the same 23rd century Ricky meant. I'd taken us to the wrong place. We were leaving. Now. "Come on," I said. "Let's just go back to that door and get out of here —"

A gasp interrupted my thoughts. We all turned to see a little girl paused in the middle of the street, staring at us. She had dark skin, chocolate eyes, and deep brown hair in a messed up pixie cut. A pale green dress draped over her tiny frame, with dirt spots staining the ends of her skirt. The only jewelry she wore was a small ring on her right index finger. The silver band glistened in the heavy sun as her fingers shook at the sight of us. Her eyes and mouth were wide as she stared at us, too shocked to scream.

"Hey," I said, "don't worry. We're not going to hurt you." I took a step toward her but she stumbled back, and I stopped before she found her voice. I bent down to look her in the eye and smiled. "Don't worry," I repeated. "We're friends. My name is Penny. Penny Grace, and these are my friends, Rich and Stranger."

The girl glanced at the boys standing behind me. "Stranger?" she asked. "Your name is Stranger?"

Stranger shrugged and flashed her a smile. "What's your name?"

The girl pursed her small lips together as she thought. I could feel her energies at work, analyzing the pros and cons. This girl couldn't be older than eight, but she reeked of cynical suspicion. Were all kids like this, or just the ones I ran into? Yet through all the cynicism, bright colors seemed to glow. Not just one, but a dozen different parts of herself which she knew and accepted. A rainbow of strength and self-love. "Name's Rosetta," she finally said, and her aura proved she spoke the truth. "My dad owns this land, so if you mess with me, he'll come after you."

"We won't mess with you, I promise." I held up my hands in surrender. "It's good to meet you, Rosetta," I said. "You said your dad owns this town? Can you tell us where we are?"

Her eyes narrowed at me. "We're on my dad's land."

"Yes, but what state?"

"State?" She laughed. "This is 2203. There haven't been states in decades."

"What? Why?"

Now her mouth gaped in disbelief. "Civil War II." She spoke with a condescending slowness. "The government collapsed. Did your tutor never give you history lessons?"

"We're from...out of town," I explained.

Her body tensed. "Which town? Benny's?" She started breathing fast. "Are you one of Benny's spies?"

"Whoa, whoa, whoa!" I shook my head. "I take that back. We're not from any of the other towns. We're just normal people passing though. We're just...um—"

"Nomads," Stranger chimed in. "We're nomads."

"Right. Nomads." I gave her another *we're innocent* smile. She relaxed, but remained suspicious. I needed to be more careful. "Listen, we're a bit lost and confused."

"Dehydrated?" she asked, and I noticed her tensing up again. I glanced around at the dusty streets, empty pots along the corners, and cloudless sky.

"No. No, we don't need any water. Just a bit too much sun. Can you help us connect some dots?"

Her liquid chocolate eyes flinted from Stranger to Rich, whom she looked up and down with interest, and back to me. "I can try," she nodded.

"Thank you. Can you tell us what state this used to be?"

"My dad says it used to be Tennessee."

Wasn't Tennessee swampier and less desert-y? I'd never been to Tennessee before, but according to Google Maps and southern movies, this was *not* what Tennessee looked like. "What's going on?" I asked. "Why's everyone so jumpy?"

"You have had a lot of sun, haven't you? Do you want your answer quick, or the one I had to memorize for class?"

"Would you mind giving us the one you memorized first?"

Rosetta sighed. "The peace in America ended in 2017, when an entire city disappeared. The country blamed both terrorists and each other. All the while the space where the city should have been kept gobbling up anyone who tried to enter it. Civil War II lasted for... er...I can't remember, but lots of years, tearing apart the governmental system. Historians think the war lasted so long because there were no answers to where the missing people went or what caused their disappearance. Fear rose in the United States until it became a house divided, like Benjamin Franklin said."

"Abraham Lincoln," I corrected. "Go on."

"Right. Anyway, no one trusted each other anymore. So the government fell. Other countries tried to help bring peace for a while, but they became afraid of what we now call the Cheyenne Circles, and everyone stayed away like we had the plague before any of their people went missing too."

"The...the Cheyenne Circles?" I asked.

"Yeah. That's the city that went missing."

"Cheyenne, Wyoming?"

She shrugged. "I think so. I don't know the old states."

My stomach plummeted with the force of an anvil. I looked at Stranger, whose eyes were already on me. He'd made the connection too. Cheyenne. Home. And where Stranger had opened the crack through time. "Why did you say circles? Why the plural?" I asked the girl.

"Because more popped up. Different cities, different states. All over the country. They still pop up every once in a while." Her voice grew sober. "My dad tries to mark them so people don't accidentally walk through."

"How do they know when a...Cheyenne Circle pops up?"

"Because it doesn't just take the people." Rosetta leaned closer. "I

189

saw one. The whole circle looks like that little bit above hot cement. All the light is shaky like that, and then…it's like it ate all the life. Leaves seared off trees, rocks melted off, and the water…." Her eyes went red like she wanted to cry, but no tears blurred her vision. "The water just flows right in and never flows out. They say that's what stopped the wars. Everyone realized what was happening all along, right under their noses. The sea level dropped a whole foot before anyone realized what it meant. Then there was the Hundred Years Pact. Everyone who survived the wars worked together to maintain the water, build dams before rivers reached the Circles, and keep the peace. They made farms and rebuilt towns. The whole country turned to hope and faith in science to save the world. Only science couldn't explain anything. There's no way to scientifically locate differences between normal land and a Circle. But the people kept hope because at least they could make dams and spot a Circle if they came across one. Only, no one could stop the clouds from rolling through, so the sea level just kept dropping.

"The Hundred Year Pact ended in 2145 when the dams lowered. Towns with peace contracts started bickering over water rations, and people started fighting again. Experts call it the Great Thirst." Then Rosetta looked me straight in the eye. Her molten cocoa eyes radiated strength, and I saw why this girl had survived this long. "My dad owns the largest glacier left in the United States. We built a dam around it to catch the runoff. My dad protects these people, and if I think for one second that you're after our water, I'll show you how we've kept it safe for three generations."

I leaned back and held my hands up again in peace. "It's okay. We aren't after your water. You can trust us."

She straightened up. "I hope so. For you. My family doesn't forgive stuff like that." She crossed her little toothpick arms across her chest. "I don't either."

I didn't know whether to call her scary or adorable. Either way, color me impressed. "All right, kid," I said. "I believe you. No messing with your town. Got it. Thank you for your time. We'll let you get back."

The moment I stood up, guns clicked their safeties off from all sides of us. Armed men and women popped out of hidden corners and formed a strong circle around us. "Yeah," Rosetta said. She raised her hand and showed me her small silver ring. Right there, hidden between her fingers, was a small button. "I pushed the emergency button as soon as I saw you."

One of the men stepped into the circle, gun aimed at me, and stood beside little Rosetta. He wore the same clothes as the rest of the people surrounding us. The only thing that made him stand out from the others was a sickle hanging off his belt. The sharp curved blade reminding me of a handheld scythe, only the blade was the wrong color. Instead of metal, it was carved petrified wood. "Good job keeping them occupied, Zetta."

The eight-year-old grinned at her father without an ounce of remorse for turning us in. The girl with the strong attitude and pixie cut hair. Who might one day grow up to become a time traveling pirate. I gaped at Rich, who glared at the girl in distaste. Then I had to look back at that eight year old as she mirrored the man with the sickle's stance with perfection. "Thanks, Dad."

Chapter 28

Getting tricked by an eight year old and kidnapped by a post-apocalyptic town? Check. Impressing the future with your can-do attitude and calm demeanor? Let's just say I'm working on it.

"Everyone just calm down. All right? There's no need for guns or...." One of the soldiers shoved me as we walked towards the three-story house along the dirt road. "Or shoving, okay? We didn't do anything wrong."

"Penny, I don't think they care," Stranger mumbled under his breath. He walked so close I could feel his shoulder against me. "We'll be fine," he whispered. I took a deep breath and swallowed my desire to babble. It was strange. Babbling wasn't my usual thing...but, then again, I'd never had a gun on me before. At least Stranger was there with me.

On my left, Rich hovered a few inches away, but I could feel his anxiety shooting out, tickling against my aura. I reached out and grabbed his shoulder, just to let him know he wasn't alone. To my surprise, it worked. The anxiety didn't disappear, but it softened to a whisper. "We're kids," Rich argued. "We're innocent kids."

"He has a point," one of the soldiers mumbled.

Zetta's dad shook his head. "Benny has sent kid spies before. Nothing's beneath that man."

"Thirst makes devils of us all." Two soldiers echoed in agreement. Stranger and I shared a look. The way they spoke that line, it was almost like a chant, a mantra. Something they said to remind themselves not to trust anyone. Geez, the future was bleak.

"Listen, we don't know who this Benny is, and we're not from another town around here," I said. "We're nomads. And we're not here to take your water."

"Nomads." Zetta's dad laughed. "How would nomads survive around here?"

I stopped walking and turned to look him in the eye. "How about we make a deal? You don't ask where we came from, and we won't ask where your dam is."

He raised an eyebrow. "You might not intend to ask, but rather sneak around and find it for yourself."

"Then keep an eye on us. Watch us. Just put your weapons down."

He studied me for a moment. "Lower your weapons." I sighed in relief as the soldiers pocketed their guns. "Do you know what today is?" he asked me. I shook my head. "It's the eightieth anniversary of the day my grandfather won the battle over our dam. Eighty years my family and friends have had water. Now, the nearest town is owned by a man named Benny Novak. He's a greedy man, and one with a passion for poetic irony. He would love nothing better than to take our water during a day of celebration. So you'll have to understand if we don't swallow your claim of innocence."

"Understandable," I agreed. "You can't be too careful. In fact, there's no reason to mess with us at all. Let us go and we'll leave."

"Nah," he said. "I figured we'd just tie ya up and get back to the party."

"Wait, what?" I snapped but the rope was already out. Someone grabbed my wrists and pulled them behind my back. Stranger grimaced when another soldier yanked his hands together. "Hey!" I snapped. "Be careful! You'll rip his stitches out. Morons." The soldier flicked her eyes at his shoulder, where the bandage bulged through his shirt, before loosening the ties.

"No," Rich said when someone reached out to grab his hands. "Nope. I'm not being tied up. I'm just a boy. You don't have to tie me up!"

"Rich, it's okay," I said. "You won't be tied up forever. We just need them to trust us before we can leave."

"No." Rich jerked his hands out before a soldier could grab them. It would have been easy for one of them to tackle him down, but instead

193

the soldiers stayed along the edge of the small circle. They didn't want to scare him anymore than he wanted to be tied down. I could sense his fear. Memories flashing of every night he'd run from the queen's men back in the 1600s. Getting trapped meant death.

"Richie," I said, and I kept my voice firm. Everyone stopped, but I knew it was only for a moment. I had to make my argument now. "This isn't like where you're from. Okay? People aren't going to treat you the same way, and getting caught doesn't mean death. Right?" I snapped at the nearest soldier.

"We would never harm a child," he promised.

"See?" I said and smiled at the kid. "They don't mean us any harm. They just need to know that we're trustworthy. Okay? It's no big deal. I'll be beside you the whole time."

"What if we get hurt anyway?" Rich argued, and his voice shook. "No one means to hurt a kid. No one says it. They just look away when it happens."

"Not here." It was little Zetta who spoke this time. She stepped between the legs of two soldiers and looked Rich in the eye. "We're good here. My dad's nice." She turned and raised an eyebrow at her dad. "Promise you won't let him get hurt while he's tied up."

"I promise," Zetta's dad said through clenched teeth. "Can we get on with this now?"

The nearest soldier moved towards Rich, but he stepped back again. "Rich," I said. "Look at me. I'm right here. And since I've been here, I've never let anything bad happen to you. Do you think I'd take you someplace dangerous?" He hesitated, but shook his head. "Of course not. So it's okay. You can trust...." I choked at the phrase. Finally, I understood why Ricky hated that saying so much. Because he did trust me, and would until I slammed a door in his face. But I still meant every word. "I'll protect you. Trust me, okay?"

His jaw tensed, but he didn't move again and they tied his hands up. The entire time they worked, Rich's green eyes stared unblinking at me. There were burns along the side of his neck, little spots of red marking the moment I'd entered his life. Small marks which would quickly heal. And yet those green eyes were the exact same ones an older man had used to glare down at me, marred with a crescent shaped scar. Again the thought came to me. How could it be better to leave this kid behind?

Then a shove told me we were again on the move, and my mind

returned to more pressing dangers. "What exactly is the plan?" I whispered to Stranger. "How do we get out of here?"

"We wait," Stranger said. "We tend to not be the only ones who go through the doors in our adventures.

"You mean The Void?"

"I'm guessing it's going to show up again. Keep your eye open, Penny. You're the only one that can see it. We might need to save and run."

"Great," I grumbled.

The soldiers led us into a house. It reminded me of an old Southern plantation home, only without the maintenance. One of the columns leaned to the side, threatening to slip right out from under the roof. The large open front doors revealed a big living room, capable of holding twenty or thirty people. But instead of luscious staining or expensive crystal, the furniture had patches to keep the holes together, while saggy cushions struggled to hold any protection from the skeletal wood. Boxes of supplies and canned food lined the walls in an organization I couldn't understand, unless they just kind of threw everything to a pile. I could understand that.

"Sit down," Zetta's dad said. The three of us took the couch. I sat in the middle and the frame dug into my sit bone, but I didn't complain. Zetta's dad pointed at two soldiers, a woman with flaming red hair and a freckle-faced guy. "Watch them," he ordered, and left to help some people outside. The two soldiers took a seat near the window and started chatting. They acted casual, but I noticed they kept their faces angled toward us, keeping us in their line of sight. More people came in and out, all in thin clothing with rolled up sleeves, and carrying homemade wooden chairs onto the front lawn.

"Is everyone okay?" I asked.

"Great," Rich snarled, and worked against his ropes.

"Stranger?" I asked.

"I'm fine," he said. "Just wondering how we ended up here. I thought you controlled where the door opened."

"I...I just wanted to see the future," I lied. "I'm sorry, Stranger. I didn't realize it would be so end of the world-like. How's your shoulder?"

"It's fine." He smiled, but I sensed a strong lack of sincerity. "I figure it'll be a few more hours before the pain meds Zetta gave me wear off. Speaking of Zetta...." He glanced at the open door where the little girl had disappeared with her father.

"Yeah," I said. "Must be a common name." I gave him a significant look, glancing at Rich to imply we needed to keep that connection under our hats.

"Geez." Stranger shook his head. "Time traveling really messes with the chronological order of things."

"Yeah, that's great," Rich interrupted us. "You two need to start talking about how we're getting out of here."

"Relax," I said. "Did you hear those people? They said there are Cheyenne Circles everywhere. Which I'm assuming is just emptiness energy collecting in one spot. We'll find it, I'll open up a door, and we can leave."

"I think you're forgetting a little something," Rich sneered, and wiggled his tied up wrists.

"I'm working on it," I bluffed. I glanced at the soldiers. "Hey, you said you've maintained the water rights around here for eighty years, right? Then how have Benny's men survived so long?"

Freckle-face looked away from the window. "We think they found some stream a few miles away or so. It's enough to survive on, but it doesn't get a lot at one time. We let them have it. We're not evil or malicious. If there was enough water in our dam then we'd share, but we get just enough to make it through the dry seasons."

"I get that." I nodded, but then hesitated as a question popped up. "I'm sorry, I have to ask. It's the 23rd century, but I don't see a lot of tech around here. How does Zetta's ring work? Is there some secret room where you protect all your awesome machinery?"

"Like we'd tell you." The red-haired woman rolled her eyes and kept talking to the freckle-faced guy.

"Is it a GPS signal? Radio? Does everyone have one?"

"Radio. It's the only thing people know how to use around here," the freckle-faced guy said. The girl kicked him in the shins. "What? Stuff like that is common knowledge. It's not like Benny's men don't live off the same system."

"Where's the rest of your tech?" I asked. "I mean, this is the 23rd century, for crying out loud. Where's the flying cars and the holograms?"

They shared a scuff and both looked at me. "You're kidding, right?" the girl asked. "What did you two say you were? Nomads or something?"

"Yeah, nomads."

"So, I'm assuming you three have been living in a cave for over a hundred years. Tech came from companies. Companies need people and materials. People need water. After the wars and the unrest, not to mention the world's complete shunning of America, we lost just about every important factor towards technological advance. Now it's been so long since anyone's taken classes or learned a thing about machine work, even if we did have the parts, we wouldn't know what to do with them."

"What about the rest of the world? Do they have Cheyenne Circles there too, or is it just America?" I asked.

"We wouldn't know," she said matter-of-factly. "We haven't had communication with the other countries in scores." She paused for a moment. "Do Benny and his men have machinery?"

"We don't know anything about Benny's men," I said. "Sorry."

"Naturally," she snipped.

"Speaking of stuff we don't know…." I gave her an apologetic smile when she glared at me. "What's with all the petrified wood everywhere? I noticed boulders of it on the streets, and your leader seemed to have a sickle made of it."

Red hair made an exasperated face at Freckles before sending it my way. "Petrified wood keeps the circles away."

My chest gave a start. "How?"

She shrugged. "No one knows. Frankly, I think it's superstition, but the Petrified Forest in Arizona never got attacked, so people credited the forest itself."

Freckles rose an eyebrow. "And everyone who brought petrified wood into their villages stopped getting sucked into the circles. Don't forget that little detail."

"There's that too," she agreed with a shrug, but then glanced out the window. "We need to do another patrol soon. I don't like the entire town in one place."

"We have patrols around the water," the freckle-faced guy said. "They'll shoot up a flare if they need re-enforcements. There's no need for anyone to be in town."

They continued talking, but I couldn't listen anymore. Petrified wood. Like the bracelet that Rich had stolen back at the Globe Theater. The Void didn't save us until Rich dropped it. I remembered the glint off the jewel as it fell below the cracks. If that little gem kept The Void away from saving us, imagine what a boulder would do. I looked at Stranger, but he seemed occupied. His eyebrows were furrowed together as he talked.

"So," Rich whispered at me, "at which hour will you start our escape plan?"

"When the moment's right," I hissed back. "Stop talking about it."

"We may have bigger problems," Stranger said.

"Oh, don't say that," Rich sighed.

"Why?" I asked.

But Stranger looked at the soldiers chatting by the window. "Hey," he called out. "When you all came to surround us, were you already in town before the little girl set the alarm?"

"No. We were all here, helping with the food and supplies for the celebration."

"Everyone?"

"Apart from the water patrol outside town, yes."

Stranger's jaw tensed and he looked at me. "Then who did we see in town?"

"What are you...? Oh." My voice trailed off as I realized what he meant. The two men in tan. The ones with knives strapped to their belts, who snuck under the shadows.

Stranger spoke up, loud enough for the soldiers to hear. "I think Zetta's dad was right. Benny's men are going to attack tonight. And I think they might already be here."

The two soldiers' faces were stone cold. Not one emotion escaped their faces as they took in the information. But I could see their auras, how their happy yellows and peaceful green emotions became stifled by the red of alert. How many times had I seen that or similar transitions the past day or so? Yet it never stopped being terrifying. One soldier leaned her head out the window. "Aziz!" she called. "Aziz! You need to hear this!"

Zetta's dad came running into the house. "What is it? The snake meat is almost ready."

"They said they saw men in town. Before Zetta called us over."

"Where? Did you see where they headed?"

"I can try, but we don't know the area well," Stranger admitted. "We could show you."

"If he's even telling the truth," Freckle-face pointed out. "Come on, they're trying to distract us so they can escape. They whispered to each other about it seconds before they *conveniently* remembered seeing someone. It's a trick."

Aziz looked at Red. "What do you think?"

"Is it worth the risk not checking?" she asked.

"And thinning out our people right before a raid?" Freckles asked. "Come on. Benny's town has used kids as a decoy before. Let's not fall into that trap twice."

"I agree," Aziz said. Red scoffed, but he continued, "We have patrols around the water, and the rest of the town is at this house, which means our supplies are safe."

"Unless they intend to ambush the patrols," Red pointed out. "Let's not be blind fools about this. You said it yourself. It would be like them to attack tonight, of all nights."

"Yeah." Aziz waved at us. "And we caught them already. Benny's men want us to split up, to be easier targets. Which is exactly what we'd be if we listened to these kids. Come on, Maggie, do you think three kids could live as nomads in this desert? If they aren't Benny's, they'd be dead. So watch them, don't pay any mind to their tricks, and let's celebrate another eighty years." He gave all three of us a stink eye and walked back out. Through the window, I saw him helping others with the BBQ. He looked up every once in a while and checked the perimeter, but otherwise showed no signs of concern.

Stranger leaned his head in his tied up hands. "Great. What if they do attack tonight?"

"Yeah, and we're all tied up," Rich added.

"We only saw two guys," I pointed out. "If they do mean harm, I'm pretty sure this town could take them."

"Sure," Rich said, and leaned back into the couch. "Let's all be thick optimists about our impending doom. I love acting as a sitting duck while a town gets raided by the desperate and thirsty."

"We don't know that," I reasoned.

"Oh?" He stared at me with angry little eyes. "Have you ever gone days without food? Have you ever been so desperate that you robbed people's houses for nothing more than bread? Because I have. And that's nothing compared to thirst. If those guys you saw belong to Bobby or Benny or whatever his name is, and they haven't had a decent drink in a while, then yeah, methinks we're in danger. Reason's one of the first things to flee, Penny. And justification? It's their best weapon, because it helps them sleep at night. It means they can do whatever

199

they want and go as far as they need to survive. It means we're not safe just because we're kids."

"Calm down, Rich," Stranger said. "We're not going to let anything happen to you."

"They have tied you up too, so I'm not comforted!"

"Hey!" Red snapped. "If you don't quiet down, I'll make you." She patted the gun strapped to her hip.

Rich flopped deeper into the couch. "I'm just telling you that we're all going to die." He pouted. "You don't have to get angry about it."

Stranger and I shared a look. Rich was on edge, but he had a point. Thirst was a familiar craving. That full-body need for hydration, like after a game or a long hike, after the sun had been blaring down your back or when you were surrounded by a fire so hot it steamed the moisture right out of you. But I'd never been *thirsty* before, not like Rich described. I'd never gone more than a few uncomfortable hours without water, and I didn't want him to feel that way again. If I left him here, would he thirst? No. I couldn't leave Richie here. It would be wrong. I'd take him with us. I'd find the right place to leave him. Ricky had only known the one future when he asked me to abandon Rich here. I could make it better. A future without the thirst. Screw Ricky's orders.

Orders.

My whole body stiffened at the sound of The Void's voice lingering within my ears. It was softer than usual, like someone had turned the volume significantly down, or perhaps like The Void was far away. No one else made any movement of recognition. Stranger studied the soldiers who kept us in their line of sight. Rich kept working against his ropes, resulting in nothing but rope burns against his wrists. I glanced over my shoulder, but couldn't find The Void anywhere.

Why should you trust a pirate? it continued.

Why would I trust a hole in the world? I retorted.

"Hey." Stranger nudged me with his shoulder. "You okay? You got tense all of a sudden."

"Yeah, just um…." I leaned in and whispered in his ear. "The Void's here."

"Great." He sighed. "Can you figure out what it wants before it burns this place down too? I'm guessing they don't have the water for a fire hose."

Penny, The Void moaned, *we don't have much time. Don't waste it*

200

chatting with your boyfriend.

How much time until what? I thought to The Void. *Until you attack us again, you mean?*

Me? Attack you? Oh Penny, you really are delusional. Tell me, are you open-minded enough to hear the truth?

I was about to snap back that being open minded when talking to a trickster was about as sane as hugging a cactus when an idea stopped me. The Void wasn't in the room itself, and its voice was distant, weak. Presumably, the blessed petrified tree trunks in town kept it at bay, which meant the only thing The Void *could* do was speak. No fires. No messing with metal and putting lives in danger. If I wanted answers without putting my life at risk, now was the time. So I put up a face of hesitant trust. *Tell me your story. I'll decide for myself if it's true.*

Then relax. Close your eyes. Go into a meditative state and I'll show you my side of the story. Don't worry. I give you my word that no harm will come to those around you while you're out. They will be protected.

And I should trust you because?

Unlike you, I do not lie.

Its words startled me. It sounded bitter. The first time I'd ever heard any hint of emotion from the thing. My gut told me not to talk to The Void, that I didn't want to hear what it had to say, but I had to talk to it. I needed to make a deal to go back home. And it knew it too. Why else would it have stolen my dad's tablet if not to prove that it could go back to that time? "I'll be right back," I whispered to the boys, and closed my eyes.

"What, wait?" Rich asked. "You're not going anywh—"

"Shhh," Stranger said.

I emptied out my mind as best I could. I tried not to think about the thirsty people of the future or the dried up rivers. I tried not to think about abandoning little Rich in this horrible, apocalyptic time, and I certainly tried not to think about what might happen if I made a deal with The Void. I focused on each breath. Inhale. Exhale. Inhale. Exhale. Until I filled my mind not with concerns or broken promises, betrayals or lost loved ones, but rather nothing. Black became the only color in my mind. Thoughts turned into empty breaths. No emotions survived this darkness. I was completely alone.

Just me and The Void.

Chapter 29

What is this place? I asked as the blackness overwhelmed my mind. It was deeper than I'd ever seen before. So deep, I questioned whether light had ever existed. I relied on memory alone to know that anything else lived. My body had gone numb, like if I tried to blink or wake up, I might not.

Home, The Void said. I couldn't see the thing as its silhouette melted in with the rest of the nothingness around me. Yet, somehow, I knew exactly where it was. Standing just to my left as if we were taking a stroll through the depths of oblivion. It felt strange feeling him there, where Stranger should be. I just had my eyes closed, right? I hadn't actually gone anywhere. But then I shouldn't be feeling this…numb. No, not numb. Like I wasn't even in my body. I was somewhere else. Or nowhere else. *Do you believe in parallel universes? Other worlds and dimensions?* The Void asked.

Three days ago I didn't even believe in time traveling, so I guess I'm open to the possibility, I replied.

You should imagine each parallel universe as a bubble, all jumbled up together. This darkness, this emptiness as you called it, is the soap to the metaphor's bubble. The material which keeps them separate and prevents them from popping at any coincidental collision with another universe. When the emptiness keeps to its own devices, no universes mix, time passes in chronological order, and life plays out as destined.

Within this anti-space, The Void continued, *there are beings much like the humans which keep the worlds in order. Beings with reason and purpose. Although perhaps without the emotions which seem to weigh the humans down. My job is to maintain order, prevent chaos, and make sure destiny is the only option. But then your Stranger decided not to let destiny take over. He wanted to change time, go back, and rewrite what was right for the world. You might understand that most of us are willing and, to use a human word, happy with our lives. We were almost all willing to let that poor boy yank his hair out until he gave in and accepted destiny's blow. Such is the reality for all beings, I'm afraid. Yet a rebel from our world saw an opportunity in this human's desperation. It snuck past my guards like some kind of criminal on the run and reached the boy's mind. It made a deal with the boy, tricked him, and escaped during the explosion. While it runs amuck through time and space, we cannot close the bubble. This reality is falling apart. People, water, and moments all spill into our little bit of between-space, and we cannot plug the holes. Like a bathtub drain, your world is leaking every last drop into our nothing, never to be seen again. We want to save this world, for its destruction would implode ours in return.*

Hold up, I thought. *I thought you were the thing that crawled out of the explosion. Aren't you the one who tricked Stranger?*

Believe me. I wish to reclaim order.

Well, that seemed not evil. *What's the catch? Why mess with me? Save it already! People are dying!*

The rebel must return home.

You trapped us in that fire. You released those dangerous criminals! Now, you're trying to convince me that you're some kind of hero?

I needed to know how human you had become.

My mind went blank. *Say what?*

You believe yourself to be human, that you care for others. It was a clever lie and well preserved. I admire your eye for detail, your cleverness, but it is time to stop.

I am human, I said. *And I have a sister who....* Who went missing when the first Cheyenne Circle occurred, when the emptiness overtook the town. Dinah. Falling into the nothing. Did she sear like the metal on Ricky's ship? Did she have time to scream? *I need to go back in time and save my sister.*

You can't trick a trickster! The Void snapped. *I know what you are! What you've done! You're nothing but a disgrace to your race, and I'm sick at the thought that we have the same genetics seeping through our veins.*

That we.... My heart screamed in my chest. I wanted to run away, to hide, just like when Stranger asked me to look into his past. Like I was getting close to something I wanted no part in, something dark. Something I needed to hide. *I am nothing like you,* I said.

You're worse. Why do you think you feel so guilty about everything, Penelope Grace? One little girl against the world, and yet you know, deep down, it's all your fault. The prison break. The fire at the Globe. Even the Great Thirst.

I tried to help. I didn't —

You did. The Void was circling me now. I felt it everywhere. Trapping me. I wanted to reach out and grab Stranger, but my arms were numb. I couldn't feel anything. *Why do you think your family can never remember you? That a loving mother could forget her child so often? I'm not the monster that whispered in that poor boy's ear to create this mess…it was you! You're the thing that doesn't belong here, that destroyed the world just by living. Because you never existed before that day in Stranger's basement! You were only a shadow, empty like me, but you wanted so much more. So you manipulated a grieving boy. You tricked an innocent girl to come to the rescue, and stole her face for your new life. You created a brain filled to the brim with mediocre memories, a meaningless life, and a family who wouldn't care if you decided to run off.* The Void paused. Although I couldn't feel my own body, my soul shook in terror. *You feel guilty, Penelope Grace, because you know it all came about because of a choice you made.*

You're crazy, I whispered.

And you're willing to let a billion people die so you can live.

You're wrong, I said. *I held that door open in the fire. It would have killed me, but that was a choice I made to save others. That's the kind of person I am.*

You are willing to die, yes. But death is a part of life. By dying, you choose life still. Tell me, are you willing to sacrifice your humanity?

BANG!

BANG!

BANG!

I gasped and opened my eyes as a rush of sensory details attacked me. The hot, dusty air against my skin. The smell of fireworks. Stranger's jeans rustling against my leg as the breeze filtered through the window. The way Rich jumped an inch off the cushion and then hid his face between me and the couch. How his body shook. How Stranger stiffened up and leaned to get a better view.

BANG!

BANG!

Red and Freckles pulled out their guns. "Where was it coming from?" Red asked.

"I don't know. West?"

She cursed. "The dam."

"Grab your weapons!" Aziz yelled from the front yard. "Prepare for attack!"

The smell of gunpowder wafted in through the open window. Fireworks. Ricky had called the smell fireworks. He must have known all along the smell came from fired guns. Benny's men were here. Ricky had warned me about a scared girl, not an armed attack!

"What do we do?" Stranger asked. "How do we save them?"

"I...." I blinked at Stranger as my mind struggled to settle back into the physical world. There was nothing we could do. I couldn't do anything against a gun or desperation. I wasn't some superhero with all the answers. I was a girl with fear shaking me to my toes. I was just as powerless as him.

Unless.... "Hey!" I snapped at Freckles. "If you want your town to survive, untie us right now!"

"And why should we—" More gunshots rang out, closer this time. Everyone ducked down against the sounds. Red cursed and pulled out a second gun for her other hand.

I can only send a little shadow to you, The Void said. *Just enough to untie your ropes. After that, you're on your own.*

After his accusations, his offer of help made me stiffen. *Why would you help me?*

Because if you die, both of our worlds end.

I smelled the burning rope before I felt the release of pressure. As soon as it fell from my skin, I stood up and let them hang free to my side. Stranger and Rich both stood up, staring at their freed hands in confusion. But it was nothing compared to the two soldiers' faces. Their shock only lasted a second though, and then they aimed their guns at us.

"I am going to save you," I said. "And it would go a lot quicker if you trusted us."

Red and Freckles looked at each other. I held my breath as I waited with my bluff, knowing full well The Void wasn't here to stop any spray of bullets. The weak tendrils of void smoke had already faded away. But then both soldiers lowered their guns. "If you're working with Benny, your backup's already arrived. We need to help the fighting," Freckles said. "There's a back exit in the kitchen behind you." Leaning down in case more bullets flew, they snuck out the front door and toward the gunshots. I grabbed the kid's hand to keep him close and ran towards the exit, Stranger right behind.

I eased the back door open and peeked my head through. I couldn't see anyone nearby, but I could hear the shouts, the fighting. My eyes were wide in search of threats, danger, any way to explain the chaotic sounds all around us. The Void had accused me of all this, claiming that the only reason the Cheyenne Circles existed was because I was in the world. But sorting through that thing's lies to get at the truth would have to wait until these people were safe. I refused to let it distract me enough that innocent people got hurt.

"Wait, stop." Rich pulled me back. Everyone paused.

"We've got to keep moving," I warned.

"Shhh," he whispered. "Don't you hear that?"

I listened, but all I heard were gunshots. I was about to shake my head when a sob interrupted the air from around the corner of the house. All three of us tilted our head around the wall. A man in tan stood crouched against a side wall of the house, gun raised and alert. He must have heard the sob too, because his eyes were wide. He turned his head one way, then the other, trying to find the source.

Just a couple of feet from him, shaking behind the skeletal remains of some bushes, hid a pale green dress. I smacked my hand to my mouth before my gasp could escape my throat. Zetta!

Stranger grabbed my arm and leaned in. "Cover the girl," he whispered, and crouched deep down, using the barrels of supplies as cover as he snuck closer to the armed attacker. I wanted to stop him before he got himself hurt, but I knew he wouldn't and I couldn't. So I steeled my fear and prepared to jump over the girl.

I looked at Rich. "Stay hidden," I mouthed. He nodded and knelt next to the house, eyes closed and hands over his ears. Stranger caught my eye and I nodded to say I was ready.

"Hey!" he shouted. The man in tan jumped, but Stranger was already on him, yanking the gun away from us. I leapt from my hiding spot and covered the girl with my body. Dry dirt stuck to Zetta's skin. Tear tracks streamed down her face like paintbrush strokes as she looked at me in horror.

"It's okay," I said over the sounds of Stranger and the man struggling. "We're here to help."

The gun went off behind me and I couldn't stifle a scream as I pulled the kid against my chest. I looked over my shoulder. The two still struggled. Stranger had the gun aimed to the sky. I exhaled in relief and turned back to the girl.

"Remember the boy that was with us? He's on the other side of that corner. Go hide with him. We'll be right there." She scurried out of sight. Stranger head butted the man and he dropped the gun. I hurried to my feet and grabbed it before anyone else. "All right, enough!" I snapped. The man paused and Stranger let go. "Now, I get it," I said. "You're thirsty. You need water. It's making you crazy. But there are children where you've chosen your battlefield."

"There's kids at home too," he snapped. "Thirsty kids."

"Yeah well…. I have the gun, so no more fighting."

"We're not going to stop," he said.

"I know," I said. This future needed to stop. It needed to be prevented. It was the only way. "Stranger, get some —"

"Way ahead of ya," he said, and pulled some ropes out of one of the supply boxes.

"Sit down," I ordered the man. He scoffed, but obliged. Stranger knelt down and tied his wrists and feet together before gagging him. Blood leaked through the back of Stranger's shirt as he tightened the rope.

I lowered the gun and went to him. "You're bleeding."

He straightened up, his face inches from mine as he got to his feet. "Just tore my stitches," he said. His fingers brushed against my elbow. "It's fine."

I nodded and tried not to think about how much worse that moment could have gone. What if The Void was right and this really was all my fault?

We returned to where we'd left Rich. Zetta had knelt down right next to him, and both looked up at us when we came back.

"Hey." I knelt down next to Zetta. "You okay?"

"Did you bring the men here?" she asked.

"No. No, sweetie, of course not. But I can help. Is there any place you can hide?"

"We have a safe base for all the kids, but people are fighting in the way. I can't get to it."

"We can't leave her here," Stranger said. "More men could come any second."

"What about in the house? Can you hide in there?"

"There's a basement, right there." She pointed behind us to a flat basement door under the sand. "But it's locked."

Stranger stepped to the basement doors and dusted the sides off. "I could undo the hinges, but I'd need some tools."

My heart stopped. "You wouldn't happen to need a small screwdriver, would you?"

"Actually, that's exactly what I need."

My shoulders slouched over in disappointment. Just like Ricky said. Which meant this really was where I ditched him. I reached into my pocket and pulled out the screwdriver, keeping my eyes down as I handed it to him. I didn't want to see his face. Or Rich's. I didn't want to think about what this meant.

Stranger started unscrewing the hinges. Zetta fiddled with her ring, twisting it back and forth, careful not to push the emergency button. "How does that thing work?" I asked.

She glanced down at the ring. "It's a walkie talkie. You push the button and tell the others where you are."

"Do you have any extras?"

"You want one?"

"Yeah. I might need to communicate with the soldiers fighting soon. So I can help them."

"There's some more in the basement."

My eyes went to the screwdriver as Stranger twirled it into a blur. If I was going to leave Rich here, I had to do everything to perfection.

"There's the last one," Stranger said. With a fist full of screws, he tilted the door open from the wrong side. "M'lady," he said with a wink to Zetta.

She scurried under the crack. I heard some rumbling through boxes and then a small hand reached out, another ring held between her pinched fingers. "Here. Please give it back. We can't get more."

"Thank you," I said, and shoved the ring into my pant pocket. Then I turned to Rich. He looked confused, scared, and ready to bolt. "Why don't you stay with her?" I suggested. "Where it's safer."

"I think I'd be safer with you," he said. "No offense, Zetta, but your family is not among my admirers. I'm not getting tied up again."

"We're not running away," I argued. "There might be more danger where we go."

His hands beat against his side in jittery fear, but he looked at me with a forced grin. "Promise?"

"Ugh," I said, and rolled my eyes. "You're asking for it, aren't you?"

"Hey, I'm not sitting in some dark corner while all the adventure happens," he argued.

Stranger laughed as he tightened the basement doors behind Zetta so no more ill-meaning attackers could find her. He dusted his hands off and patted Rich on the back. "Yeah. He'll fit right in with us." I wished he hadn't said that.

"Let me just find out where we need to go and then I'll lead the way," I said.

I turned around and closed my eyes, searching for any excess emptiness from traveling here. I could sense the fear in the citizens as they tried to protect their water. The mind-numbing thirst which urged the invaders onward. The whole town was red in desperation. People willing to die cornered by people willing to kill. But the beacons of petrified wood kept the void energy far away. In all the red here, where was the black?

Chapter 30

Using the darkness was the only way I could help these people. Take away my ability to manipulate the nothings leaking into this world and I became just about the most useless person here. But it had to be here! It was everywhere! Zetta said there were circles of the stuff throughout the country, eating up their resources. Surely there were some just outside town, hopefully within a quick jog's distance. But that wasn't the only problem. I needed to know directions, but the guns were still firing, people screaming, and Stranger bleeding. I couldn't calm down enough to meditate. I needed action. Somewhere to run, something to do. Some way to save the day.

I tried blocking the fear and desperation out, shooing it away with my mind so I could get a better view. Like ripples in water, the red waved back and forth, separating just enough to give hints at what lay behind. The flickering survival of plants starving for hydration. Dots of solitude where no human stood to fight their battles. And a smoky trail, slithering through the people like a water snake on the prowl. "That way," I said.

"That's away from the town." Stranger looked at me with furrowed eyebrows. "What exactly is your plan?"

"We need some of the void energy. Just trust me, okay?" I said, and started running. Away from the shooting, the yelling, calls for help, or orders to keep each other calm. Away from the thirsty Tennessean town and into the dried up remains of what used to be a swamp. Tall, thick tree trunks scattered across the desert, teetering against the heavy wind. The dried up moss crunched under our feet, crumbling into dust and blowing away with each step we took.

Until the swamp's skeleton came to an abrupt end. Singed branches marked the danger zone less than three steps in front of me. "Stop!" I screamed. Stranger and Rich screeched to a stop. Only Rich stumbled over a dried root and fell into an uncontrolled tumble right into the circle. I reached out and grabbed his shirt collar. Rich stopped, eyes wide, with heavy breaths, and his nose almost parallel with the singed ends of nature. I pulled him back and helped him to his feet. Stranger grabbed a handful of dried moss and tossed it in. The mess burst into flame, but not even ash hit the ground. It just...disappeared. The three of us stared at the space in silent horror. And they didn't even see what I saw. Because the space wasn't blank. There was more than just dust and air. The whole circle was filled to the brim with storming emptiness, fighting against unseen restraints.

What would happen if I poked a hole right in the middle of that bubble? Could I control it? Take out what I needed and shove it back in after I was done? Could I close the crack I'd made before all the nothing spilled out and destroyed these thirsty towns? Did I have a choice?

"Hello?" Rich asked. "Are you seeing something we're not?"

"Always," I answered. I turned to Stranger and handed him the ring. "At my command, push the button and tell everyone to drop their guns."

"Their...what?" Stranger snapped.

"Their guns. And to hit the ground fast."

"Why in all the times on Earth would they do that?" Rich asked.

I reached out and called the darkness to me. A stream filtered through the circle, singeing the upper twigs above our heads as I pushed the darkness out. "Because all the guns are about to get very, very hot," I said. Rich's eyes went wide as he stared at me.

Stranger mouthed "oooh" and he put the ring to his lips. "Listen up, town of Aziz. When I say three, I need you all to drop your guns and hit the ground like an angel's coming to take down your enemies."

"Why on Earth!" Static blurred the voice, but it came from Aziz himself. "Is that one of the kids we caught? Maggie!"

"You needed backup!" Red snapped back through the comms. "I'm not apologizing for that!" A wave of gunfire shot through the ring's speakers and Red cursed.

"There's not much time," Stranger urged. He glanced up at me. Pulling the emptiness out weighed on my body. My muscles strained to keep the destructive force in place as I gathered it out of the circle. I ordered the smoking energy out and toward the town, towering arches of darkness snaking their way to the battlefield. I took deep, careful breaths as I tried to control the force, but my blood started pumping fast from the effort.

The petrified wood. My stomach flopped as the strong, earthy aura of the tree trunks fought against the void energy. I'd forgotten about that. And the more I struggled to slip the smoke through the petrified wood's hold, the more I understood why it didn't work. The two were exact opposites. The void energy, a vague whisper of something which existed outside of life and death. And petrified wood, the perfect embodiment of both as something which once lived and breathed and then became stronger as it embraced death.

The boulders scattered in town were strong, but I knew it was possible to sneak past. If The Void could get some tendrils through the petrified wood's hold enough to break our ropes, I could do this. Because I wasn't like The Void. I was human. I was born on this earth. A child with parents and a sister and blood pumping through my veins. The petrified wood didn't have to fight against my will. All I had to do was sneak the void energy through too, and yet never before had moving the void energy been so difficult. Back at the prison ship, the problem had been too much compliance. Now, there seemed to be resistance from every angle.

Finally, I'd covered the town in smoking clouds no one but me could see. A whimper escaped my shaking lips as I fought against the petrified wood's continued defense. "You have to trust us," Stranger continued into the ring/walkie talkie. He kept his pale blue eyes on me in concern as he spoke. "If you want to keep your weapons in working order, drop them, and your angel won't break them. All guns touching skin will be destroyed as soon as I say three."

"Yeah, and we're just going to disarm ourselves on the word of some random kid," Aziz said. "Town, don't listen to him."

"Dad." Zetta's voice silenced everyone. "They saved my life. They want to help."

"Sweetie, you don't understand," Aziz said in his soft, dad voice.

"Daddy, you know my instincts are never wrong! I see what you don't, and I know these kids are good! Especially the girl. I saw a power

212

in her, Dad. She could pull this off."

I remembered with a sigh of relief what Ricky had told me about his wife. She was a natural. Like me, she saw the soul. Now for the test. Did her family trust her, or were they like mine, cynical and tired of so-called meaningless rants? The energy continued to struggle against my strength. A bead of sweat dripped down the side of my face, cool against the hot wind. I grimaced and clenched my teeth together.

"We don't have time for this," Stranger snapped. "If you want to live, hide, and be ready to disarm. One."

I closed my eyes and felt the energy of the town for metal. For the smell of fireworks and the smooth curve of bullets. "Two." The shaking finger against a trigger. The bead of sweat telling the soul not to shoot, how much it needed to shoot. I nodded at Stranger.

"Three!"

"Dad, please!"

Streams of black sprang toward the town, single droplet sized trails sneaking through the air at my command. They wrapped around every gun in touch with skin, like black ribbons wrapping into the inner workings of the machines. I clenched my raised fingers into fists and the black ribbons squeezed. It seared through the metal, separating the pieces until the guns popped into harmless parts. The dismay, the horror…the relief taking over half the red desperation of the town.

I opened my eyes and shared nervous faces with Rich and Stranger. "What happened?" Rich asked. "Did they let go?"

"I don't know," I admitted. "I took out the guns."

Stranger looked to the town. "If they didn't let go, they wouldn't have the edge. The whole thing would have been pointless." We waited in silence. Had I just made it worse? What was going on? I wanted to run back into the town just to get a glimpse of what I'd done, but the weight of the loose blackness was too much. I couldn't move. I could only wait.

Static leaked out of the ring. "West end secure."

"Center of town is secure."

"Dam's secure."

"Anyone hurt?"

"Some flesh wounds, but I think we'll all survive. We're taking the prisoners in."

The three of us sighed in relief. Zetta had said she saw a power in me. Heck yeah, there was! I felt unstoppable as I pulled the emptiness back up into the sky, away from the town, and back to the circle. The crack I'd created strained to free more emptiness. I reached out and smeared the fluid edges together until they melted back into one strong restraint.

The second the connection was lost, my vision blanked out. Emotions blared into view, like someone had turned the volume on high and silenced the constant that was reality. Stranger's sunshine aura shone uninhibited as he started laughing. The Cheyenne Circle to my side whirled and churned like a trapped thunderstorm, fighting against the edges. In that mess, I swore I saw a solid form the same color as all the emptiness around it, and yet deeper. It watched me, and I thought maybe it grinned.

It was the same thing that had happened on the prison ship, after I used the void energy to scare everyone away. And after that talk with The Void, I had a sneaking feeling this wasn't just a side effect. But what exactly did it mean? That I was human and something messed with my head? Or that maybe I was something else and wasn't supposed to see the world through human eyes in the first place?

"Good work, Penny."

Stranger's voice knocked me out of my own confusion. I flashed a smile in the general direction of his aura and blinked rapidly to get my vision to return. Stranger had one arm draped around Richie's shoulders, and both beamed in celebration. We did it. We saved the town. The battle was done. This moment was not a tragedy. The smoking emptiness had slurped back into the circle with ease.

"Is it gone?" Stranger asked.

"It's gone," I grinned, and leaned over in near exhaustion. Stranger caught me. His strong arms wrapped around me and I closed my eyes, treasuring the moment as I wrapped my arms around him. We'd won. Finally. I'd saved the day. I started giggling in disbelief, and Stranger laughed with me.

"Wow," Rich said. "So that's how you save the day. You wiggle your fingers around and things magically fall into place?"

"Was that how it looked?" I asked.

Stranger laughed as he let go. "Pretty much."

"There was a lot more to it, I promise," I said to Rich.

"So what do we do next? Please tell me it includes accepting the town's grateful and plentiful rewards."

"Rewards?" Stranger chuckled.

Rich rolled his eyes. "I'm going to have to set some ground rules if I'm going to travel with you."

"Zetta, where are you?" Aziz's voice came from the ring.

"In the basement."

I tuned out the rest of the banter, the orders, and exclamations of relief. Zetta was safe. Ricky's Zetta. The girl of his dreams. That strong time-traveling mother. Who knew how to stitch up wounds and turn a prison ship into a home. The Noble Pirate. It was time to make that future come true.

I grabbed the ring from Stranger's loose fingers. "I promised to give this back to Zetta. They can't replenish this stuff." I handed it to Rich. "Why don't you give it back to them as a sign of good will? Get a head start on that reward for us. We'll meet you in town."

Rich took the ring from me. For a moment he looked confused. Then he shrugged and started running off. To his future. And, if I could change time like Ricky the Pirate claimed, then I would change this. I would make sure that the boy running off in the distance would never go thirsty. Somehow.

The problem was I didn't know what to do next. The plan before had been vague, but at least I knew my place in it. I'd go down swinging. Clear and to the point, if not majorly depressing. But this new possibility was even worse. The Void claimed I was like it, a monster who'd manipulated Stranger and tricked him into trapping Dinah so I could, quote-unquote, steal her face. Gosh, that was ridiculous. Were there no twins where The Void was from? And all those other lame excuses to make me doubt myself. How my parents never remembered me, how I never fit in, how....

How I could control the darkness like no one else. How only I could change destiny, as if I was some creature somehow connected to it. How my life never quite fit into place, as if I knew all along it was a false memory of a life I never had. Or how, when I reached into Stranger's mind, I heard the memories of The Void as though they were my own, when Stranger himself could never have had those memories. The fear deep in my soul at the thought of uncovering something in those memories that might destroy everything. Uncovering a fresh start.

No. That was ridiculous. The Void was a trickster, plain and simple. I never should have talked to it. It got in my head, messed with me. All it spoke were lies.

215

But then why couldn't I find any evidence against it? It was true, my parents couldn't remember me. I didn't fit in at school. If I didn't exist, my story wouldn't change much.

Except I couldn't always see the void energy. If I had, I would have been able to tell something was strong with Stranger's house earlier on, before it was too late. Then I remembered. That searing pain in the school parking lot, as if something had attacked my eyes. That's when I first saw The Void. And then I could manipulate the void energies themselves, not before, only doing so made me lose my connection with the physical world, if only for a moment. But what if the longer I played The Void's games, the worse the symptoms got? It literally messed with my mind. What if it was trying to turn me into the villain?

I couldn't reach my birth certificate, being in another century, and I couldn't reach the one person in the world who could prove it. Dinah. The Void could take away all of Stranger's memories, so it could definitely take away all the memories that proved my existence too. The accusation was too convenient, and from too untrustworthy of a being. Which, to me, just proved the lie to its story. The Void was the one who manipulated Stranger and tricked me, not Dinah, into the house.

The plan came into place like a zipper intertwining. The Void wasn't the only one. It had confessed that much to me itself. There were others, and they needed to close the gap. Which meant The Void was the criminal who'd opened the gap and hid here in our world. If it wanted the others to leave it alone, it needed a scapegoat. It was trying to blame me for its own crime so it could enjoy its precious fresh start. Already it was playing with me, forcing me into situations where I had to use The Void's energy in order to survive. The more I played along, the more I looked guilty. If I confronted The Void now, I could stop all this before it finished its work. Because I was still all me. Who knew how many more *adventures* it would take before the others would believe I was the guilty party? And multiple Voids? I shuttered at the thought. No. Best end this now.

I turned to the Cheyenne Circle. We couldn't just go anywhere. We needed to be somewhere with an advantage over the void energy. Somewhere with a lot of petrified wood. Where was that Petrified Forest Zetta had mentioned? Arizona. *All right, let's do this thing.* I closed my eyes and envisioned a door opening up to the Petrified Forest, with all the strong, earthly stones. It was easier this time. I was confident.

216

Finally, I understood. I opened the door.

"Whoa, whoa, whoa." Stranger grabbed my arm. "Aren't you forgetting someone?"

Richie. Stranger didn't know the plan. He couldn't until it was over. "Stranger." I grabbed him by his shoulders and stared him straight in the eye. "I can't explain right now, but you have to trust me. It's what's best."

"What's best?" He shrugged my hands off and looked at me like I was the stranger. "What are you saying?" I gave him a significant look and his face hardened. "In what universe is this apocalyptic town what's best? For anyone? Let alone a ten-year-old kid?"

"Stranger, please just come with me and I'll explain everything."

"I've put a lot of faith in you," he said. "I've trusted you."

"I know, and I'm so grateful. I just need you to do it again."

He stepped back. "No. Not this time. Not without an explanation."

I leaned my head back and grunted in frustration. But when I looked back at Stranger, I saw him in the distance. Rich. He had turned around, and he was standing there, staring at us, at the door. He mouthed no, and I knew he'd put two and two together. Here it was, what I'd been dreading. Leaving a poor kid alone in the desert. But not without Stranger. "Come on," I begged. "Please. Let's just go. Let's just get out of here."

"Not without Rich."

Rich was getting closer every second. He called out to us against the background of a chapped desert, and Stranger turned around. When he turned back to me, his face was stone cold and stubborn. We'd lost the luxury of time to argue.

"Let's go," I said, and opened the door.

"No—"

"I said let's go!" I snapped, and pushed him through the door. I didn't mean to grab him by his bleeding shoulder or to put pressure on his wound. By the time I realized what I'd done, he'd already stumbled through the frame.

I stepped through and turned back. Rich was steps away, his small hands outreached. "Wait for me!" Rich yelled.

"I'm sorry," I sobbed, and slammed the door in his face.

Chapter 31

As soon as I slammed the door closed, I knew something was wrong. The air was too cold for Arizona, and the trees breathed life. The strength of petrified wood was nowhere to be seen. And Stranger was not happy. "What did you do?!" he yelled as he shoved me aside and yanked the door open. But it was too late. Rich was gone. I'd done my part in the kid's happy ending. And Stranger had done his. Now, if Rich ever saw him again, he could trust Stranger. The time traveler who didn't betray him. I had done everything right. So why did I feel so messed up?

Stranger looked in horror at the other side of the door. Trees blocked his view. Fresh and hydrated trees with sap seeping down their bark. "What did you do?" Stranger asked again. Only this time it was a whisper. It felt worse than the yelling.

"I kept a promise," I said.

"To whom? The Void?!" He spun around and gaped at me. "Are you that desperate to go home that you'd ditch some kid to make a deal?!"

"It wasn't a deal, okay! I promised Ricky!" Stranger blinked, and some of the anger faded to confusion. "Ricky made me promise to ditch him there! That's where he gets to know Zetta! He fell in love with her! For crying out loud, they ran away together and made that perfect life on some stolen ship! He didn't want that ruined, so he made me promise to ditch him, to make sure it happened. And guess what?! It worked! I did everything just like he asked, and now Ricky and Zetta and Shreya and that whole big pirate-y family get to live in peace, floating around on the water like they've never been thirsty in their lives!"

Stranger cursed and combed both hands through his hair. "Come on, Penny, would it kill you to warn a guy?" He cursed again and leaned over, hands still in his hair. "You nearly gave me a freaking heart attack."

"It had to happen that way. Ricky said he needed to trust you. It was the only way he'd get back into time traveling, which means it had to look like you were just as betrayed as he was."

"Well, points for that one," he snapped, and stood back up to look at the sky. "Geez, Penny."

I left him alone to go through his shock and looked around. We were in a forest. Pine trees lined us like scattered, half-finished walls. The floor was wet with rain and pine cones. Wherever we were, it was the past. Back before the Great Thirst. What I'd done hit me like a hot brick. How many times would Rich thirst for water, go crazy with dehydration, before he got his prison ship? How many sleepless nights and hate-filled days had I just cursed over him?

I hadn't realized I was shaking until arms wrapped around me. I leaned into Stranger's chest. His fingers tangled in my hair as he held my shaking neck, rubbed my back, and said, "It's okay. I'm sorry I yelled at you. I'm sorry I didn't trust you. Next time I will. I promise. Whatever you say, I'll believe it. I swear. It's okay," he whispered into my hair and held me closer.

I couldn't decide if I needed to cry or scream. Both. I wanted to do both. I wanted to scream the pain away and cry until the memory dried up, but only a few silent tears escaped. I lifted my head from Stranger's chest and wiped away the tracks. His hands dropped to my arms. He rubbed the warmth back into them as he gave me a smile.

"Your stitches—" My voice caught in my throat, but I swallowed the shock down, "They're still opened, and I...I didn't mean to shove you there."

"It's fine." He shook his head. "I think it was only one stitch. It's already stopped bleeding."

We were quiet for a moment. I didn't know what Stranger was thinking. I didn't want to look. All I knew was that I couldn't waste time pitying myself or the people I'd hurt. We hadn't landed where I'd wanted, which meant The Void had messed with the connection I had with the Petrified Forest. Could it know my suspicions?

"Stranger, we need to get back home."

"The Circle." Stranger nodded. "Yeah, I put that together too. I broke the world." He gave one cold, half laugh. "Who would have guessed it could be that easy?"

"We can fix it." I looked him in the eye. "I can fix it. Whatever The Void did to me, it made me see the energies, to be able to control them. I think it's trying to turn me into a Void too. But that was a bad choice, because if it hadn't, we would have been helpless. But now? I can take it, Stranger. I know I can. All I have to do is get home and close the gap with The Void still inside. Then it's done."

Stranger frowned. "We can't close the gap," he said.

"Why not?"

"I...." He paused, and his frown turned to frustration. "I don't know. I just get this feeling like we're not done yet. Like there's something big we're forgetting."

"And we're not going to remember anything or know truth from fiction until we get that void out of our heads."

"That's what makes me so mad." Stranger rubbed the back of his neck. "I feel like I should know. It all happened in my basement, right? My experiment gone wrong. But that thing, whatever it is, stole what I needed to remember. And it didn't just steal my memories of the experiment. It stole every single one."

"I get it, and I'm sorry—"

"No." He grabbed my arms again. "I'm not trying to start a pity party here. I'm saying it wants us to have no other choice. That thing has been calling the shots since the second we woke up on the deck of the Lusitania. Everything that has happened since then has played out exactly like it wanted. Even the crack in my basement, Penny. Probably you and Dinah getting there too. What if fighting it is just the next step in its grand plan?"

"It won't kill us. It needs us alive for the plan to work."

You're wrong, you know.

My muscles tensed at the voice.

"What's wrong?" Stranger asked.

"It's here," I whispered. "Listen, Stranger, I know what you mean. I've got this, but I need you to trust me. No questions asked."

His eyebrows furrowed together. His thumb massaged a circle

along my bicep. "I don't have a choice," he said, and his voice was soft, sad.

"What?"

"I can't see it, Penny. I can't hear it or communicate with it. I have no option but to trust you."

"It's okay." I smiled. "Just…." Without moving against his grip, I bent my forearms up and held his elbows. "Stay by my side, will you? I think I can save the world, but I can't do it alone."

Stranger's lips twitched into a small smile. "You save the world. I'll save you. How does that sound?"

"That sounds good." I wanted to lean in and kiss him, to let his touch drown out the uncertain. So I smiled back and stepped away. Because this wasn't the time to ignore the unknown. This was the moment to dive in and hope for the best. True, I didn't have the petrified wood with me, and even worse, The Void had isolated us in this forest. There were no people. No one to save or justify us being here. No, The Void knew I meant to fight. One way or another, this was the moment. I could only hope I was strong enough. Stranger's fingers trailed down my arm and held my hand as I closed my eyes to read the energy around us.

"All right, Void, I'm done messing around with you," I said, calling The Void out so Stranger could get at least one part of the conversation. "You said I wasn't human. You're trying to blame me for your mistakes."

The Void chuckled as it slipped between two trees, careful not to touch the delicate bark. *You told me you were open-minded, and yet your delusions are still too strong. Tell me, Penelope Grace, do you really think you can take me?*

"I'm not going down for your crimes."

The world is collapsing into the cracks you created in your selfishness. Now you blame me so you can live with your guilt. And yet, the only way your little Richie can live in a world without thirst is if you surrender yourself. Let the world return to its peace without you.

"Without…." I paused. The Void didn't just want to frame me. It wanted to take me in itself, to the nothingness. But if I wasn't a Void like it, the action would destroy me. Maybe Stranger shouldn't hear everything. I continued the conversation in thought. *You said you needed me alive.*

I didn't want you to die. There's a difference.

221

You want me to dissipate? Go into the nothing?

I want you to come home.

You do realize that'll kill me, right?

Penny —

No, thank you. You're a manipulator. You mess with people's heads. I'm not going to let you mess with mine.

Can you live now, Penelope Grace? Knowing what you know? Knowing the world would be better without you in it? Trust me. In the end, I'm doing you a favor. The shot of darkness came at me too fast, aimed straight for my head. I hadn't expected it — I barely had enough time to duck — and screamed as it passed my ear by just a hair. A tree trunk behind me seared as it took the attack.

"Is it attacking?" Stranger shouted.

"Apparently!" I grabbed his arm and ran.

"I thought you said it didn't want us dead!"

"Obviously I was wrong!"

We jumped as a tree fell to our right, a great big scorch mark slicing it in half. "'Trust me,' she said," Stranger half teased as we ran. "'It'll be fine,' she said."

"Oh, shut up," I answered, and veered him to the left as The Void came rushing to the other side. Stranger tripped on a tree root and we both went down hard. I looked over my shoulder even as I was scrambling to my feet, but then I froze. The Void stood over us, blocking our escape. I shoved Stranger to the ground with a sorry, and didn't blink as I kept my eyes on the monster. "You kill us, your plan won't work."

On the contrary, it'll work perfectly.

It reached down, wispy fingers stretching toward us, just like in Stranger's basement. I leaned over, blocking Stranger from the attack. Maybe I couldn't get him home, but at least I could buy him time.

And then the great blackness of The Void split in two, like a lightning bolt through a night sky. The two sides dissipated like a weak cloud in the wind, and there, in its place, was Richard Noble. Full grown and holding a sickle with a petrified wood blade in his hand. "Did I get it?" he asked.

I released a shaky sigh and relaxed with a nod. Stranger wrapped one arm around me as he sat up. "You came just in time," I said. "We were almost —"

"Yeah, I bet." Ricky twirled the sickle in one hand. He kept his eyes down or at Stranger, never quite looking at me. His aura was thick with distrust and confusion. A murky green struggling against rage-filled red and blue tinged betrayal.

"Which Ricky are you?" I asked.

"What?"

"When was the last time you saw me?"

He rose an eyebrow. "Let's just say we didn't end on the best of terms."

"Oh." I glanced at Stranger, who cringed. "Well, you look good," I said, trying to soften the tension. "Apocalypses suit you."

He scoffed. "Gee, thanks."

"How did you get here?" Stranger asked.

"Didn't mean to. A door popped up, right near that circle where you ditched me. I heard screaming so I went through. Then I saw Stranger. I don't hate Stranger, so—" He shrugged.

"Thank you," I said. "You saved our lives."

"Is it dead?" Stranger asked. "Is it over?"

A horrible thought came into my head, even as a deep chuckle echoed in my head. "It can't die. It's not living," I said. "But I think Ricky bought us some time."

"Time to do what, exactly?"

I glanced at Ricky's sickle. "How strong is that thing? How far does it keep that void…er, I mean the Cheyenne Circle energy away?"

"Not much if I have to slice through it. The sickle is mostly symbolic. If you want to keep that energy away, you need something thick and strong, like a tree trunk."

"Dang it." I brushed my fingers through my hair. "I think I can navigate through the unstable energy enough to get home, but I need time. The Void keeps messing with it. Like here, I meant to go to the Petrified Forest in Arizona, but it interfered." My voice trailed off as something stirred behind Ricky. I narrowed my eyes and looked around.

Darkness. All around us, in a complete circle, like hungry walls ready to eat forests to get at us. "It's back. And we're already surrounded," I said.

"Quick," Ricky said. "We can get back to my time before—" The door snapped in pieces in the distance as the wall closed in. "Ah…. My wife is not going to be happy about this."

"Penny?" Stranger said. "You think you can take this thing?"

I closed my eyes to focus. The black was closing in fast, and with a vengeance. I imagined reaching out and pushing against it, stopping it in its tracks. The wall sped up. "Well, that didn't work," I said, and opened my eyes. "I think I made it mad."

Ricky hesitated. "I can't believe I got pulled back into this. I might have an idea."

"What is it?"

"It's a meditation my wife and I have been working on. You see, everything has an aura, even if we can't see it."

"Skip to the end," Stranger said. "What's the meditation?"

"Well, it's the basic protection wall. Usually a person just puts it around their aura so outside energies can't interfere. But what if the wall went even farther? And if the mental wall was made out of petrified wood—"

"The Void couldn't get in." I nodded. "That's a great idea, but do you think you can mimic petrified wood's aura that exactly?"

"That's what we've been practicing," he said with an unconfident shrug. "Problem is, the energy usually catches on pretty quickly, starts fighting back. But it might give you time to make an exit."

"Bait," I whispered. "You want to play bait."

"No," Stranger said. "Hard no."

"I'm not saying I like the idea," Ricky snapped. "What other option do we have?"

Stranger gaped at me. "Please tell me you're not considering this."

"I...." All I needed was a little time, a little distraction. Then I could do it all. Hopefully. "I can't do anything with The Void focused on me."

"Penny!"

"No. It's okay," Ricky said. He looked back and forth between Stranger and me, as if almost not recognizing us. "You two look like kids. In my memories you two were both so much...." He looked down at us. "Taller. Listen, we don't have much more time. You should know, my life—"

"Was it good?" I asked. "Did you marry Zetta? Do you have any kids?"

He blinked in surprise. "How did you know that?"

"I know more. You won't have to live in an apocalypse forever. I promise. I'll send you someplace where you'll be surrounded by water. Your very own ship. And you'll have your own time traveling door.

You and your family can go anywhere you'd like."

"What are you talking about?" Ricky asked.

"I swear to you, Richard Noble, everything I've ever done has been for your own happy ending."

"She's right," Stranger said. "Trust Penny and all your dreams will come true. Apparently."

Ricky gaped as us like we were crazy and opened his mouth, most likely to argue, when a tree crashed down, making us all jump. "We don't have much time." Ricky handed Stranger the sickle and sat down on the ground, his back straight and his legs crossed. "As soon as I start, the attacks will get worse. So, for the love of petrified wood, be fast, Penelope Grace." He closed his eyes.

The energy changed in a second. Instead of the cold emptiness that sucked the life right out of the forest, there came a warmth of life. Ricky's aura turned a thick amber, which inflated like a balloon around us, covering the three of us completely. The dark wall hadn't reached it yet, but it would soon.

Stranger gripped the sickle, but looked terrified. "I can't see it," he said.

"So feel it," I suggested. "The temperature's changed. You feel that, right?" He nodded. "Trust your gut. When it gets cold, swing." He widened his eyes like that was the worst plan ever, but I knew he had it in him. If Ricky could learn to create a petrified wood aura around us, Stranger could do this. The hardest part would be trusting his gut when it warned him.

I gave him one last nod of encouragement and closed my eyes. The war in front of us came into sharp focus. The blackness hit Ricky's solid amber aura with a hard slam. Ricky leaned to the side but stayed sitting up. A small tendril slivered through the amber, going straight for Ricky. "Stranger, to your left!" I yelled. He didn't hesitate but swung. The tendril dissipated like smoke in wind. But there were more. Coming from all directions. "Right!" I said. "Straight ahead! Above your head!"

"I got it!" Stranger half smiled. "I think I can feel it. Do your thing, Penny. I'll protect Ricky."

Right. I tore my focus away from the boys. Geez, if anything happened to those two.... *No, focus. We've got to get out of here.* I waited like a fishing hook in the water, still and silent as the prey came closer. A tendril of smoke shot past me, reaching for Ricky to stifle his powerful energy, but I was too fast. I gripped the tendril with my mind and pulled it around us, gathering more and more tendrils as I went. They fought and beat against my grip to get at us, but once I had a hold of them, there was nothing they could do.

Ah, Penny, you're trying to escape, The Void sneered. *You think you can go where I don't allow?*

I think I'm stronger than you, I said, and even as I spoke, I swirled the tendrils around us, the edges just barely scraping against Ricky's aura, as if we were in the eye of a tornado.

Stronger than me? The Void chuckled. *This is why you had to run away from home, why you dreamed of life on this earth. Because you're weak and want to live among the weaker.* A force slammed against the amber aura. Ricky groaned and the strong color faded. The darkness was all around us, but I couldn't tell where The Void itself stood. We didn't have much time left.

I tried to think of home. Of Dinah and the windy state, full of life and hope and chances. I thought of my forgetful parents, and a dad who didn't yet know he needed to ground his daughter for losing his tablet. Of Stranger's basement and his grieving home. I got only static back. I gritted my teeth. *You know what I think? I think you need me. You're literally nothing, and without me you have no meaning. I think you want to kill me because you hate the fact that your plan went wrong. You wanted to be among the living, but it didn't work. You're still you, still nothing, and now you're a wanted criminal on top of that. The only way you can return home is by tricking people into thinking you were just the first one out to save the day. That someone else messed up as royally as you truly did. Because the fact is, it's you who doesn't belong in your home. You who feels guilty because your selfishness will implode your own world.*

The slam came harder this time. A tendril tore through Ricky's aura. "Stranger, your ten o'clo—!" But Stranger was already swinging. The sickle sliced through The Void's arm. In that second, the static silenced. Home called out to me like a beacon. Dinah's voice calling out. The swirling tendrils whirled into solidity. A rotating door. Because we needed to go two different places.

Keeping my grip solid on home, I quickly connected with the prison ship, just a week or two before Stranger and I arrived. Ricky might hate me for a little longer, but he'd get over it. I gave one last look at the grown up saving our lives, and yet he was still there, that little ten-year-old who trusted us. Who wanted freedom and safety. I'd never see that kid again, or the pirate hero either. But he'd be happy. I was sure of that. Ricky must have felt the darkness ease from his aura as we connected with the prison ship. He opened his eyes and looked around at the grimy ship deck. "Oh," he said, and looked at me in exasperation. "You've got to be kidding me."

"Don't worry," I grinned. "You'll thank me later."

The door rotated once more and suddenly it was just Stranger and me, going back home. He grabbed my hand.

That's when the rotating door shattered around us. Darkness pooled in like water on the Lusitania, swallowing us whole.

Chapter 32

I swam in nothing. I saw nothing and I felt nothing. As if nothing else existed. Love and hate were imaginary. My memories were right up there with dragons and happy endings. I couldn't feel the loss. No more Stranger or Dinah. No more chances for Mom and Dad to remember my favorite meal was fish tacos, because I couldn't feel the hope that they ever existed. That I could ever go back.

But then…if I was nothing, how did I think? What allowed me to remember? Had my spirit survived? Was that all I was now? A ghost haunting the gap just between realities? I wanted to cry but had none of the tools. I hadn't fought through time and space to become this. To fade away and never know. Did The Void close the crack? Did the world end thirsty? Did Dinah scream when the emptiness took her? Did she know she wasn't alone?

Dinah. Such a good person. She wanted so much to make a difference in the world. To have someone like that just…fade. It was more than a waste. There was a word for it, but I couldn't remember. Maybe no one had ever invented a word strong enough to cover the loss of losing a girl like that. Maybe the world would never know.

I was drowning in the darkness. Being pulled down by the weight of everything I couldn't have. Everything I wanted. Humanity strangled me. Choking me. A pressure thicker than water pushing me down. Down. Down.

"Help!"

A sound. It didn't just echo through the nothing. The voice rang sharp and clear against the backdrop of blackness. Dinah.

"Somebody get me out of here! Please!" My muted mind took a moment to react. All I could think was that Dinah did scream in her last moments. Right next to the crack. I wanted to scream back, tell her I was coming, to Marco Polo my way to her, but the only thing that came out was a thought. *Dinah.* So I searched through the sea of empty for one sign of goodness. If I could just get back to that moment and push all that emptiness back where it belonged before it could do any more harm. I just need a fresh start.

There. A splinter of light no bigger than my hand. I rushed to the only thing that was real. And then I saw her. My sister. Alive and well and cowering, terrified, in a corner. All I needed to do was go to her. I reached out, stretching through the hole.

Only, my arm didn't reach out. No skin and bones. Just a smoky silhouette. Dinah screamed and bent deeper into her crouched position, trying to be smaller. But I wasn't trying to hurt her! I was there to save her! I pulled my hand in and she choked back a sob. Emotions were sharper near the crack, like I was feeling reality for the first time. And the panic overwhelmed me. What was I supposed to do? I needed my body! I had to have my body!

Maybe if I just focused. My emotions were coming back. I could bring my body back too. So I focused on what I once was, chestnut hair and tanned skin, freckles on my arms, and wearing Shreya's clothes. Nails cut too close to the skin and ignored cuticles. Blood pumping and organs working. A little chub around the waist, and barely any curve of muscle along the arm. This was me. This was what I wanted back.

I reached for Dinah again. Fingers struggled for air as I forced myself through the crack. Then an arm. A weight by my side, like I was pulling something with me. I held on tighter and kept working my way through. Air flooded my lungs in a painful gasp as my head freed itself from the emptiness. I groaned through clenched teeth as I pushed through. One hand still tied down by the weight, I used my other to grip the frame and used it to push myself out.

I collapsed on the hard basement floor, skin raw against the sharp evening air. Right next to me, Stranger let go of my hand and struggled to his feet. He coughed in some air and took in the sight, the crack leaking out. My lungs were dry, my chest still burning from where The Void had stabbed me. Every cell struggled against itself, like it

229

knew it wasn't supposed to form me. My hands shook. I tried to get to my feet, but my knees went out from under me and I fell again, my forehead hitting the floor with a hard smack. I whimpered and looked at Stranger and Dinah. They stood in frozen horror, not just at the crack but at me too.

Oh no, it's fine, I thought as I worked my arms under myself again, preparing for another attempt to stand. *I've got this. Don't inconvenience yourself.* I grimaced against the shaking and forced my weight to my legs. My head spun at the movement. I felt dizzy, but I forced the nausea down and turned to the crack. The blackness spilled out in a smoky haze, and everything from the books to the metal shelves sizzled at its touch. The puddle of spilled Mountain Dew began to boil.

I stepped in front of Stranger and Dinah before reaching my hand out. I pushed the smoke back. For a moment it just paused, and then it fought back. It wanted out. Like gravity. The Void's voice echoed in my head, but it was weak still from Stranger's blow. *You need me,* it taunted. *You're nothing without me either, Penelope Grace.* In one big wave, it slammed against my grip and I slipped back. Dinah screamed.

"This world is not for you," I said through clenched teeth, and pushed back. "You don't belong here!" I stepped forward and the emptiness slid back. With each step I gained momentum, forcing more and more back through the crack, like a vacuum sucking the smoke back through the makeshift door in the middle of the room. Until I stood in front of that door, with only a few small wisps of fighting smoke left.

All the nothing, I thought, *get all of it out.* The last tendril of smoke slipped into the crack. It was so strange, seeing the crack from this side. A floating strip of space splitting reality apart. I reached out to seal it closed. Then the outline of my hand blurred, like it was losing solidity.

I yanked my hand away and stumbled back. When I looked again, the hand was back to normal. But the crack was still open. If I let go, the smoke would just spill right back out. I ran back to the crack and reached out again, careful not to overlap my fingers with the crack itself, but rather to come at it from the edges, smearing reality back together like I had in Tennessee. The way the colors blurred into the crack seemed like smearing icing on cake until the colors connected.

I stepped back in breathless awe. The crack was gone. Just like that. We'd tricked The Void and gotten home. We'd stopped the Cheyenne Circles. We'd saved the world. "We did it." My voice burned my throat and I seriously needed some painkillers, but…we'd done it. A giant smile of relief split across my face and I turned around. Stranger and Dinah still stood there, in the corner, staring in confusion. Dinah, alive and well and completely safe. Stranger, confused and shaken, but home. I couldn't help it. I laughed. But no one joined in. No one else looked relieved. They just stared at me.

"Everyone's okay, right?" I asked.

Stranger blinked. "Um…yeah, I'm fine." He looked like he couldn't decide if he was going to have a headache or throw up or both, but at least he was alive.

"What the freak just happened?" Dinah snapped. "What was that?!"

"It's a long story," I said. "I'll tell you everything, I promise, but first I just want to go home. Tell Dad his tablet is officially lost forever," I teased.

Dinah's eyebrows furrowed. "How did you know I lost my dad's tablet?" Dinah asked.

"I…."

Dinah stepped closer. She leaned in and studied my face. There was not one ounce of familiarity in her face, no love in her aura as she looked me straight in the eye. "What are you?" she whispered.

Being consumed by the darkness had hurt less than the way she looked at me. "What are you talking about?" I stumbled. "I'm…. Dinah, it's me. Penny. Your twin sister. Stop playing games."

She looked taken aback. "I don't have a sister," she whispered.

"Dinah, that's messed up." My voice cracked. "I just went through hell for you. Now's not the time to start making practical jokes."

"I agree," she said. "So why'd you steal my face?"

"What? Come on, we're twins. We're identical. Stranger, tell her."

But Stranger didn't seem to hear us as he looked around the mess of his basement.

"He's processing," Dinah guessed. "The guy must have gone through a lot."

"No kidding," I said. "You seriously don't remember me?"

Dinah looked me up and down. "Sorry. First time I saw you was when you crawled out of that…thing and pushed it back. Which, you know, thanks and all, but…." She shrugged at me.

Shrugged. She freaking just shrugged? People shrug when they don't know the answer to a math problem, or don't know where they left their keys. People don't just shrug when they deny knowing their sister!

I wanted to get mad. I wanted to scream at her, but a core truth silenced me. Because Dinah would never deny me like this. Something was wrong here. I couldn't ignore that. The Void had messed with Stranger's memory once. It wouldn't be a stretch to learn he'd done it again with Dinah. I had to find out how it messed with people's memories. How The Void stole this memory and kept that one. Twisting reality to meet its own ends. The thought of facing The Void again made my stomach churn and my gut twist. I thought I had won, but somehow, it still held all the cards. I had to stop it. I had to get my family back.

Then Stranger whispered something, so softly that I couldn't make out the single word, and yet it sounded heavy, weighted with grief. He stepped back and exhaled sharply. His face had gone pale.

"Stranger?" I asked. "What's wrong?"

He looked at me, and for a second I thought he'd forgotten me too, but then he stared at the space where the gap used to be. He ran over to the still smoking machinery. "No, no, no, no," he chanted as he checked the broken wires and dented metal. When he looked back at me, his face was desperate. "Open it back up."

"What? Why on earth would I do that?"

"Because I remember," Stranger half whispered, half pleaded. "I remember who I need to save."

Acknowledgements

When I first imagined becoming a writer, my mind went straight to the romanticized hermit in the mountains, sending off works of literary art and never speaking to a soul. Since then, I've learned that the art of writing and publishing depends heavily on a strong social and supportive system. With that in mind, I want to thank all those who helped make this book possible.

First, I want to thank Kimberly Durtschi, for everything from talking to me at my first writer's conference to introducing me to my editor, and for creating the gripping book cover. People will pick up my book because your art caught their eye. I would also like to thank my editor, Ashley Gephart, for her great advice which turned my rough ideas into a story. And a special thank you to proofreader Skye Bassett for making sure my stuttering fingers didn't type up another "dairy diary debacle."

And no "thanks for your support" speech can be complete without thanking my family. Mom and Dad, thanks for your support and never doubting me even when I was a little kid who didn't know what plot meant. Thanks to my siblings Clint, Heather, Cade, Shane, Brook Summer, Misty, and Skye who have inspired and supported me from all over the world and even The Other Side. Thanks to my nieces and nephews for being my guinea pigs and listening to my geeky rants. We're all stuck with each other for eternity, so someone start the popcorn.

Aspen Bassett works at a library, telling stories and suggesting books. When she's not working, she's usually sipping hot cocoa and wondering what would happen if she had superpowers. She's been published in multiple anthologies including Oomph: A Little Super Goes a Long Way and Inaccurate Realities.

Aspen grew up learning about chakras and auras and the true power of imagination which slips into her writing whether she intend it to or not. In college, when she wasn't busy working on her degree in Creative Writing, Aspen also got her certificate in Women's Meditation (basically general energy work). Now, she's working toward a diploma in Integrated Healing Arts with a certificate in Hypnotherapy.

www.ingramcontent.com/pod-product-compliance
Lightning Source LLC
Chambersburg PA
CBHW020938180626
46814CB00003B/848